# THE LIKES OF US

## A SCRAPBOOK
## OF THE SHEEHANS

William J. Duffy

ISBN-13: 978-1983878978
ISBN-10: 1983878979

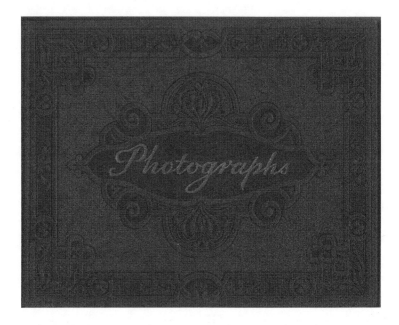

If a snapshot in a photo album could speak to us, what

story would it tell?

# The Sheehan Scrapbook

## 2019

Anne Genovese sat at her kitchen counter sipping tea. She held in her lap an old photo album with a fake leather cover, one of several she had brought with her when her family came to Australia thirteen years earlier. She sometimes wondered why she kept these things, these photos of faces she did not recognize, of people who died before she was born. But as she grew older, now approaching fifty, she felt an urge to revisit them.

"Mother, whatcha up to?" asked Jane as she entered the room. Jane was home from university for the Christmas holiday. "Digging into the family crypt again?"

Anne laughed. "Yes, I am. Don't you give me grief about it."

"Which tomb have you opened this time?" her daughter asked, reaching into the refrigerator for a coke.

"The Sheehans. My mother's family. Your father's family has been in Australia for more than a century now. We have lots of information about his parents, his grandparents, even his great grandparents." Her hand stroked the cover of the scrapbook. "But on my side—well, it's all muddled. Maybe it's the challenge of the hunt that makes me go digging. I've managed to find out a lot about the Oldmans, my father's family, and the Sheehans." She laughed. "I'd bet that at this point I'm the world's foremost expert on both those families. In fact, I probably know more about them than any single individual in either family ever knew."

"That's because nobody else cares," Jane said.

Anne gave her a sharp look. "Somebody should care. You should care. We all don't come from nowhere. They're your people, too."

Jane held up her hands in surrender. "I'm sorry, Mother. That was flippant. I admire you digging up the family tree. I just meant, it's only important to us."

Anne took another sip of tea. "Not only us, but all the other people descended from these same folks. I wonder if any of them are doing family history."

Jane pointed at the scrapbook. "So, who do you have there?"

Anne lay the book on the counter. "This is a Sheehan album from the 1940s. I've thrown in some photos I've acquired in my online researches. You know, in the old days, people only took photos on special occasions. It wasn't like now when everybody posts a dozen photos a day to Facebook or Instagram. They took photos for special occasions: parties, anniversaries, weddings, graduations."

Jane rolled her eyes. "I may be only twenty, Mother, but I do have some understanding of life in the previous millennium."

Anne's frown quickly turned to a grin. "OK, I've officially become my mother. My point is, photos then were rare things. I'm not sure how someone your age can understand that. You didn't carry a camera around with you all the time, and you didn't just take a bunch of pictures and then delete the ones you didn't like. When people took them, they had to send them off to get developed, and then a week later they got them back, and maybe they stuck the halfway decent ones into a photo album. Like this one. Someone made the effort to put this album together, even marking the date on some of the photos. Unfortunately, that someone didn't bother to attach any names. Still, they're our family, or strangers important enough to our family to have their

3

photos included."

She opened the album. "Look at any one of these pictures. I like to try to imagine what was happening when it was taken. The person in it – he or she had already had a whole life before they stood in front of the camera, a whole life yet to come. I like to think about that."

"Now you're getting metaphysical."

Anne closed her eyes a moment. "I just wonder what stories attach to these people. I know better than to think they're all happy stories. But some of them were."

Jane looked at the pages to which the scrapbook was open, a dozen photos of two young couples, the men looking like brothers, each couple with an infant daughter. "I never thought of it like that, Mother." She pointed at a photo lying loose on the page. "This one looks a lot older than these others. He's certainly not wearing 1940s clothes. Is it one of those you found? What's his story, do you think?"

"Oh, that one," Anne said. "That's the oldest picture I've got. Well, I mean, it's only a copy of the original photo, but the original was taken 150 years ago. It was in a box with a bunch of other loose photos."

"But who is it?" Jane persisted.

"I don't know."

"Then why do you keep it?"

"Because he looks like my uncles."

4

## Bound for Amerikay

### 1870

He would leave this land. He had always wanted to leave this land. The morning mist cool on his face, Jack Sheehan turned away from the new cathedral and looked down the hill, down to the harbor below. Strange how the sounds floated up, all the noises of the sailing ships, the steamships. The English called this place Queenstown, because their queen had passed here twenty years earlier. No true Irishman used that name. It was Cobh. Before today he had never seen this place, after today he'd never see it again. His country lay thirty miles and more north of here. Like all those who had gone before him, all those to come after him, Cobh would be his last sight of Ireland. A sorry sight it was, a warren of shops and houses lining streets going up and going down, all of them leading to the docks below, all full of people out to separate him from his last farthing. And why wouldn't they try, impressive as he was in all his finery, togs the likes of which he'd never had before? Knee breeches, knitted wool stockings, a fine white linen shirt, a blue swallow-tailed top coat, a tam o'shanter atop his head, and brogues upon his feet. The finest clothes he'd ever owned. Sure, all second-hand. If only these too tight brogues hadn't blistered the feet.

He had never thought this day would come, dream of it though he did. Thought he'd go the way of the others, dead, dead in the Great Hunger even before his mother bore him, or the others in the years since. Brothers, sisters, uncles, aunts. All dead or gone. Family talk filled with "your Aunt Margaret, God rest her soul" or "your brother Patrick, Holy Mother, pray for him." Joseph off to Canada, and Mary with her man and babes to Australia. What became of them?

Those early years, wandering the lanes, his parents no land of their own, drifting from workhouses to shanties to the open road. They died a year apart, m'athair first. Ten years old he was, just him and little Annie left together. The parents gone, he and Annie living a life even worse, two

6

waifs roaming an empty country, empty farms and villages, gach duine gone to the next world or to the new one. Every day a struggle.

He would have given up and died himself, without Annie. She needed him. He had done what he had to keep them alive. He was a small man, but with a strong back and his father's way with words. He saw them through. Let the priests worry about the right or the wrong of it.

But for the Irish Republican Brotherhood they'd have perished after all. He had played his part in the Fenian Rising, the Rising that was going to rid Ireland of the Sasanachs once and for all, if only the IRB leaders had had a plan and informers had not filled the rebels' ranks. He had never thought much of the IRB's prospects, but they gave Annie and him food and shelter. Now the IRB was giving him one final reward: passage to America.

Jack thought back to the American wake his friends had held for them a few days earlier at Keane's shebeen just south of Mallow on the Cork road. Annie sat by the peat fire sipping her tea with the other women while the men stood around the dark, smoky room drinking good whiskey and bad poteen and smoking their pipes. The murmur of conversation filled the low-roofed room.

"Sure and won't we be missing ye, you and Annie, when ye have gone your way?" Liam Keane said to him. "'Tis a wonderful thing the Brotherhood does, sending ye both to Amerikay." Keane puffed on his clay pipe.

"We are the both of us grateful."

"Will you be joining with our American brothers when wunst you are there?"

"The Fenians? That I will." Jack held the glass to his lips and relished the whiskey fumes.

"'Tis good to hear you say so." Keane tapped out his pipe and turned to refill it. "You will be repaying the Brotherhood's generosity, you will."

"That is so, me being the one to insist they pay for passage for the both, she being the only kin left me in this world." What was the point of the trip, if not for Annie?

"Musha, and how could we expect you to leave and Annie not be gone with you? What kind of future is there in cruel Ireland for a colleen as pretty as she?"

"You have the right of that. Whatever will become of this shitehole of an island?"

Keane paused to relight his pipe with a brand and drew a puff. "Someday we will drive out the English. And then we will turn on each other."

Jack laughed. He had no great expectation that life in America would be any easier. He knew about "No Irish need apply" and "mick" and "white nigger." But would the Americans treating him like shite in their country be any worse than the English treating him like shite in his own?

He turned to his sister. Annie had made the climb with him to the cathedral and stood off to the side. The rough texture of her woolen skirt and felt blouse did not conceal the beauty of her features. "Annie, when wunst we are over there, we must have you a proper American cloak."

She smiled at him, wrapping her faded plaid shawl more tightly against the wind. "That would be glorious, it would!" she said.

"Let us go down then, and find our ship, and be away from here."

Annie hesitated. "Will we ever regret leaving?"

"Wisha! I think not. What of this land is ours, other than the bitter memories?"

The Sheehans made the ten-day voyage to New York on the *Abyssinia*, a new steamship 400 feet long and forty feet wide with a smokestack and (should the coal give out) three sailing masts. Until Cobh, they had never seen a vessel larger than a fisherman's currach. Two hundred mostly English passengers occupied first class. The thousand travelers in steerage were fellow Irish, half on board at Liverpool and half at Queenstown, a mix of families and young people displaying varying levels of poverty and varying degrees of hope. Still, the *Abyssinia* in 1870 was not a coffin ship from the 1840s. Jack and Annie made the crossing in relative comfort.

Cork and Cobh, the biggest cities in their experience, had amazed them, so many people, so much activity, so much energy. Both were country crossroads compared to New York City. They found it a relief when at last they escaped the city's noises, smells, and strange languages (even the strange American English) and tumbled into the quiet of the train that would carry them from Jersey City to Philadelphia. Then the engine started to make its own hideous noises, and the train jerked forward. It moved slowly at first, but quickly gained speed, soon going faster than they had ever moved before. Annie huddled back in her seat, her eyes shut tight, her complexion pallid. Jack's initial panic gave way to exhilaration. He loosened his grip on the armrest and craned his neck to take in the passing landscape. Maybe America would offer them a glorious future after all!

He had decided on Philadelphia as much on a whim as anything else. He liked the sound of the name and the meaning "City of Brotherly Love." He did not want to live in a "New York" or a "New England" or any other place with an English association. But his limited knowledge of England's geography failed him when he found a place to live across the river from Philadelphia in Gloucester City, New Jersey.

They had two rooms to themselves in the attic of Sheila

O'Hara's, a large, run-down boarding house on a quiet street that offered two good meals a day and clean sheets weekly. Jack got work on the docks and Annie became a scullery maid for a Protestant family.

When they first arrived, Jack had some dealings with the local Fenians, but he quickly grew tired of their unrealistic expectations for Ireland's future. Finding he could get by without their help, he drifted away from them, their contacts becoming little more than an occasional pint together in Kelly's Saloon, a dark, narrow establishment with a long wooden bar running along one wall and a row of tables and chairs opposite it. Even then, he found their company and conversation less of a reason to visit Kelly's than the opportunity to talk to the barkeep's daughter, Meg, a dark-haired beauty with a steady banter to tame the rudest customers.

In time it became a given that Jack and Meg were courting, old man Kelly's disapproving frowns notwithstanding. When Meg got in a family way, Kelly abandoned his objections and insisted on marriage. Jack accepted the inevitable with neither eagerness nor reluctance, and the wedding took place in Saint Mary's Church.

He stood at the altar uncomfortable in his borrowed suit, wondering, when had he last stepped through a church's doors? He never would again, except for the children's baptisms. First Lizzie, who arrived three months after the wedding, then Patrick, Dan, John, Ellen, Charlie, and Mary, one every year or so, with a few others scattered among them who either didn't survive the pregnancy or died early on.

Jack's sister Annie blamed Meg for trapping her brother into marriage. The bitter feelings between the sisters-in-law hardened. As soon as Annie met a young man of her own, Tom Flanagan, the two of them married and went west to Detroit.

Jack settled his growing family into a rented two-story house on Burlington Street in Gloucester City. The years passed, Jack and Meg grew older, the children grew up. By the time Jack became too old and stiff from the arthritis to handle the life of a dockworker, his boys were able to find jobs themselves on the docks. The family never grew prosperous, but they never went hungry either. Work became harder for Jack to come by. He would shave ten years off when skeptical foremen asked his age.

His last job was in the pipe shop at the Camden Iron Works, every day the work a struggle. One winter morning shortly before the noon hour, with the pain coursing through his body, a ten-foot pipe he was attempting to maneuver slipped and crushed him. He died instantly, his back, ribs, and leg all broken.

# The Streets Paved with Gold

## 1885

Fifteen years after Jack and Annie's departure, Johanna and Liam Danaher stood with their seven children in front of the same Cobh cathedral. The family had just made their confessions and attended Mass. They had walked the seventy miles from Tipperary, all their possessions carried in bundles at their sides. Sometimes one of the older boys would carry little Maggie, the youngest, when she became too tired to keep pace. Johanna looked at her flock, all poorly dressed and poorly shod.

"Do you think this is the right thing we do?" she asked Liam. "I fear that the greatest sorrows are yet before us."

He looked at her. The shame of the ejectment remained

13

a raw wound. They had watched, the family all huddled together, as the landlord's crowbar brigade stove in the roof and knocked down the walls of their cottage. Cottage, shed, hovel—her English was insufficient to describe what the Danahers had called home. But it was home.

What were they to the landlord? He had never even set foot in Ireland. But he raised the rent through years of bad weather and bad crops and took all their money.

Then the landlord's men had set the ruins on fire. That angered Johanna most of all. What was the point of it? The Land Leaguers would see no one else lived there.

"Mavourneen," Liam said softly, "you know we have no road back."

"Mayhap we should have gone to Australia with your brother after all." She sought any path that would give them the power to decide.

He glared at her. "We had not the money then. Now we have it from your brother in New Jersey. Do we have young Liam write him, 'Thank you very much but it's off to Australia for us instead?'"

America, Australia, wherever—they had to leave Ireland. Tipperary had been home to their families for generations. They did not own the land now, but it had once been theirs and would be again, or so they had hoped. How many times had Liam said he wanted to die in that place?

14

Johanna looked at her husband's face. She knew he thought he had failed them, and now they had to leave, dependent on the charity of a brother-in-law he had yet to meet. If only she could take that pain away!

"The die is cast," he said. "We have a future in America, or we have none. Now we will go down, and board our ship, and be off."

The Danahers made the crossing on the *Spain*, a small ship crowded with hundreds of others in similar straits. The food was bad, but enough. High waves and high winds accompanied them every day of the crossing. Johanna wept as all the Danahers, adults and children alike, fell sick from the rolling ship. Some began to show the first coughing symptoms of the trouble that would stalk them even after their return to dry land.

In New York's Castle Garden, they survived the inspection of an indifferent immigration officer. With their remaining money, they made their way to Philadelphia by rail and caught the ferry across to Gloucester City in search of Johanna's brother. After a few hours of questioning passersby on the street, they found him, to their relief if not his, even less to his wife's.

"Johanna, I have done what I can for youse," the brother said. "I sent youse the money for the passage without telling Addie about it, more than I could spare, and she has not forgiven me. I have no more to give. All I have I need to support us and the children, and that is not enough."

They stood on the street in front of his house, his sullen wife in the doorway, her arms folded tight across her bosom barring entry. The other Danahers waited a few yards off.

"I understand, mo dheartháir mór," Johanna said. "I thank you for what you have done for us. At least now my children will live in America."

"Come, Johanna," Liam called. "Say goodbye. We will go."

"Tá brón orm," the brother called after them as they walked down the street. "Try Father O'Malley at St. Mary's Church."

The church was easy to find, its spire the highest point in Gloucester City. Father O'Malley greeted them warmly, more warmly than his housekeeper. He had long experience with immigrants. He ushered them all into a small waiting room and bade the housekeeper bring them tea and bread. Johanna noted the woman held a handkerchief to her nose as she did so. Well, neither they nor their clothes had seen water to wash in since they left Ireland.

"Your husband and your older boys should be able to find work on the docks, or over at the lumberyard," the priest said. Something encouraging at last. "But for now, all we can offer in the way of housing is a shack behind the Sheehan place."

Johanna despaired when she saw the shack in an alley behind a house on Burlington Street. Nothing but a tar paper shed scarce big enough to hold them all standing up. How she missed their sturdy stone cottage in Tipperary! With no other choice, the Danahers took the shack. The yard had a water pump and an outhouse, shared with two other families occupying equally wretched hovels off the alleyway. When the winter came, the flimsy walls did nothing to keep the cold out, such cold as they had never experienced in Ireland. The small brazier generated as much smoke as heat in the room.

The Danaher men found jobs, but too much of the money went to the doctor. The symptoms of consumption that had appeared on the sea voyage flowered into full-blown disease as the winter wore on. One by one almost all fell sick, Johanna last of all.

The others recovered, her illness lingered on. More and more she took to lying on one of the straw mattresses they had crowded into the shack, leaving the running of the household to the older children. There came a time when she could tell from the night sweats and the fever and the look on the doctor's face that her end was near. She died on a New Year's Day morning, coughing up blood, Liam by her side.

Revolution in Mexico, President Diaz overthrown /
Amundsen reaches South Pole / *Come on and hear, come
on and hear Alexander's ragtime band* / Indian land for
sale / Ty Cobb hits in 41 straight games! / *Oh, you
beautiful doll, you great, big beautiful doll* / 1st
transcontinental air flight, New York to Pasadena, only
82 hours / $15 for this genuine Victrola.

## A Child Is Born

### 1911

Margaret Sheehan lay back on the bed, both she and it drenched in sweat. The waves of pain had stopped. She reached up and Mrs. Wagner put the baby into her arms. The midwife wiped perspiration from her brow. She's done almost as much work as I have, bringing this baby out, Margaret thought.

"He's a right handsome one, all right," Mrs. Wagner said. "Whattar ya goin' to call him?"

Until now Margaret had known this creature only as a

presence in her belly, and here he was with his own face and arms and legs. "We'll name him after his father. Daniel Joseph Sheehan, Junior."

"Well, Daniel Joseph Sheehan, Senior, is downstairs in the parlor and begging to be let up to see his son."

"Oh, I don't want him to see me like this!" Margaret said. "I need to wash my face and comb my hair!"

Mrs. Wagner laughed. "Doncha worry. You look as fresh as if you'd just woken up from a nap! The girl'll get you a basin of fresh water and a comb, and I'll straighten the room before we let him up."

The girl took the water basin and headed downstairs while Mrs. Wagner picked up the dirtied towels. "And then I'll fill out the birth certificate. Quite amazing, when you think of it, November 11, 1911. That's eleven, eleven, eleven. There must be some luck in that! You both are new to Rahway, aincha?"

"Yes," Margaret said, her gaze focused on young Daniel's face.

"From Ireland, I take it?"

"Yes, that is so."

Mrs. Wagner raised the shade to let in the afternoon light. The leafless branches of the trees swayed in a stiff wind. "Been here long?"

"Six months in Rahway."

20

"Well, you don't have much accent, lucky for you. Any kinfolk hereabouts?"

Margaret looked at her. "What did you say?"

"Kinfolk. Family."

"No, we have no relatives here."

The girl returned with a basin of fresh water and put it on the small table next to the bed.

"A pity the child'll grow up not knowing his grandparents or his uncles and aunts, if he has any," the midwife said, rearranging the sheets neatly on the bed.

Margaret considered the comment. Whether Ireland or New Jersey, it made no difference. Her parents and most of her brothers and sisters were dead. And Daniel's family — well, that was water under the bridge.

The baby started to cry. "There, there, little one. Don't you be afraid because you'll never know your grandparents! Your father and I will take good care of you."

"Let me hold him while you wash up a bit and fix your hair." The midwife took the baby into her arms and rocked him while she sang, "*I am a poor, wayfarin' stranger, a-travelin' through this world of woe. There is no sickness, no toil, no danger, in that bright land to which I go.*"

A curious choice of lullaby, Margaret thought, as she rubbed a little soap onto a dampened towel and wiped her face and arms. How strange to feel comfortable again, to focus on some sensation other than the presence of the baby inside her. She took a dry towel and patted the moisture away. Then she ran a brush through her hair and, after glancing at her reflection in the hand mirror, said with a laugh to Mrs. Wagner, "Will you please ask Mr. Sheehan to attend to me and his son at his pleasure?"

"Go and fetch the new father," Mrs. Wagner said to the girl, who laughed and went skipping down the stairs. The midwife handed the baby back to his mother.

Margaret soon heard the heavier step of her husband. He burst into the room, his face alive with joy. She loved to look at his handsome face and his mop of jet-black hair. Three years of marriage had not lessened her love for him. Now, with the baby, she wondered whether she would ever again be as happy as she was at this moment.

Daniel approached the bed and kissed his wife on the forehead. Then he stroked the baby's face. "He's beautiful, Margaret!" He looked at her and smiled. "And so are you! Birthing little Daniel has only made you more beautiful! You're a vain one, all right, making yourself up before letting me up." He always kidded her about her vanity.

"Daniel, we have a child at last!"

"Well, not for want of trying!"

"Oh, Daniel, you say the most awful things!"

"Ahem! Me and the girl will be going now!" the midwife

22

said, picking up her things. "I'll stop in tomorra to check on you and the baby and get my pay."

After the women had left, Margaret fretted. "Daniel, what are we going to do now? Mrs. Harrigan said we could only stay till the baby arrived."

"Well, you can't blame her for not wanting a squalling baby to bother all her other boarders, even if he is our handsome son!"

"But where will we go?"

Daniel lifted the baby from his wife's arms and rocked him as he walked around the room. "No need to worry. I was talking to Keenan down at the shop yesterday. He has a brother looking for a good cooper and willing to pay."

"What does that have to do with where we're to live?"

He laughed. "The brother's in Philadelphia."

"But we've only been here a few months!"

"All the less to hold us in this place, then."

She agreed there was nothing to hold them here, but the prospect of moving so far with a newborn baby did not appeal to her. "I thought you liked your job here."

"I do. But it pays barely enough for us to afford this one room in a stranger's house. Now with the baby, I need to do better."

"Why doesn't Keenan go work for his brother if it's such a good situation?"

"Keenan's already settled with his wife and children. He has no interest in moving."

Margaret reached for the baby. "Is there no other way?"

"No doubt there is. But I do not know what it is."

Margaret knew what he was thinking. They had come to Rahway at her urging, not through any desire on his part. She was silent for a moment, stroking little Daniel's head. "Just promise me one thing, Daniel. Promise me that this young boyo will not end up a cooper like his father."

She could see her husband stiffen. "A cooper I am, a good one. Nobody I know can match my skill with the barrel. What is there wrong with the profession?"

She smiled at him. "Nothing, my love, for our generation. But where would the world be if sons always followed their fathers? Where would you be? It's 1911, still early in a new century. We need to plan for the wonders that this century will bring to the lives of our children."

"Perhaps you have the right of it, Margaret. Here's to Daniel and our other sons finding employment we cannot even imagine."

"Our sons? And what about our daughters?"

"Pshaw! The daughters will need to find husbands, not employment."

Sacco and Vanzetti sentenced to death / *Don't forget your promise to me. I have bought a home and ring and ev'rything* / Extra! Extra! Black Sox not guilty of fixing the 1919 World Series! / *The Sheik* starring Rudolph Valentino: see it today! / Oil your teeth with Chlorox Tooth Paste / 21 whites, 60 coloreds die in Tulsa race riot / Margaret Gorman crowned the first Miss America / *It's three o'clock in the morning, we've danced the whole night through* / Anglo-Irish Treaty divides Ireland into Irish Free State and Northern Ireland.

## A Puzzle in the Making

### 1921

Daniel Sheehan sat hunched over his tool bench. The small work shed's thin walls did little to cut the December chill. Other than the bench and the stool and a few tools hanging on the walls—mainly discards Daniel had brought home from the cooperage—the shed was unfurnished. He was gluing a page out of a recent *Saturday Evening Post* onto a one-inch thick block of wood. The page pictured a winter scene in an idyllic countryside, complete with a horse-drawn sleigh, snow-covered hills, and a charming farmhouse.

"Well, Danny Boy," he said to his son standing next to him, "you have to remember not to rush the process or you'll

26

leave creases and bubbles."

"And then we cut it into the jigsaw?"

"No, one step at a time," Daniel said without looking up. "Then we let the glue dry. And after we let the glue dry, we lacquer it so the picture will last. And after we lacquer it, we let the lacquer dry. And I will borrow a fretsaw from work, and then we will cut it into a jigsaw puzzle."

"You mean we won't finish it today?"

"No, Danny Boy. Not today. But it will be ready for Christmas." Satisfied with the gluing, Daniel set the block of wood aside and looked at his son. Oh, Danny, such a handsome little man. But he'd be a short one, for sure. In a few years his two brothers would catch him up in height. Theirs came from their father; his must have come from their mother's side.

The ten years of the boy's life had brought the Sheehans both tragedy and happiness. Margaret Mary had arrived a year after Danny, and Mary Ann two years after her. Neither girl survived the birth. Margaret Mary entered the world already dead, and Mary Ann survived just long enough for the midwife to splash water on her head and cry, "Mary Ann, I baptize thee in the name of the Father, and of the Son, and of the Holy Ghost."

Daniel found that his grief over the deaths overwhelmed him. He understood the dangers of pregnancy, but he had thought they meant nothing to his family. Surely all his children would arrive like Danny Boy, with a few hours of labor and a minimum of fuss. In response to his daughters' deaths, he refocused his attention on his son, his namesake, and put all his hopes for the future on him. His wife seemed to resign herself to the deaths. She never spoke of the girls.

Joseph Daniel arrived when Danny was five years old, and Edward Timothy a year after that. Daniel didn't like to think that he favored his eldest son over the other two. He told himself that it was only natural that young Danny should be his favorite. He was the first, after all, and he had had a five-year head start to work his way into his father's heart. Daniel loved his other sons, but his grief over the baby girls lay like a shadow, and every day he feared that death would snatch them away too.

"So, do you think your brothers will like their present?"

"Yeah, I guess so."

Daniel raised his eyebrows. "What? Is there something else you're wanting to give them then?"

"Naw, I just wanted to finish it today. It takes so long!"

Daniel laughed. "All good things come to those who wait. See," he said, pointing to the block of wood, "the glue is drying nicely." He turned back to his son. "Tell me, Danny Boy, do you like your brothers?"

"Yeah, they're alright, I guess."

"Well, that's not a very enthusiastic response, I must say. Aren't you happy to have younger brothers?"

"I s'pose so. But Ma always makes me take them with me when I go out to play, and they're too little to do what me and my friends like to do."

"Mmm, yes, I can see that could pose a difficulty. But you're their big brother. They look up to you. You need to set them an example, show them how it's done."

"I like it better when it's just you and me, like now, here."

Daniel frowned. "Well, we're done here in the shed for now. Why don't you run along into the house and see if there is something you can help your mother with?" He ruffled the boy's hair, as black as his had been until the grey began to creep in the last few years.

Danny left the shed and crossed the half-frozen mud of the small yard to the house's backdoor. The Sheehans rented an old, close, two-story row house on Gladstone, a narrow street down by the Philadelphia docks. It had a parlor and kitchen on the first floor, two bedrooms and a bath upstairs, and a furnace and coal bin in the basement. Out back was a small yard with a laundry line and the work shed. Twenty steps out the front stoop lay the neighbor's door across the way. This, not the tableau in the *Saturday Evening Post* picture, was Danny's world.

He wiped his feet carefully before stepping inside. The

29

kitchen was uncomfortably warm from the heat of the stove. His mother stood at the sink washing the lunch dishes. Joey and Eddy sat hunched over at the kitchen table playing cards.

"Joey, do you have any aces?" Eddy asked.

"Naw. Go fish," Joey answered.

Their mother glanced at Danny. "Looking for something to do? You can help with the drying."

"Yes, Ma." He got a clean towel out of the drawer and picked up one of the cups on the counter to wipe it.

"Eddy, do you have any threes?"

"Here's one."

"Do you have any fives?"

"Go fish."

Margaret Sheehan watched her son as he worked. She had thought Danny's arrival after three years of marriage was a sign of a bright future that awaited her and Daniel. Then came the two hard pregnancies and the two dead girls. It made her realize she would never escape the hardship and misery she had known as a child. But she had a husband and she had three sons. She would do her duty for them.

"Careful, there, Danny," she said as the boy almost dropped a plate. "Don't be thinking you'll get out of drying the dishes by breaking them!"

"No, Ma."

"Eddy, I've got a book of aces! What do you think of that?"

"Danny," she asked, "what would you like to be when you grow up?"

His face lit up. "A radio man!"

"Radio? Wherever did you get that idea? Have you ever even seen a radio?"

"Yes, Ma, down at Lit Brothers. And I read an article in *Popular Mechanics* about how to build a crystal set. It's like looking into the future! Do you think we'll ever have a radio?"

His mother laughed. "Radios are toys for rich people, not for the likes of us."

"I don' wanna play no more!" Eddy wailed as he threw his cards on the table.

"Ah, gee," Joey said, "just because you're losing don' mean ya hafta give up!"

"Hush, you two!" their mother said. "You've been playing long enough. Take the scuttle down to the basement and get some more wood for the stove."

She turned back to the sink as the two boys trooped down the stairs. Without looking at Danny, she said, "It's good to have dreams. It's good to have hope for the future." For all the good it would do, she thought.

# A Morning Coffee Break

## 1926

Margaret Sheehan removed the last of the breakfast dishes from the kitchen table and carried them to the sink. This was her favorite time of the day, just after Daniel had gone off to work and the boys to school. The back door was open, allowing a gentle breeze in. When the day got hotter, she would close it.

She had the radio turned on low, just for the sound of the conversation flowing from it, not to listen to. She only used the radio when no one else was home. After two years, its presence in the house still angered her. Returning from the corner store one afternoon, Margaret had arrived home to find an ugly wooden box with something like a tuba sticking out of it sitting on the gate-leg table. Daniel insisted the radio was becoming a necessary part of modern life, like electricity or the telephone. When he told her (only after her repeated prodding) that the thing had cost one hundred and fifty dollars, she had had to leave the room. One hundred and fifty dollars? The price of a used Model T! Even now she refused to join him and their sons when they gathered around the radio in the front room for an evening of listening. She kept herself busy in the kitchen instead or went upstairs to sew.

She heard a knock at the front door. Brigid Kelly from across the street was peering through the front window. Brigid could see Margaret as easily as Margaret could see her. Now Brigid was smiling and waving her fingers. Margaret set down her coffee and went to open the door.

"Oh, Margaret!" Brigid said, putting a hand to her breast. "What a relief to see you! I was so worried!"

"Worried? About what? Valentino's death?"

"Isn't that just dreadful?" Brigid replied. "So young and handsome and talented! I couldn't believe it when I saw the paper this morning!"

Margaret sighed. "Would you like a cup of coffee?"

"Don't mind if I do."

They went into the kitchen. Brigid sat at the table and chattered on while Margaret filled a cup with the leftover breakfast coffee and set the milk and sugar in front of her. Margaret tried to pretend she was interested in the conversation, interjecting an occasional "You don't say?" or "I see." Brigid's prattle was almost like having a second radio playing in the background.

"Well, I told Denis he really should ask for a raise. He's been with the company for ten years now, and some of the younger ones are making more than him. He's too good for them."

Margaret nodded and ran down her mental checklist of the chores for the day. She had to finish cleaning the kitchen, tend to the pile of laundry in the basement, get to the bank for grocery money. The iceman was scheduled to make a delivery and the windows were overdue for a thorough washing. If Brigid stayed too long, Margaret would just have to finish cleaning the kitchen around her.

"And did I tell you what Father McIntyre had to say about how good little Paddy was, learning his Latin responses to be an altar boy? We are so proud! Maybe Paddy will become a priest himself someday."

All she did was talk about her husband and her boys. Had she nothing of herself to discuss?

"But, Margaret, I completely forgot why I came over this morning! Did you see the paper?'

"Well, yes, just to glance at it. What about it?"

"Well, it gave me quite the start!"

Margaret knew her face must have a baffled look. "Valentino's death? We already talked about that."

"Well, yes, no, that of course, but I mean the obituary page. Mind you, I don't normally read the obituaries, I was looking through the paper to see when the back-to-school sale starts at Lit Brothers, and lo and behold there was *your* death notice!"

Margaret felt a chill. "My death notice?"

"Yes, it said 'Margaret Sheehan.' My word, I thought, and I remarked to Denis I had just seen you a few days ago and you seemed in perfect health."

"As you can see, here I am." Why did Brigid have to come bother her with this?

"Well, then I noticed it was for an old woman, about seventy, I think, a widow. Was she any relation of yours? Or I guess I mean, of Daniel's?"

Margaret looked at her a moment before answering. Of course, Brigid might wonder about that. "Philadelphia is full of Sheehans. We belong to none of them. None of them belong to us."

"Still, how odd to recognize a name on the obituary page!"

Margaret laughed. "We're both still young enough not to have to worry about checking the obituaries every morning

35

to see which of our friends made it through the night."

Brigid sat back sharply in her chair. "I'm not sure we should joke about death."

"Why not? Death will have the last laugh anyway. Would you like another cup of coffee?"

"No, thank you, I've taken up enough of your time and I have so many things to do. I'll be going now." Brigid looked offended, but if a joke about death put her on her way, Margaret had no qualms.

Margaret walked her to the door and watched her cross the street to her own row house. She returned to the kitchen. The morning's *Inquirer* still lay on the counter where she had put it when she cleared the table. She thought for a moment. Daniel had read the paper as he always did at breakfast, but he usually focused only on the sports and the national news. He never looked at the paper when he got home, preferring to listen to the radio.

She paged through it until she came to the death notices. Scanning them, she quickly found the box with the heading "SHEEHAN, MARGARET."

"It's so small, how did it ever catch Brigid's eye?" Margaret muttered. The whole piece read: "SHEEHAN, MARGARET (nee Kelly), aged 70, widow of JOHN. Wake and Rosary Wednesday 7:00 p.m. at Lynch's Funeral Parlor, Trenton Ave., Funeral Mass Thursday 10:00 a.m. at St.

Mary's, Gloucester City, interment St. Mary's Cemetery."

The family certainly didn't waste its pennies with drivel like "beloved wife and mother" or listing survivors, she thought. When my time comes my children will do right by me and spend some money on a real notice.

She threw the paper into the waste bin.

# Family Photos

## 1928

"Come, along, boys!" Daniel Sheehan called toward the house. "I'm waiting here with Mr. Kelly's Brownie to take some pictures! We haven't got all day."

His wife stuck her head out the back door. "They're coming, Daniel! Keep your shirt on!"

"And you too, Margaret, I want a picture of you too." He thought how simple life had been when he was single. When he wanted to do something, he did it. After he got married, everything took twice as long to accomplish. Then, as the children arrived one by one, even simple excursions out of

38

the house became major expeditions. He decided to put those thoughts out of his mind and focus on something he could control: the camera.

Kelly had assured Daniel the camera was as simple as pie to operate. "You push the button, we do the rest," as the slogan had it. But Daniel had only used a camera once before in his life, the last time they had used a neighbor's equipment to take family pictures.

"Whattara you up to?" Daniel turned to see his neighbor Frank Davenport leaning over the stockade fence between their two yards. The Davenports had lived next door for a decade, one of the non-Catholic families on the street. They were about the same age as the Sheehans and their two boys about Eddy's and Joe's ages. The two families maintained a polite relationship, although it never occurred to either one to invite the other over for a visit.

"How are you? I'm just taking some family pictures. I hope." Daniel continued to fiddle with the camera.

"Howasabout I take them for you?" Davenport offered. "Hardly no point, ya taking pictures and you not in them."

Daniel considered the offer. It would be easier to have Davenport do the work, but then he'd control the results as well. Convenience won out. "You wouldn't mind? It would be nice to have a shot of the five of us together for once! I don't think we've ever done that."

"Would be my pleasure," Davenport said, gracefully leaping the fence. Daniel started to show him how to work the camera. "Doncha worry! I know how to work a Brownie! You just leave it to me!" He took the box out of Daniel's hands and looked it over. "This'n yours?"

"No, I borrowed it from Kelly across the street."

At last the boys began to straggle out of the house, looking relatively presentable for a day other than Sunday. Margaret came last, smoothing her hair and wearing a colorful tea party dress she had sewn herself. She had resisted most of the Jazz Age fashions, such a break from the voluminous clothes she had grown up wearing, but she wasn't beyond going with a more modest modern style.

"All right, you Sheehans," Davenport said, casting a look around the bare small yard, "this here ain't no Hollywood set, but we're gonna make it look real good. Howasabout ya all stand there next to the work shed?" He looked through the viewfinder. "Wait, no, on second thought, let's have the parents sit on this bench here and the three boys stand behind. That'll look more respectable."

Daniel and Margaret carefully positioned themselves on the unpainted bench that had already seen too many winters, and the boys formed a line behind them, each boy's face reflecting their parents' features. Daniel put his arm around Margaret's waist. He was pleased when Dan put his hand on his father's shoulder.

"Well, no doubt you're all related!" Davenport commented. "Now, hold still while I frame the picture!" He looked through the viewfinder. "Joe and Eddy, stop making faces! Your father didn't waste good money on film for you to clown around." Margaret turned to give her sons a chastising look. They responded with gestures of innocence. "Now watch the birdie!" Davenport pressed the button. He managed to take a few more shots before the orderly scene dissolved and the boys ran off in different directions. Margaret stood up to go back into the house. So much time to get them organized, Daniel thought, and no time at all for chaos to return.

"I'd hate to have to try to get them to sit still in one place again today," Daniel said to Davenport. "Thanks so much for your help!"

"My pleasure. It's good to see you all out and about. It's a shame. Here we are living next ta other all these years, but we hardly ever see ourselves."

"It's comforting just to know you have good neighbors," Daniel said.

"I mean, even our boys—they're pretty much the same age, right?—even our boys don't do all that much together. Course, it might be different if they went to school together."

Daniel thought it an odd comment. Of course the boys

41

didn't go to school together. The Sheehans sent their boys to Catholic school. At twenty-five dollars per child per year the expense took more of the family finances than Daniel would have liked. But they could hardly put them in the public school. American Catholics knew "public school" meant "Protestant school," where the teachers led the students in Protestant prayers and read to them from the King James Bible. The nuns at Our Lady of Mount Carmel would make sure the Sheehan boys absorbed the One True Faith.

"You've got a point, there," Daniel said, and realized that, even after all these years, he didn't know whether he was on a first-name basis with Frank Davenport.

St. Valentine's Day massacre in Chicago—7 men dead /
General Electric presents the first All-steel Refrigerator /
*Wings* named the Best Picture of 1928 / Vatican City now an
independent state / *Happy days are here again, the skies above
are clear again* / The new Dodge Brothers Six, anticipating
the needs of the woman who drives! / *Graf Zeppelin* passes
over San Francisco on round-the-world voyage / Babe Ruth
hits 500th homer / Screen grid Radiolas — the sensation of
the Radio Year! / No end to Wall Street bull market? /
Richard Byrd reaches South Pole.

# Graduation Day

### 1929

The early summer heat arrived in time for graduation day at Roman Catholic High School. Dan Sheehan fanned himself with the graduation program as he and the other soon-to-be graduates waited listlessly outside the auditorium with their parents and teachers. His father tugged on the unfamiliar dress collar and then fingered the fedora in his hands. His mother, shaded by the wide brim of her straw sailor hat, looked more relaxed, happy to show off a new flowered dress she had sewn herself.

"Your mother and I are both very proud of you, Daniel," his father said. "I believe you're probably the first Sheehan or Danaher to finish high school. Isn't that so, Margaret?"

"Probably so."

"But you are only the first. Both your brothers and your children will follow."

"Oh, Daniel, let's not get ahead of ourselves. Let's focus on young Dan's graduation today!"

"It's never too soon to plan for the future, Margaret. We must take care that our children are ready to face the world we live in."

An older man with flowing white hair, also wearing a cap and gown, approached them. He smiled at Dan. "Dad, Mother," he said nervously to his parents, "you remember Mr. Cieskowski?"

Mr. Sheehan nodded curtly. "Hello, Mr. Cieskowski."

"Hello, Mr. and Mrs. Sheehan!" Mr. Cieskowski said. "And congratulations, Daniel. This is a wonderful day for you and the other graduating men."

"Thank you, sir," he replied. "Thank you for all you've done for me."

"It was my pleasure, Daniel. What I wouldn't give to have another group like you and your friends under my tutelage! I hope you won't forget me too soon."

"That's very kind of you," his mother said.

45

"Where to from here, Daniel?" he continued with a smile.

"I've been accepted at the Drexel Institute. I'm going to study electronics."

"Ah, good for you! You always have shown a knack for such things. I wish you all the best."

The auditorium's heavy wooden doors swung open from inside and the crowd started to move forward.

"It looks like it's time to go in then," Mr. Sheehan said, ushering his wife and son.

"I hope to see you all after the ceremony," Mr. Cieskowski called as they moved away from him. Dan nodded in his direction.

"Come, Daniel, let us find our seats," Mrs. Sheehan said. "And you, young man, had better find your place up on the stage."

"Yes, Mother," her son answered, breaking away.

As the Sheehans moved down the aisle, the fans overhead and the open windows did little to make the auditorium any cooler than the outside.

Mr. Sheehan muttered under his breath, "I never did like that man."

"Hush, Daniel! He's a good man who worked hard on our son's behalf. We should be thankful to him, and to all the teachers who helped him."

He exhaled. "Yes, you are right, Margaret, as always. That's why I married you."

She placed a hand on her husband's sleeve. "Yes, I have the wisdom of Saint Brigid. That's why I married you. Now, let's sit here and focus on this happy day."

They slid past several people who had already taken the seats closest to the aisle, in a row about halfway back from the stage. "I hope we will be able to see him from here," Mrs. Sheehan whispered.

"Look at this program!" Mr. Sheehan said as he finally took the opportunity to open it. "We'll be here half the day! An invocation, 'The Star-Spangled Banner'—I still don't understand why we sing it instead of 'America the Beautiful,' an English tune instead of an American one— 'Pomp and Circumstance' —and the boys on stage already!— a speech by the Rector, speeches from the valedictorian and the class president, a keynote speech by the cardinal, and then at long last we get to the conferring of diplomas."

"Oh, stop!" his wife scolded him. "Daniel has worked four years for this. It's a milestone for our family. We can take an hour or two to enjoy it while we can! Oh, look, there he is, up there on the stage, to the right, in the third row! Daniel!"

"Margaret! Don't make a spectacle of yourself," Mr. Sheehan said, looking around. "They'll think you got off the boat yesterday. He can't hear you anyway. I doubt he can

47

even see us."

The Rector came out on the stage, fanning his hands to quiet the crowd. "Take your places, please!" he announced in a loud voice that cut through the noise of conversation. "We are about to begin the ceremony!"

"They must give priests special training at the seminary to talk like that," Mr. Sheehan whispered to his wife.

Everyone sat down and the room quieted as directed. "I welcome you all to the Roman Catholic High School graduation ceremony for 1929," the Rector continued. "Now it is my great honor to ask His Eminence, Cardinal Dennis Dougherty, Archbishop of Philadelphia, to offer the Invocation." He gestured to one side of the stage, and Cardinal Dougherty appeared, dressed in scarlet from head to toe: the biretta, the cassock, the cape of watered silk, the sash, and the satin shoes on his feet. A large pectoral cross hung around his neck.

"Which came first?" Mr. Sheehan whispered. "Cardinals the bishops or cardinals the birds?"

"Enough, Daniel!" his wife whispered back.

When the cardinal reached the center of the stage, he faced the audience and said, "Please rise." The crowd rose as one. "Let us pray. Heavenly Father, we are gathered here today to celebrate and give thanks for every student here. Thank You for leading them in their learning, for keeping them safe as they studied, and for watching over them in their final exams. May today be a memory that burns bright as they embark on life's great adventure. Amen."

"Amen," the audience echoed. The cardinal walked to one side of the stage where a chair appropriate to his rank awaited him. The audience sat down.

"Please rise and we will sing 'The Star-Spangled Banner,'" the Rector said.

"What are we? Jack-in-the-boxes?" Mr. Sheehan grumbled. His wife ignored him.

The Rector turned to a cassocked man sitting at a piano. "Brother McMurray, if you please."

Up on the stage Dan thought about his future, a future that seemed to hold nothing but promise. The horrors of the Great War lay more than a decade in the past, the whole world at peace. The major powers had even outlawed war. Mr. Hoover, the new president, was a great humanitarian and engineer, not a politician like the men who usually ran the country. A decade of economic growth had made the United States the most prosperous country in history. It even seemed possible, as President Hoover had said, that poverty would soon be a thing of the past.

Dan looked forward to Drexel and his electronics studies. He admired his father, but he was a man of the nineteenth century. Dan would be a man of the twentieth. If his father were the best cooper in Philadelphia, Dan would be the best electrical engineer. When his father was born, there were no phones, no electric lights, no planes, no radio. Soon he would turn fifty. What new wonders would the world have when Dan turned fifty, in 1961? What would the world look like then, after three more decades of peace and economic growth? Would Dan live to the end of the century, maybe see the twenty-first century?

He was so caught up in his musings he didn't hear the Rector call his name. An elbow from his neighbor brought him back to June 1929. He sheepishly stood up and walked across the stage to receive his diploma.

# Eddy Has a School Report

## 1930

Dan Sheehan was helping his father take down the summer screens and put up the storm windows. It was autumn 1930. His father was trying to pry loose one of the second-floor window screens, while Dan stood at the ladder base to hold it steady. This was not how he had planned to spend his Saturday afternoon, and Dan would have preferred that he do the work and his father hold the ladder. But his father at fifty was not about to display any doubt he was still up to the job.

"I'm just thankful to have a job," the older Sheehan was saying. "People need working plumbing no matter what! Hopefully this rough patch will blow over soon and the economy will get back on track. We've had depressions and panics before. Sooner or later the market will right itself."

"So you think things will be OK by the time I finish at Drexel?"

"Oh, yes, without a doubt," his father called back, the screen at last coming loose. He passed it down to Dan and moved to the second window. "Bad business conditions like this never last more than a year or two."

"But your old boss Keenan went out of business, right?" Dan replied.

"Well, it's the changing times. The barrel industry isn't what it used to be. Lucky I got into plumbing when I did." The screen on the second window proved even more difficult than the first.

Thirteen-year-old Eddy came out of the house. Already he was almost Dan's height, and Joey was taller than both of them, a fact Dan did not appreciate. "What? Your shadow not with you?" he asked.

"Joey's helping Ma clean." Eddy looked up the ladder at his father. "Pa, can I ask ya somethin'?"

Mr. Sheehan peered down at him. "I'm a little busy right now, Edward, but what is it?"

"I've got a school report to do. All us kids have to prepare reports on our family history." Mr. Sheehan continued to struggle to loosen the screen.

"I said I hafta do a report on our ancestors."

Suddenly the screen popped free and fell to the ground, narrowly missing the two boys.

"Jesus, Mary, and Joseph!" Their father shimmied down the ladder, almost losing his balance in his haste. He assessed the situation. "No damage done? No bops on the head to smack some sense into you? Good. Your mother would be none too pleased if our winter preparations resulted in a doctor's visit."

He smiled and brushed himself off. Then he turned and looked seriously at Eddy. "In answer to your question, Edward, your mother and I agreed years ago it was best to leave the past in the past and not to talk about our lives before we got married. It's enough to know that for better or worse we have lost contact with the families we left behind so many years ago. So that's that."

Both boys looked at their father in amazement. His attitude seemed so out of character, so unlike the man who eagerly helped his sons with school projects and other life difficulties. "Is that understood?"

"Y-yes, sir."

"Good. Now go and help your mother while Dan and I finish destroying the screens."

Eddy went back into the house. Dan looked at his father, who was now bent over assessing the damage to the screen's wood frame. It occurred to Dan he knew nothing about his parents' history.

That night, as the three brothers prepared to go to bed in the small barracks-like room they shared, the beds lined up along the wall and a foot of space between each one, the subject of family history came up again. "Why all the secrecy?" Joey asked Eddy.

"Secrecy about what?" Dan asked as he sat down on his bed by the window and pulled off his shoes.

"The family. Eddy said you were standing right there when Pa told him to lay off with the questions."

"Yeah, what of it?"

"Here's the thing," Eddy said. "Before I hit Pa up for the info, I made the mistake of asking Ma. If looks could kill! Even for her it was somethin' to see." He mocked her tone. "'Why do you want to know that ancient history? Those were hard times, best forgotten. We're here now and that's all that matters.' End of discussion."

Dan leaned back on his bed. "Maybe there's some deep, dark secret back there. Maybe Dad ran off with another man's wife?" He warmed to the subject. "Maybe he was an Irish revolutionary and the English put a price on his head. Maybe Sheehan's not actually our family name!"

"Aw, who cares, anyway?" Joey said. "Nobody wants to know about what happened years ago in Ireland. It's ancient history. I'm just glad we live here in the good old U S of A."

"But what'll I do about my report?" Eddy wailed.

"You'll think of something." Dan reached up and turned out the light bulb hanging from the ceiling. "Now let's go to sleep before Ma starts yelling, 'Don't make me send your father up there!'"

"Yeah, Eddy," Joey said, "You never have any problem making up stories."

# The Davenport Gossip

## 1936

Daniel Sheehan tapped tobacco into his pipe as he settled back into his easy chair. The *Bulletin* lay open on his lap. His three sons sat around him, Dan and Joe on the sofa, Ed on the floor. Margaret Sheehan was in the kitchen, cleaning up after dinner.

"Your mother made you a very nice birthday dinner, Joseph," he said.

"But maybe we're getting a little old for paper hats and the Charlie McCarthy doll," his son replied.

"You can say that again!" Ed agreed.

"Now, now," Mr. Sheehan countered, lighting his pipe,

"you may all three be grown men, but you'll always be your mother's baby boys. It doesn't hurt you to humor her."

"Yeah, Ed," Dan said. "When your birthday comes along, be sure to tell Mother you want to forget the kid stuff."

Ed recoiled in fake alarm. "Not me, brother!"

Mr. Sheehan chuckled. "And, Dan, I'm sure you were sorry not to be here for your last birthday. It's good to have you home, at last."

"It's good to be home, for good, Dad." Dan had just returned from a three-year stint with the Pennsylvania National Guard, a job he took when jobs were hard to find.

"It's not so good, all three of us crammed back in that bedroom together," Ed said.

"Oh, hush, Edward," Mr. Sheehan said. "That'll take care of itself once we sign the papers on the new house."

"So, you think you're going to make it on your own, Dan, with your own business?" Joe asked.

"I plan to. Between Drexel and my National Guard experience, I think I know just about anything about electricity and radio a fellow can know. Drexel gave me the theory side; the Guard the experience side."

"We wish the best for you, son," their father said. "Times are hard, but they are getting better. This may be a good time to start a business."

"Other than the technical stuff, what did you like about

the Guard the most?" Ed asked.

"Just the experience of travelling all around the state. I never thought about it much, growing up, that all I knew about the world was Philadelphia."

"Don't forget that week in Atlantic City in '29!" Joe said.

Ed laughed. "That kind of proves his point, doesn't it?"

Dan ignored his brothers. "Now I've seen most of Pennsylvania, with all the exercises and maneuvers we did. It's a big, beautiful place, between the mountains and the rivers and the forests. But it has its ugliness. Pittsburgh's location is naturally beautiful, the way the rivers come together. But the smokestacks spew black smoke around the clock and the sun is practically blotted out of the sky. And some of those mining towns up in the mountains — they make Gladstone Street look like the Main Line!"

"But, son, that's because they have the industries we depend on. Imagine if nothing were coming out of those smokestacks, or if the mines were still shut down."

"I know, Dad. But still, it's depressing to see what we've done to nature."

Daniel Sheehan pointed his pipe at the radio. "Joe, it's time for my program. Please do the necessary."

"Yes, Dad." His son turned the radio on. Static crackled from the speaker as the machine came alive. Joe tweaked the dial until an announcer's voice emerged from the static.

" —bring you *The Golden Hour of the Little Flower*, with Father Charles Coughlin. If you wish to join the Radio League in defending the principles of Christianity and Patriotism, please mail your one-dollar membership to the Radio League of the Little Flower, Woodward at Twelve Mile Road, Royal Oak, Michigan. And now, Father Coughlin."

Unlike most listeners, Mr. Sheehan did not hang on the Radio Priest's every word. He preferred to listen with one ear, the fiery voice in the background.

Mrs. Sheehan came in from the kitchen. She picked up her sewing basket and sat down on the sofa, Dan and Joe making room for her. Mr. Sheehan puffed on his pipe. "Margaret, the boys and I were just commenting how much we enjoyed dinner tonight."

"Well, I always like to make a little fuss for their birthdays." She extracted her needles and thread from the basket.

"Yes, Mother," Dan said, looking in Ed's direction, "Ed was just saying how much he's looking forward to his birthday party!"

Mr. Sheehan started to pick up the newspaper but put it back down. "By the way, Margaret, I saw our neighbor Davenport on my way out this morning."

"Did you now? And what is new with the Davenports?"

"He finally got called back to work. So, he was a much

happier man than I've seen him in a while."

"That must be a relief to Mrs. Davenport and the boys. They've had a hard year of it." She turned to the pile of socks needing darning.

Coughlin's voice filled the silence, " —strike against Communism, because it robs us of the next world's — "

"Dad, may I ask you a question?" Dan asked, stirring uneasily in his seat. "Well, it's not really a question. It's more a concern. Why can people be so two-faced, acting all nice one minute and then so mean the next when they think you can't hear them?"

Mr. Sheehan wondered what Dan was getting at. "Is that such a bad thing, not always blurting out mean thoughts? Would you rather they were mean to your face as well?"

He scowled at his father. "That's not what I mean."

"Then what is it you do mean?"

As Dan hesitated, the radio voice went on, " —faults of the governments of Herr Hitler and Signor Mussolini. But we must recognize they offer an antidote to — "

"All right then. I'm talking about the Davenports."

"You're not talking gossip, are you? We'll not have gossip. The Davenports have never been anything but polite to us."

Dan ran his hand through his hair. "I'm not talking gossip. I'm talking what I overheard today. I wasn't even going to bring it up, but then your mentioning them made me think maybe I would."

" —Russian Revolution was launched and fomented by distinctively Jewish— "

"Daniel," Mrs. Sheehan said, threading a needle, "you shouldn't be eavesdropping."

"I wasn't, Mother." He looked out the front window. "Blame it on the breeze, maybe. I was in the back yard, weeding in the garden like you asked me to. The Davenports were sitting on their back stoop, but I couldn't see them because the fence was between us, until I heard Mrs. Davenport say, 'There goes the young O'Connell girl.' I peeked up and Annie O'Connell was walking down the alleyway. I was surprised to hear the Davenports talking, because they had been quiet up till then. So, I paused for a second. Just as I was about to get back to the weeding, Mr. Davenport said, 'Whattaya mean, *the* O'Connell girl? There's three of 'em, ain't there? Not to mention how many boys.'"

"Go on, Daniel," Mr. Sheehan said. "But there's no need to mimic Mr. Davenport's voice."

"Well, I was just so surprised—all right, here's where I started eavesdropping!—but they were talking about our neighbors, Mother! And Mrs. Davenport said, 'Well, you know the breeding habits of Irish Catholics.' I'm sorry, that's what she said! And he said, 'Not just the Irish. All those

61

Catholics think they need to bring as many brats into the world as possible.'"

"Daniel!" Mrs. Sheehan. "I don't think your brothers need to hear this!"

"It's not news to us," Joe laughed. "We've heard the same from their lunkhead sons, haven't we?" He turned to Ed for confirmation.

"They've got a point, after all," Ed said. "The O'Connells have enough kids to fill a pew and a half at church. What is it with us Catholics and all the babies? I'm just glad there's only the three of us. That's plenty, don't you think?"

The ball of thread fell out of Mrs. Sheehan's hands. "Edward!" Mr. Sheehan said. "We will have no talk like that in this house. It is not up to you to judge others' families. Only the good Lord decides how many children a family has." He looked at his wife. "Are you all right, Margaret?"

"Yes, yes, just a little clumsy," she answered softly as she bent to pick the thread up.

" —blame for the Depression at the feet of the Jewish – "

Mr. Sheehan sighed. "Anything else, Daniel?"

"Well, no, I was so shaken up I just knelt there. I waited till I heard the Davenports go into their house before I got up. I couldn't very well stand up and let them know I'd overheard everything they'd said."

"Sometimes ignorance is bliss," Mr. Sheehan said. "This

will make it a little harder next time I have occasion to wish either of the Davenports a good day."

"Surely you don't think it's just the Davenports, do you, Daniel?" Mrs. Sheehan asked her husband as she resumed her sewing. "I'm sure any number of our other good Protestant neighbors harbor similar thoughts."

"And we shall let the Good Lord judge them for that," Mr. Sheehan said, returning to the *Bulletin*. "We shall not."

" —Gentile self-defense in the face of Jewish —"

"Joe, please change the station. I think we've had enough of Father Coughlin for one evening. Find us some light music."

Glenn Miller's "In the Mood" tops Hit Parade / Always buy Chesterfield cigarettes! / Nazis crash into France / Hattie McDaniel wins Academy Award, first colored woman to do so / 338,000 troops evacuated from Dunkirk / *When you wish upon a star, makes no difference who you are* / Flash! France surrenders / Joe Louis TKO's Godoy, wins heavyweight boxing title / Dogfights above England! / First-ever peacetime conscription law / Roosevelt reelected, unprecedented 3rd term.

## My Little Margie

### 1940

Dan Sheehan loved Margaret O'Sullivan from the first day he saw her. He stopped in his tracks when he saw her shuffling sheet music behind the counter at Lit Brothers. She had the pale skin and black hair of many Irish women, just like his mother in pictures taken when she was young.

He brushed off the front of his tan work jacket and did a quick check of his breath before strolling over to her.

"Top o' the morning to you, Margaret!" he said.

She gave him an unfriendly look. "Excuse me? How do you know my name? Do I know you?"

"Well, I assume that nametag you're wearing is yours.

65

Or are you travelling under an alias?"

The other salesgirl, whose nametag read "Rose Smith," giggled.

"How may I help you, sir?" Margaret asked.

"Do you happen to have 'My Little Margie'?"

"Yes, I believe we do! But isn't it a bit old-fashioned for a hepcat such as yourself?" She flipped through a stack of music and pulled some sheet music out. "Here it is."

"Why, thank you very much." Dan took the music from her with his left hand, cleared his throat, thrust his right arm out, and, to the delight of Rose and nearby customers, began to sing in a whiskey tenor voice, "*My Little Margie, I'm always thinking of you, Margie, I'll tell the world I love you.*" He continued until he came to the end of the verse. The watching customers applauded. He bowed in their direction and handed the music back to Margaret, a big smile across his face. She stared at him stonily.

"Do you want to buy it, sir?"

"No, no, I want to buy *you* dinner."

"Sir, this is a workplace."

"Yes, and we're both working." He pointed at his own nametag. "I'm actually here on an electrical job, not here shopping. And we both need to get back to it. Just say you'll go out with me."

She stared at him. "I don't know you. I don't even know

your name."

"Dan, Dan Sheehan, Sheehan's Electrical Service, at your service! Just like it says on my nametag. It's a meeting of nametags! So, is it a yes? Don't say no."

"Oh, Peggy," said Rose, "go ahead. Say yes!"

Peggy continued to stare at Dan. "Fine. Give me a call."

"What's your phone number?"

"We're in the book."

Dan put a finger to his lips. "You're going to have to help me out here. Do you know how many O'Sullivans there are in Philadelphia?"

"Too many. But we're the only O'Sullivans on Pomona Terrace in Germantown." She almost smiled. "Before we go out, you'll have to pass muster with Himself. And with the four brothers."

Dan tipped his workman's cap and walked away, saying, "I'll ring you up." He hoped neither girl had noticed the sheen of cold sweat on his face.

He quickly made his way to the bank of telephone booths in the basement. He pulled out the city directory. "K, M, N, O, O," he mumbled as he flipped through the pages. "O'Callaghan, O'Connor, O'Donohue, O'Keefe, O'Leary," he murmured as his finger moved down the pages. "Jesus, are there any Irishmen left in Ireland? O'Sullivan, O'Sullivan, O'Sullivan. Ah, here it is, O'Sullivan, Timothy on Pomona

Terrace! Victor 6392." He jotted down the number and went back to work.

Dan waited until the family had finished dinner and his mother had disappeared into the kitchen to do the dishes before he asked, "Dad, may I use the telephone?"

"Certainly, son. I'm not expecting any calls," his father replied, lighting his cigar. He sat in his easy chair in the corner of the living room and opened the *Bulletin* to read.

Dan's brothers Joe and Ed were there, too, fiddling with the radio dial, trying to find a program. Dan looked at the candlestick telephone sitting on the little table midway between his father and his brothers. At least at Lit Brothers he had an audience only of strangers to witness his possible humiliation.

Dan picked the instrument up and cradled the receiver on his shoulder as he dialed the number. It rang twice before a girlish voice answered. "Hello?"

"Hello? Is that the O'Sullivans'?"

"Yes."

"This is Daniel Sheehan. May I speak with Margaret, please?" Ed and Joe stopped playing with the radio to watch their brother. His father kept his eyes on the *Bulletin*, but Dan had no doubt his father's ears were ready to hear all that passed.

"One moment, please."

Dan could hear a man's voice in the background, "Who is it, Madeleine?"

"A man for Margaret, Papa."

"Does he know Margaret?"

"I don't know, Papa."

"Well, ask him!"

The girl's voice came back full volume in the receiver. "Do you know my sister?"

"Yes, I do. She's expecting my call."

"What did you say your name was?"

"Daniel. Daniel Sheehan."

The girl's voice drifted away from the receiver. "It's a Mr. Sheehan for Margaret, Papa. He says she's expecting his call."

"Well, go and call her then."

Dan could hear male voices discussing the Philadelphia Eagles' dim prospects for the coming season. Those must be the brothers she mentioned. Maybe he should just pretend she wasn't home and hang up. He was on the point of doing so when he heard a female voice.

"Hello?"

Dan straightened up and squared his shoulders. "Hello, Margaret? It's Dan. Dan Sheehan."

"Who?"

"Dan Sheehan. We met today at Lit Brothers. You said I could call you and we could have a date." Joe and Ed started to make faces at him. He turned his back to them and tightened his grip on the mouthpiece.

"Oh, yes. How could I ever forget that serenade?"

"Shall I sing it again for you?" Dan grimaced. What if she said yes?

"No, I'd really rather you didn't."

Dan's brothers moved into his line of sight. Ed knelt in front of Joe and spread his arms wide, a pleading lover. Joe looked toward the ceiling and put the back of his hand to his forehead, a reluctant damsel.

"But you will go on a date with me?"

"Well, I don't know whether I should or not."

"But you promised!" How desperate did he sound?

"Does a promise under duress count?" she answered coyly. "But yes, I'll go out with you. But only if you promise not to sing."

Dan let out a long breath. "How about Saturday I pick you up at seven?"

"Saturday at seven? Well, all right. I take it you know the address?"

"That I do. Goodnight, then. See you Saturday at seven!"

Dan felt like he had just successfully made his way through a National Guard obstacle course. He returned the telephone to its stand and turned on his brothers. "Why don't you two grow up? You'd think you were still a couple of teenagers rather than men in their twenties."

"Ah, we're just having a bit of fun witcha," Joe said.

"And what a born Casanova you are," Ed put in. "Right to business, no sweet talk. Hello, goodbye."

Dan's shoulders dropped. Had he been curt? What must Margaret have made of the conversation?

"Say," Joe added. "Mary and I are going out Saturday night. Wanna double-date?"

"On a first date? No, thank you. Mary and I had our share of dates together. On a double-date she might forget she's with you and not me now and that would be awkward."

"A first date?" came their mother's voice from the doorway. "What is this about a first date?" She came into the room, drying her hands on her apron. Over the years her jet-black hair had faded to grey and all her frowns had resolved her face into a tapestry of wrinkles. She looked at him with her usual skeptical countenance. "Who might this be you're taking out?"

"A girl I met, Mother. Her name's Margaret O'Sullivan."

"A good Irish name, at least. What do you know of her?"

"Not much. She works at Lit Brothers and lives with her family in Germantown."

71

She scowled. "A secretary? A clerk? What is she? How did you meet her?"

His father put down the newspaper.

"She's a salesgirl in the music department. That's how I met her. I'm doing a job over there."

"Nothing but a salesgirl? And you know nothing about her family?"

"What's to know? They're probably shanty Irish, like us. I don't see that we should go putting on airs."

His mother put her arms akimbo. "We're respectable people. Just make sure any woman you go out with is one whom you would be proud to bring home with you. I don't need to remind you that you haven't always done well in that department!"

"Don't be so harsh on the boy!" his father said. "Dan has brought home some very nice girls. He found Mary for Joe!"

"This time will be different, Mother. We'll have you to the wedding!"

His mother shook her head and left the room. Dan and his brothers watched her go. His father smiled at Dan and returned to his newspaper.

"She's going to give it to you one of these days, Dan," Ed whispered.

"Hush, Edward," their father said. "Will you two knuckleheads stop playing around with that radio and put on *The Jack Benny Show*?"

When he called at Pomona Terrace, Dan found a row of nineteenth century duplexes lining a bricked street. Like its neighbors, the O'Sullivans' house had two stories with a narrow porch extending over the front. It was separated from the sidewalk by a small yard and a low rolled-wire fence.

Standing at the gate, Dan checked his double-breasted suit to make sure it hadn't gotten smudged on the streetcar. The summer humidity had broken, and the first hint of fall was in the air. Not that that made him feel any more comfortable. He tugged at the knot of his necktie. Did he have the courage to go through with this? He squared his shoulders and stepped through the gate and up to the front door and knocked. A medley of voices came from within. A young boy opened the door and showed Dan into the living room where much of the family (but not Margaret) awaited him. He was relieved to discover that Margaret's brothers were high school and grade school age and not hulking dockworkers.

After a flurry of introductions, he suddenly found himself standing alone in the room with Margaret's father, who sat in an old Morris chair. *Glenn Miller on the Air* played quietly on the radio.

Mr. O'Sullivan was a tall, thin man, about sixty, with a

full head of graying hair and old-fashioned spectacles perched on an aquiline nose and hooked over prominent ears. He looked relaxed, as if he found the moment amusing.

"Margaret will be down shortly, Mr. Sheehan," he murmured as he puffed on a pipe. "Why don't you have a seat?"

Dan sat in an adjoining chair. "Please call me Dan, sir."

"So, tell me about yourself, Mr. Sheehan. Where do you and your people come from?"

"Well, I was born in New Jersey. My parents both came from Ireland, of course." Dan shifted in his chair.

"Of course from Ireland. But which counties?"

"I really don't know. They both came over some time before I was born, and they met here. Ireland is a small country, after all. I never thought to ask."

"Small, yes, compared to Pennsylvania, for example. But that doesn't mean it's all the same. We O'Sullivans are from County Cork. Our family has a distinguished history in Ireland, although perhaps not so much in more recent centuries. Mrs. O'Sullivan's family, the O'Callaghans, are also from Cork. Curious how she and I both came such a great distance only to meet here. We had some Sheehans in the county, I remember, but I don't know from where the sept hails originally."

Dan opened his mouth to speak, but then thought better

of asking what a sept was.

Mr. O'Sullivan continued, "I came over in May of 1912. Sailed out of Queenstown, on the *Laconia*. Just a month after the *Titanic* took the same route to disaster, mind you. Fortunately, I was a wee bit slow getting my affairs in order, so I did not have the misfortune to be on it." He smiled in Dan's direction as he paused to relight his pipe. "I had been to America once before, to escort my sister Mary here safely and ensure she did not fall in with the wrong sort. Well, she fell in with the Catholic sisters and became a nun herself. My work done, I returned to Ireland. But as the song goes, 'How Ya Gonna Keep Them Down on the Farm Once They've Seen Paree?' So back I came. My last night at home I took a knife to the kitchen cupboard and carved 'TO'S May 1912' inside it. My mother was none too pleased, but I wanted to leave some memory behind me." He blew into the pipe to make the bowl glow. Dan wondered if Mr. O'Sullivan were always so chatty when a man called on his daughter.

"My last sight of Ireland from the deck of the ship was of St. Colman's Cathedral, on the hill above Queenstown." He took a couple of puffs. "Its soaring spire somehow made me think of the angel with the flaming sword guarding the gates of Eden, as if driving me out, with the Statue of Liberty ready to welcome me on the other side. When I reached Philadelphia, I lived in my cousins' small extra room, so cramped the bed partially blocked the doorway. I didn't like being here, much, at first. I missed the lush green Irish countryside, and the more sedate pace of life in Kanturk. But then I met and married Mrs. O'Sullivan. That made everything alright."

He took another puff. "You should ask your parents about their history, Mr. Sheehan. It's important to know where you've come from and what they've been through. We don't each of us just burst on the world as a blank slate."

"No, sir."

"And what about yourself?" Mr. O'Sullivan asked as he dropped the match into the ashtray. "Where did you do your schooling?"

"I went to Boys Catholic and the Drexel Institute."

"Good schools, both. My boys go to Saint Joe's Prep. The Jesuits do them good. A couple of them are talking about entering the priesthood."

"That's wonderful."

"You're in the electrical business, I understand?"

"Yes, I have a repair service of my own. Besides Drexel, I learned a lot about electronics and radio during my time in the National Guard."

"Ah, the National Guard. Good experience is good to have. When was that?"

"I was in from thirty-three to thirty-six. I'm thinking

maybe to reenlist, what with things being the way they are in the world. Especially if we're going to have a draft anyway."

"Yes, these are troubled times." Mr. O'Sullivan sat quietly, apparently focused on his pipe.

Dan wished Margaret would hurry up. Ordinarily he felt comfortable making casual conversation with other men, but a conversation with a date's father was never casual.

"I've been crazy about electronics all my life," Dan began, just to make conversation. "I guess I got that from my father. I remember when he bought our first radio, in 1924, an RCA Radiola. Gee, was it expensive! Dad said he wanted it for the Republican National Convention. Said we'd be listening to history with the first broadcast from a political convention. But we all knew he just wanted to have a radio in the house. Who didn't? Boy, was it a beautiful machine! Not just the wood case but all the wires and tubes and wax inside that somehow pulled sound out of the ether. I was hooked. Of course, Dad almost killed me when he got home one evening and found me disassembling it to see how the whole thing worked —"

Mr. O'Sullivan was peering at him over the rim of his eyeglasses. "I'm sorry, sir. I guess I just let my enthusiasm get the better of me. I didn't mean to run on like that. Sometimes I forget not everyone shares the same interests that I do. I didn't mean to bore you."

"Not at all, Mr. Sheehan, not at all. We do indeed live in a time of great technological wonders. I myself saw neither a telephone nor an electric lamp until I was twenty years old. Our family lived in the countryside in Ireland. Sometimes with all the commotion the telephone causes around here, I almost wish it had never been invented."

Margaret entered the room and smiled at Dan. She wore a short-sleeved turquoise green dress belted at the waist with puffy shoulders. A small heart pendant hung from a chain around her neck. She had covered her hair with a turban hat.

"Well, daughter, don't you look lovely this evening!" Mr. O'Sullivan said. He looked from Margaret to Dan. "What do you think, Mr. Sheehan? Do you not agree?"

"Yes, yes, indeed I do," Dan managed to reply, taken aback by the transformation of the pretty salesgirl into a knockout.

"And what will you two be up to this evening?" Mr. O'Sullivan asked, a hint of fun in his voice.

"Well," said Dan, "I thought a little bite of dinner and then maybe a movie. *Knute Rockne, All American*, I think. If that's all right with Margie."

"Margie, is it? Well, that's no worse than the Peggy her girlfriends inflict on her. A movie about the Fighting Irish of Notre Dame. An excellent choice, although I was never clear on which county the Rocknes were from. Perhaps one of the northern ones."

Dan laughed politely while Margaret said, "Oh, Papa! That was silly the first time you told it!"

"Yes, daughter, I know. Have a good time, you two! And Mr. Sheehan, you will have Margaret home by midnight."

"Yes, sir."

Dan breathed a sigh once they were out on the street. Margaret laughed at him. "Papa's actually very sweet. He just likes to get the gentleman callers off on the right foot. He wasn't too hard on you, was he?"

"No, not at all. But even under the best of circumstances it's nerve-racking to make small talk with the father of the woman you're taking out."

"Oh, have you had a lot of those circumstances?" she smiled at him as they turned to walk down the street.

"Well, once or twice, maybe," he answered, abashed. "Is the *Rockne* film OK with you? I forgot to ask you the other night."

"Well, I'm not sure it's the most romantic movie for a first date . . ."

"Would you prefer to see something else?"

"Rose at the store said she really enjoyed *The Broadway Melody of 1940* with Fred Astaire and Eleanor Powell."

"Then *Broadway Melody* it is!"

From the beginning, Dan made it clear he intended to marry Margie. Margie made it equally clear she was not about to rush into anything.

One night, after they had been dating for almost a year, the couple was having dinner at Pasquale's, the little Italian restaurant that had become their regular spot. Outside, the wind gusted, and rain drummed against the windows. But inside, the mood was romantic with red-checked tablecloths and soft light from candles in straw-wrapped chianti bottles.

Dan placed his hand on Margie's. "Margie, you know I want to marry you. But you keep putting me off. Maybe I started in on you too quickly and that's scared you off. But that's the way I am. I make up my mind and stick with it. I'm serious. I love you and I want to marry you. You've told me you love me. Now please, please tell me you'll marry me."

Margie tried to draw her hand away, but Dan tightened his grip.

"I just don't know," she said. She reflected on their times together, good times. But was it the basis for a life together? She wasn't getting any younger, as her mother had pointed out more than once. Some of her friends rushed into marriage as if they were picking out a new dress. Why couldn't it be that easy for her?

"I do love you, Dan, but maybe it's just too soon to know."

"Too soon? You're twenty-four. I'm about to turn thirty." He looked away for a moment, then put both his hands on hers. "I've made up my mind. I'm not leaving the table tonight until I have an answer, one way or another. The whole world's at war, and America's going to be part of it soon enough. I can't drift along like this. Margie, will you marry me? Wait!" he said hurriedly as she started to speak. "It's a simple question with only two possible answers: yes or no. No maybes, ifs, ands, or buts. Will you marry me?"

Without thinking, he tightened his grip until she was tempted to cry out in pain. "Dan, I don't know what to say."

"Will you marry me, yes or no? Just to be clear, I will live with either answer. It's your choice. If it's yes, I'll be the happiest man in Philadelphia. If it's no, we'll pay the bill, go home, and I'll say goodnight and goodbye."

"You mean goodbye for good?"

"Yes, I mean it's over, if you say no. I want you to say yes."

Margie sat, not breathing, looking at him in silence, her eyes brimming with tears. He was a good man. She had no doubt he would make a good husband. If his patience had now run out, it was only because she had been happy to let the relationship drift without direction. Now she would have to decide its direction.

"All right," she exhaled at last. "Dan, I do love you. I will

81

marry you."

"Ah, My Little Margie, it does me good to hear you say that!"

British sink Nazi battleship *Bismarck* / Exciting new Nash Hurricane Power! You flash from 15 to 50 M.P.H. in 13 seconds! / Lindbergh accuses 'the British, the Jewish, and the Roosevelt Administration' of leading US to war / *Citizen Kane* flops at the box office / America runs on Bulova time / Roosevelt and Churchill release Atlantic Charter with postwar goals / Blended 33 times to make one great beer! Try Pabst Blue Ribbon and prove it! / Germany invades Soviet Union! / Roosevelt orders the seizure of all Japanese assets in US / Germans surround Leningrad.

# Wedding Bells

## 1941

"Ego conjungo vos in matrimonium in nomine Patris et Filii et Spiritus Sancti. I join you in matrimony: In the name of the Father and of the Son and of the Holy Ghost."

"Amen."

"May you be blessed in your children and may the love that you lavish on them be returned a hundredfold."

"Amen."

When the nuptial Mass ended, Dan and Margie turned to face the church pews. Dan wore a navy-blue suit, a white shirt, a paisley tie, and a white carnation boutonniere. Margie had on a knee-length velvet skirt and jacket and a wide-brimmed tam hat, all a deep lavender, and a white blouse. She had pinned a corsage of yellow carnations to her left lapel. Dan's best friend Guy Alfieri stood at his side as best man, and Margie's friend Rose Smith was her maid of honor.

There in the front row sat the two sets of parents, each flanked by their children. There were no other relatives on either side. Scattered among the remaining pews were friends and coworkers of the couple.

Hand-in-hand, Dan and Margie nodded and smiled their way down the aisle toward the ornate front doors. As they passed, people emptied the pews into the aisle behind them. Once the newlyweds reached the porch in front of Saint Madeleine Sophie's, they turned to greet the emerging well-wishers. The September day was warm with overcast skies.

"Best wishes! . . . Congratulations! . . . It was a lovely wedding! . . . You make such a lovely couple!" All the rote phrases, full of love and warmth and sincerity.

Father Lawton emerged from the church, still wearing his white vestments. He went up to the newlyweds and took Margie's hand.

"Ah, Margaret, I baptized you in this very church twenty-five years ago, and now here you are, all grown up and married! And to such a fine young man as Daniel! I am so happy for the both of you."

Margie smiled at the priest.

Dan, seeing his parents standing to one side, went over to them. His father smiled at him; his mother's face showed no expression. "So, what did you think?" he asked.

"You have our blessing, son, of course. We are very happy for you," his father said.

"I still think you should have asked Joe to be your best man," his mother commented, a little too loudly.

"Mother, we've been over it a thousand times. There is nothing that says a guy has to have his brother as his best man. We weren't all that close growing up, and we're not close now. Given our history, having Joe up there might have raised a snicker or two."

"But he's your brother!"

"Yes, he is. And Guy Alfieri is my best friend. I wanted him standing next to me. It's all water under the bridge, anyway. The wedding is over."

"Well, have it your way," she sniffed.

"Oh, Margaret," his father chided her, "don't spoil the beautiful day. You know how happy this day makes you, to see a son get married. First Joe, and now Dan, and no doubt Ed will soon follow behind them."

A beautiful day, no thanks to you two, or to Margie's parents, for that matter, Dan thought. For reasons that were not entirely clear, both sets of parents had resisted the marriage. Dan's mother didn't like the fact Margie worked as a salesgirl at Lit Brothers, or that her father ran the maintenance department there. She always managed to mention that Joe's new wife Mary's father was a lawyer with an office downtown. She was even willing to overlook Mary's family's English roots. La di da, Dan thought, and my father (your husband) used to make barrels for a living and now he's a plumber. So we can't really get our noses too high in the air, can we? We get enough of that from Mary's family.

Dan's mother also appeared to have developed a personal dislike for Margie, beyond her disregard for Margie's family. She had gotten the idea that Margie had a "loose" reputation, based upon a chance remark about the musical group that Margie had belonged to for a couple of years after high school.

His mother's seemingly innocent asides about her future daughter-in-law came to a head during a discussion among Margie, Mrs. O'Sullivan, and Dan's mother about the wedding dress. Dan didn't know exactly what transpired, but Margie was still furious when next she saw him. "Your mother as much as called me a tramp!" she exclaimed. "Of course, she did it in that way of hers that didn't leave me or Mama any room to respond, or if we had she'd just have gotten all innocent and say, 'Oh, my dear, I'm sure you misunderstood me.' Your father is a dear and it's harsh of me to say it, but I don't know how he has put up with her all these years."

"Yes," Dan agreed, "Mother does have her ways. It's nothing personal, really. She's that way with most people. And you're marrying me, not her."

"Yes, I am. But if she wants to treat me like a scarlet woman, I'll show her."

Dan looked across the church porch to where Margie now stood, looking aloof and serene, oblivious to the conversational chatter of the friends around her. She showed his mother, all right. He almost passed out when she bought that purple outfit and said she would get married in it. It left his mother speechless when she saw it. Dan wondered how many of the cheery folk here at the wedding were secretly wondering whether her choice of purple over white had some hidden meaning.

Margie's parents, less vocal with any objections, also showed little enthusiasm for their prospective son-in-law. They seemed to like Dan well enough when he and Margie were just dating, but their attitude turned a little cool when the couple announced the engagement.

Both the O'Sullivans and the Sheehans even hinted (separately, of course; they didn't talk to each other) that they might not attend the wedding, or that they would perhaps sit in the back of the church if they did come. Dan and Margie each made it clear to the parents that either action would be unforgiveable. Dan believed what finally got them into the front pew was the thought of the gossip they would cause otherwise.

Down at the curb, Guy and Dan's brothers and some other friends were tying cans and old shoes to the back bumper of the Packard sedan Dan had borrowed from a friend for the weekend.

Dan moved away from his parents, who were now talking to some neighbors, and crossed the porch to Margie. In passing, he heard Mary remark to Rose, "Yes, it was quite pleasant and intimate. I don't think the O'Sullivans could have afforded a big wedding. Now for Joe and me, my parents insisted . . ." The conversation faded behind him. That's Mary for you, he thought.

He took hold of Margie's elbow. "About time we hit the road, don't you think, wife?"

She turned to him with a smile. "Yes, husband. Let's go."

"We better say goodbye to all the parents."

The O'Sullivans smiled at them as they approached. Mrs. O'Sullivan had tears in her eyes. "Mama, Papa," Margie announced, "we're off." She put her hand to her neck. "Suddenly I'm surprised how emotional I feel."

"Yes, my dear," her mother said, stroking her arm and nodding towards Dan. "Your whole life has changed now, leaving our home, the house you've lived in your whole life, to set up a home with this man who is now your husband."

"May you know nothing but happiness from this day forward, the both of you," her father said. He embraced her, and then shook hands with Dan while she hugged her mother. "Be a good husband to our daughter, Dan. We know you are a good man."

"May all your troubles be little ones and all your little ones be trouble-free," Mrs. O'Sullivan added, clutching a linen handkerchief to her lips. She turned to her children who had gathered around. "Say goodbye to your big sister, all of you. She's Mrs. Sheehan now!"

Dan smiled and nodded and stepped back to guide Margie over to his parents and his brothers. At least they're smiling, too, he thought.

"This is it, Dad, Mother," Dan said. He kissed his mother on her forehead and shook his father's hand, and then gave his mother a second kiss.

"Best wishes to you both," his father murmured. "This is a very happy day."

"There's an old Irish saying, 'A man's best friend is his mother, until he meets his wife,'" Mrs. Sheehan said, putting her arms around Margie, who stiffened slightly as she cast a pleading eye in Dan's direction. "I will keep you both in my prayers."

When Mrs. Sheehan released her, Margie smiled and turned to shake hands with Mr. Sheehan. Dan shook hands with his brothers and Margie kissed each of them.

The couple found Father Lawton standing behind them, beaming. Margie said, "Thank you again for everything, Father. And, Father, before we go, will you give us one final blessing?" In some way she felt as if this blessing would be as important for their future as the wedding vows themselves.

"Certainly, Margaret."

The couple knelt on the steps. Father Lawton made the sign of the cross over them, saying, "May almighty God, Father, Son, and Holy Ghost, bless you, my children, for time and eternity, and may this blessing remain with you forever."

"Amen," they responded. The couple stood and headed down the steps toward the car.

Rice came flying at them from all directions. Guy ceremoniously opened the car's rear door and ushered them into the back seat. Dodging the rain of rice, he trotted around to the driver's side and got in. As he pressed the starter button, he turned to face them. "Ready?"

"Ready," Dan answered. He could hardly believe how happy he was at this moment, how lucky to have Margie as his bride. No matter what might come, he would always remember this day with joy.

Margie looked straight ahead with her hand on his left shoulder. Guy put the car into gear and drove off, the sounds of the rattling cans and bouncing shoes quickly drowning out the cries of the well-wishers left behind.

"Next stop, Atlantic City!" Guy said.

WILLIAM J. DUFFY

Stalingrad battle ends with Nazi surrender / Have you bought his ticket home? Buy War Bonds! / *Don't know why there's no sun up in the sky, Stormy Weather* / Mexico sentences Trotsky's assassin to 20 years / When you ride alone you ride with Hitler! Join a car-sharing club today! / German and Italian troops surrender in North Africa / 25,000 workers walk off line at Packard Motors to protest Negroes working alongside whites / Yamamoto, planner of Jap sneak attack on Pearl Harbor, killed when plane shot down / Meat is material of war. Use it wisely / Army troops move into Detroit to end 2 days of race riots.

## A Surprise for Margie

### 1943

The Japanese attacked Pearl Harbor a few months after Dan and Margie married. Dan went back into the National Guard, which allowed him to stay at home most of the time. They settled into a small apartment not far from the O'Sullivans' house. Little Peggy arrived a little more than a year later.

One day, Dan decided to buy a complete set of the

*Encyclopedia Americana*, all thirty volumes. As he carted the three boxes home in a taxi, he went over the various explanations to justify the expense: the good price, all this knowledge at their fingertips, handy when the kids went to school.

The taxi driver helped Dan unload the boxes onto the sidewalk in front of their building. When Dan got the first box up the stairs to their third-floor apartment, Margie was sitting in the cramped front room giving Peggy a bottle. She looked at him quizzically as he put the box down. "Dan, did you get the new ration book?"

"Yes, dear. Here it is." He handed it to her.

"Good. We're all out of sugar and coffee. By the way, your brother called. Mary's going to have a baby!"

"A cousin for little Peggy! That's great! I'll be right back." He hurried out of the apartment to collect the second box. On his return, Margie had put Peggy into her "crib," the bottom drawer of their bedroom dresser. By the third trip up with the heavy boxes, Dan was panting for air.

"Dan, what's in these boxes? Are they something for work?"

"It's an encyclopedia. For us, for Peggy, for our kids."

Margie frowned. "You must be joking."

"No, no, seriously. Tomorrow I'll pick up the two bookcases for them. They're included in the price!"

"How much did all this cost?"

"Fifty dollars."

"You spent fifty dollars on an encyclopedia?" Margie cried. "That's crazy! We can't afford that."

"Yes, we can. I saved this money special. I want to give our kids better opportunities than we had. When I was a kid, we had almost no books at home. My parents had no real education themselves. Your parents were the same. Mine wanted us to better ourselves, but they really didn't know how to go about helping us do that. We worked hard to learn. I just want our kids to be smarter than us. You do too, don't you?"

"Holy Mother of God, Dan, can we at least do that in some kind of logical order? Worrying about their school reports is a bit down the road, don't you think? Other than Peggy, we have to get them born first. Talk about putting the cart before the horse!"

Peggy started to cry. Margie went to her, shutting the bedroom door behind her. Dan sat down in the living room, his head in his hands. She always focused on the present, he thought. If only he could convince her to look to the future!

She came out of the bedroom to prepare another bottle for Peggy.

"Honey, I'm sorry," Dan said.

She ignored him and returned to the bedroom, again

closing the door. He sat there, staring at the three boxes.

When next she emerged, Dan looked up and asked, "Margie, what's for dinner?"

"I wouldn't know," she said, not looking at him. "Why don't you decide it for yourself?"

The next day, Dan went back to the store. The same clerk who had sold him the encyclopedia greeted him. Dan explained he would have to return it. The clerk expressed regret and said he could replace any defective volumes. Dan said there was nothing wrong with the books, it was just that the Sheehans had decided now was not the right time to buy an encyclopedia. The clerk reminded him that all sales were final, with no refunds or returns. He also helpfully recapped Dan's own arguments in favor of the purchase. "And remember," the clerk concluded, "the *Encyclopedia Americana* will send you an annual update, for a nominal fee, in perpetuity. I'm sure your wife will come to appreciate that, in the long run, you have made an excellent purchase!"

"I hope you're right. Thank you for your time."

Margie did not speak to Dan for two days. She took care of the baby and left everything else to him. Dan had many fine qualities, she thought, but it distressed her to know they came as part of a package with less desirable traits, such as a willingness to let hope substitute for reality. He would do things she objected to, and then make her feel guilty that she was not as carefree about the results as he was. The encyclopedia was a perfect example, something he'd probably joke about in years to come. "I bought this set for you kids," he would tell them one day. "Your mother didn't want me to. But I was planning for your future when you were still in the future!"

On the third morning, as Dan sipped the coffee he had boiled too long, Margie came out of the bedroom. Without any reference to what had happened, she resumed the normal life of the Sheehan household. Dan didn't know what to say, so he said nothing.

Nationalist Chinese flee to Formosa, Reds take mainland /
Philadelphia Eagles defeat Los Angeles Rams 14-0 to win
National Football League championship / Soviet blockade
of West Berlin ends / Don't miss *On the Town* with Gene
Kelly and Frank Sinatra! / Russia has the bomb / Jackie
Robinson named National League's Most Valuable Player /
Hi ho, Silver! ABC brings *The Lone Ranger* to television! /
Great Britain recognizes full independence of Republic of
Ireland / *Some enchanted evening you may see a stranger.*

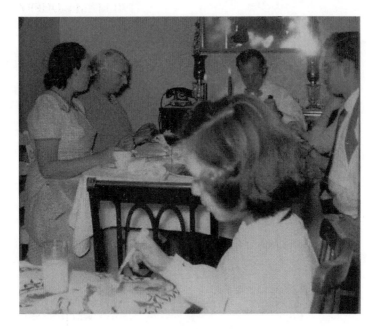

# A Christmas Story

## 1949

Margie was determined to make Christmas Day a success. She and Dan had at last escaped apartment living. The house they rented was a red brick colonial duplex, a yard both front and back, a first floor with a living room, dining room, and kitchen, and upstairs three bedrooms and a bathroom. Best of all, it had room enough to have people over, and today for the first time she was hosting her family in her own home. Already the cooking smells filled the house and brought back memories of earlier

Christmases on Pomona Terrace.

They were all here—her mother, her four brothers Michael, Denis, Joe, and Tim, and her sister Madeleine—all except Eileen, off to her fiancé's family for the day. And their father.

Timothy O'Sullivan had died in the spring of a bad heart. He went into the hospital one day, and two days later he was gone. He had his family around him when he died, except Margie, who was at home pregnant with Danny, the roughest of her three pregnancies.

"At the end, Papa couldn't speak," her mother told her later. "He looked around the room from one to the other of us with a puzzled look, as if something were missing. I think he was missing you, Margaret."

Danny had finally arrived in September, joining Peggy, now seven, and Jane, four.

Margie surveyed the downstairs. The dining room table was covered with the fine Irish linen tablecloth she had ironed and starched until it could stand on its own if necessary. Laid out on top of it were her best dishes and the new Waterford crystal. The table would hold eight, everybody except the two Sheehan daughters, who would sit at a card table in the living room. If little Danny were awake for the festivities, his crib awaited him in the corner.

The Christmas tree sat in the front window, a sad little

tree, but the lights and ornaments and tinsel Dan had decorated it with added all the magic necessary. Opened presents surrounded it. There were practical gifts like a new school uniform for Peggy and her first children's missal, and jumpers and blouses for Jane. Santa had also brought the girls a dollhouse, a Donald Duck xylophone pull toy, and Yakity Yak Talking Teeth (Dan's idea). Margie had gotten Dan some new work shirts and a few tools he had asked for, and he had splurged for the Waterford goblets now sitting on the table. For Danny, there was the American Flier train set which Dan had set up to encircle the tree.

Margie still couldn't decide which was crazier: the encyclopedia he bought Peggy when she was a year old or this train set for a three-month-old infant. She looked over to the encyclopedia in its bookcases. As long as the Sheehans had lived in an apartment, it had sat in its unopened boxes in the closet already too small to hold the clothes in it. Only when they moved into this house had Dan opened the boxes and set the books up. Margie had made no comment.

Her eye drifted to her mother, wearing a colorful Christmas apron over her plain dress. She had just come into the dining room from the kitchen to dish the canned cranberry into the cut glass dish on the table. How old her mother looked. Margie had never noticed that. How strange that you could see someone all the time, but never realize

102

they had changed, and suddenly you really saw them, as they were now, not what your memory remembered.

Mrs. O'Sullivan lifted her head and smiled in Margie's direction. "Come, Margaret, don't just stand there! I think everything is just about ready and time to serve."

Margie nodded in agreement and moved toward the kitchen. The rest of the family—Sheehans and O'Sullivans alike—had gone out front to build a snowman, leaving Margie and her mother to prepare the meal. "Will you call them all in, Mama? And get them all seated?"

"That I will. And don't worry—Madeleine and I will help serve."

Soon the quiet of the house gave way to a babble of conversation as the family came in and took their seats. Margie hoped the bedlam would not awaken little Danny upstairs.

"Dan, will you carve the turkey, please? And Tim, will you see that all the wine glasses are filled?"

Soon they were all seated, admiring the dishes of food arranged before them. A sudden quiet by unspoken agreement came over the group.

"Dan, will you say the Grace?" Margie asked.

Dan nodded toward Michael. "I know as head of the house it is my place, but I think on this special occasion we should ask Father Michael to do the honors."

There were murmurs of agreement around the table.

Michael, ordained a Franciscan priest two years earlier, appeared about to demur. But he bowed his head and said, "O Almighty God, the Savior of the world, Who hast nourished us with heavenly food, we give Thee thanks for the gift of this bodily refreshment which we have received from Thy bountiful mercy. Through Christ our Lord. Amen."

"Amen."

The hum of conversation resumed as the food got passed around. When everyone's plate was full, Dan stood up with his glass of wine. "I want to welcome you all to our home, our first Christmas in this house, hopefully the first of we hope many more. This has been an important year for our families. First, we lost—too soon—a good man, a good husband, a good father, Timothy O'Sullivan. Now he has gone to his Maker, and we will not forget him. Here's to Himself! May he rest in peace!"

"Amen." They all followed him as he took a drink.

"And God does not close a door, but He opens a window. This year He blessed us with young Daniel Joseph Sheehan, the Third."

"Hear, hear," the O'Sullivan brothers said.

Dropping his air of formality, Dan continued, "Now, Margie and I thought about naming young Danny in honor of his late grandfather who has just left us. And we thought that my father, even if it would have disappointed him, would have understood the sentiment."

He paused dramatically. "But then we considered what my *mother* would say —"

Peals of laughter engulfed the table.

"So it's Daniel Joseph Sheehan, the Third, after all! Now, now, quiet down." Dan fanned his hand. "But we promise you this — the next Sheehan boy will be Timothy John Sheehan!"

"Bravo!" they chorused.

Everyone turned their attention to the food.

"So, Michael," Dan asked, "when do you leave?"

"I sail from New York in early February and arrive a week later." Michael was on his way to Brazil to teach in a local college.

"When Denis gets ordained in the spring, we'll have two priests in the family," Madeleine said.

"What about you two?" Dan turned to the other brothers, who were both in college. "Will Holy Mother Church get dealt four of a kind with the O'Sullivan boys?"

"Not us!" Tim replied. "I think the O'Sullivans have given the Church our share of priests."

"Somebody has to carry on the O'Sullivan name," Joe added.

"Daniel," Mrs. O'Sullivan said, "how are your parents?"

"They're just fine. They're with my brother Joe and his wife Mary today."

Peggy's voice came from the other room. "Grandmother Sheehan likes them better than us."

"Quiet, Peggy!" Margie said. "No comments from the peanut gallery!" Even if they were true, she thought.

"Give them my regards when you speak to them," Mrs. O'Sullivan said, as if there had been no interruption. Suddenly tears filled her eyes.

"Mama, what is it?" Margie asked in alarm.

Mrs. O'Sullivan waved her hand dismissively. "Oh, don't mind this old woman. I'm all right. I'm just so very happy to be here with you all, and just so unhappy Papa is not here with us."

"That's the way we all feel!" Margie said, nodding at her siblings to agree.

"To think of it! This is the first Christmas since I married your Papa that we are not having Christmas dinner on Pomona Terrace. That first Christmas, it was just the two of us. Of course, we had no money then. But we were so happy! The second Christmas, you had joined us, Margaret. You were only a month old, then, and we were both amazed at this new creature God had given us. As the years went by, the rest of you appeared, one by one. And I think of your brother John, who only Margaret knew because he died so young, that last Christmas before he died, with Michael just a little baby — it's just that I have all these memories washing over me. And here I sit with you all at my daughter and her husband's table, and all of you all grown up and getting on with your own lives. And my Tim gone from me."

Margie wrapped her arms around her mother. "We love you, Mama. We are so happy to have you here. And we all miss Papa terribly."

"Mama, tell us again how you met Papa," said Madeleine. "It is a Christmas story, after all."

Mrs. O'Sullivan laughed as she wiped a tear from her eye. "That it is, indeed. And one you've heard a million times. But why rehash what you all already know?"

"Because it's Christmas!" Tim said.

"Because I've never heard the story," Dan added.

"Oh, very well, humor an old woman!" Her face lit up as the memory came back. "It was Christmas Eve, 1914. I was working as a live-in housekeeper for a family in Rittenhouse Square. They were good enough to let me out of the house for a few hours to meet my sister Margaret Mary (God rest her soul these twenty years) at Lit Brothers so we could exchange presents. Margaret Mary worked at a fine house out on the Main Line, so we rarely saw each other. But when I got to the store, it had already closed, early, it being Christmas Eve. How silly of us not to have thought of that! I didn't know what to do. We had planned to meet in the tearoom. I could wait for Margaret Mary on the street, but by which entrance? Just then, the door near where I was standing opened and out came a tall, good-looking young man."

"Papa!" the O'Sullivan children chorused.

"Excuse me," Dan said, bewildered. "Are you telling me you met Mr. O'Sullivan at Lit Brothers?" Mrs. O'Sullivan sparkled with mirth. "I've seen that movie!"

"No, dear," Margie said. "You saw the 1940 remake, with Fred Astaire and Ginger Rogers playing the two of us. Go on, Mama."

"He walked right up to me — swaggered, really, like the cat with the canary — and said, 'Would you be wanting some assistance then, Miss?' Well, his tone was almost insolent, and I had half a mind to tell him to take his cheek elsewhere when he added, 'Perhaps you'd care to step into our tearoom where your sister awaits?' But of course Margaret Mary had arrived before me, and Mr. O'Sullivan — who was busy locking up, him being in the maintenance department — saw her in her distress and had let her in. When she explained, he sat her down in the tearoom and wandered from entrance to entrance until he found me.

"So, there we sat, the whole empty building to ourselves, having our cup of tea courtesy of Mr. O'Sullivan and exchanging our little presents. It was grand! Of course, the tea was weak—your Papa never could make a decent cup—but never the mind."

"But, Mama," Madeleine said, "there were the two of you. How did Papa end up choosing you over Aunt Margaret?"

Mrs. O'Sullivan huffed. "Him choose? *I* did the choosing! Margaret Mary already had her beau, your Uncle William, God rest his soul, although it would be another year before they married. But your Papa made quite the impression on me that first day, that he did. And then we discovered we had lived no more than ten miles apart from each other back in Ireland! And us never meeting until that Christmas Eve!"

"What a lovely story!" Dan said. "Shall I tell Margie's and my story?"

"Not if it involves another rendition of 'My Little Margie,'" his wife said as she passed the mashed potatoes for second helpings.

Later that evening, with the O'Sullivans departed and the Sheehan children in bed, Margie and Dan sat on the sofa, their arms around each other. The bulbs on the Christmas tree provided the only light in the room.

"It was a beautiful meal, Margie."

"I'm glad it went so well. I was so nervous."

"Nothing to be nervous about! It was all family. It was just like previous years at your parents' house, only in a different location."

She punched him in the shoulder. "That's easy for you to say. All you had to do was tell people where to get their drinks. And joking around with those stupid talking teeth! I mean—first of all, none of us has ever had Christmas without Papa before! I think we've already gotten pretty used to his absence from our everyday lives after all these months, but on a holiday like today! It was the same way at Thanksgiving. Happy and sad, all at the same time. And I hope Mama didn't think I was trying to push her out of the way and take charge by having dinner here."

"Let me reassure you on that front. You mother told me how proud she was to see you come into your own like you did today."

Margie leaned her head on his shoulder. "It was lovely, wasn't it? And fun. And our own house! I do love it. I can see us being happy here for many years to come."

Dan kissed her on the forehead. "I can too, dear."

Supreme Court declares separate but equal public schools unconstitutional / I dreamed I was at a masquerade ball in my Maidenform bra! / Senator McCarthy investigates US Army, says soft on communism / Hey, kids! What time is it? It's Howdy Doody time! / Fallout from A-bomb test in Nevada reaches as far as St. George, Utah / *Life could be a dream (sh-boom) if only all my plans would come true (sh-boom)* / Ellis Island, longtime gateway to the US, closes / *It's delightful, it's de-lovely, it's DeSoto!* / French defeated at Dien Bien Phu, unlikely to hold Indochina.

## Dan Gets a Job

### 1954

D an wanted to parlay his knowledge of electronics and radio into a better paying career. His brother Joe had gone to work at Chrysler's Newark Assembly plant in Delaware in 1951, a couple of years after it opened. Joe told Dan that Chrysler was hiring and the jobs paid well. So one morning, with the girls off to school and the next-door neighbor ready to watch Danny when he got home from kindergarten, Dan and Margie, with baby Timmy in her lap, drove down U.S. 1 to Newark in the Willys-Overland panel truck with *Sheehan's Electrical Service* on the side. The bare-

112

bones truck was uncomfortable, especially on a long drive, but it served his business purposes.

Dan pretended to play with a nonexistent radio, punching imaginary station buttons on the dashboard with his fingers while warbling "That's Amore" and "Stranger in Paradise." Margie kept her fingertips on the dashboard to steady herself as the truck went around curves. She wished he would stop the antics and focus on his driving. She hesitated to say anything for fear it would only encourage him. And Timmy enjoyed watching his father perform.

Dan had on his Sunday-best suit and tie. Margie wore a nice dress with hat and gloves, as if she were on her way to shop at the big stores downtown. She didn't know why she had decided to come — maybe just the chance for a little road trip on a beautiful day or to escape the daily grind of running a household.

When they reached the plant, Margie and Timmy waited in the truck while Dan disappeared inside the sprawling facility. It was a pleasant spring day, with fleecy clouds scattered against the blue sky. Margie enjoyed the cool breeze that blew through the window as she watched Timmy occupy himself with the buttons and knobs on the dashboard.

After a couple of hours, she started to fret and he started to get fussy. What could be taking Dan so long? She regretted coming. She had wasted the day, and Timmy would almost certainly make the drive home an unpleasant ordeal. She was about to get out of the truck and go in search of Dan when he returned, a dazed look on his face.

"They hired me!" he said.

"That's wonderful, Dan!" Her surprise overcame her frustration.

"It's more than wonderful. They didn't hire me to wire radios or lay phone lines or work on the factory floor. They hired me for an office job, an engineer job. A white-collar job! We were talking about this and that and I went into my engineering background and my radio work with the National Guard during the war, and suddenly the interviewer stopped me and said I was too qualified for the position we were talking about. He offered me a full-fledged engineer's job, on Chrysler's missile program."

"Missiles? Oh, my word! Who would have thought?"

"There's one called the Redstone, which I guess we cribbed from the Nazis' V-2, and they're starting one called Jupiter. It's like the science fiction stories I read growing up. I may even meet Wernher von Braun someday!"

"It all sounds so World of Tomorrow."

Dan's smile faded. "Just one other thing. The job's in Detroit."

"What? Detroit?" She tried to keep the tension out of her

114

voice. They had never discussed anything about moving halfway across the country.

"I'll be working at the Chrysler Tank Assembly in Warren, outside of Detroit."

Margie looked at him blankly. She had been born in Philadelphia. She had grown up in Philadelphia. She had always assumed she would die in Philadelphia. "But I don't want to uproot the children. I don't want to leave my family."

"But the opportunity is just too good. I can't pass it up."

Margie fidgeted with Timmy's shirt. In the end, Dan would do what he wanted. "Let's go home," she said.

When Margie's mother heard the move announced at a family gathering, she commented, "So, Margaret, you'll get to Michigan at last."

Dan was about to ask what she meant when his own mother asked querulously, "What about the Indians? Won't it be dangerous?"

In the ensuing laughter, Dan said, "Mother, this is the twentieth century. Things have changed since you came over from Ireland a hundred years or so ago! There are no Indians in Michigan."

# Moving to the Motor City

## 1954

Dan went to Detroit ahead of the rest of the family. For the first time he had a steady job with good pay, benefits, and a pension, and a new-fangled title of aerospace engineer.

He settled into a motel that had just opened near the Chrysler plant. As soon as he cashed his first paycheck, he went out and bought a brand-new cream-colored Plymouth station wagon. He would have preferred a Ford, but in Detroit you could hardly work for one of the auto companies and drive a competitor's product. Still, he was pleased with the size of the car – plenty of room for the whole family!

He and Margie had decided to rent a house at first, to give them time to get to know Detroit and save some money. He talked to realtors all over the metropolitan area.

"Renting to a family with four children, well, that really complicates things," they told him.

"How can that be legal?" Dan asked.

"Property owners can decide who they want to rent to. They don't have to give a reason."

One day Dan stopped at a new subdivision in Royal Oak on Woodward Avenue just north of Thirteen Mile Road.

He had quickly learned Woodward's importance in Detroit's geography. Starting at the Detroit River downtown, its twenty miles of pavement rolled northwest past skyscrapers, stores, restaurants, old mansions, gas stations, factories, parking lots, motels, and parks, all the way to downtown Pontiac. It split the city and its suburbs into the East side and the West side. For its entire length it was a broad thoroughfare with four busy traffic lanes in each direction. North of Six Mile Road, Woodward became a boulevard, with the lanes separated by a median strip. In some areas, the median was paved for customer parking for the stores lining the street. For most of its length, it remained a grassy strip dotted with trees.

Detroit had other major avenues, all also radiating out from the downtown: Jefferson and Gratiot on the east side,

Michigan and Grand River on the west. But Woodward Avenue was Detroit's main street.

In the subdivision Dan now pulled into, rows of almost identical brand-new Cape Cods and cottages lined the straight streets. Some lawns were covered with grass and some were still just mud and construction debris. A small elm sapling sat in front of each house between the sidewalk and the curb. Three old-fashioned two-story houses towered among the newcomers, representing the remnant of an earlier development that had failed in the Great Depression. It was a sunny day in early summer, a pleasant contrast to the cool, wet weather Dan had mostly experienced since his arrival.

The sales agent greeted him as he walked into the model home on Darby Road, the first house off Woodward. "Welcome! I'm Henry Gavin. Looking to move to the suburbs from the big city, are you?"

Gavin was a short young man, a little on the heavy side, with well-shined shoes, a suit in need of pressing, a wrinkled white shirt, and a flashy bowtie.

"Dan Sheehan," Dan replied as they shook hands. "No, we're coming here from Philadelphia."

"Welcome to Detroit! You couldn't have come at a better time. The whole area is booming! The 1950 census said Detroit had 1.8 million people. It's probably up to two million by now. The suburbs have another million and a half people. Construction everywhere! Some big urban renewal projects in the city, cleaning up the slums. And they're building a Civic Center down on the riverfront. That dairy farm you probably passed at Woodward and Thirteen Mile? That's going to become a shopping center, with a J.C. Penney and a Kroger's. Just beyond it will be the new Beaumont Hospital. You'll want to check out the big Northland Shopping Center that just opened up over in Southfield. It's incredible! Nothing like it anywhere in the country. Practically an entire city of shops! Maybe you saw the articles about it in *Time* and *Look*? The J.L. Hudson store there is almost as nice as the main store downtown."

"The Hudson store? You mean, the car company?"

Gavin hesitated a second before he grasped the source of Dan's confusion. "No, no, Hudson's, the big department store downtown, not the carmaker. But old J.L. Hudson did give some financial backing to the car company when it started up. Will you be working downtown? They're building expressways to cut down the drive time between here and there."

"No, I'm over at Chrysler in Warren."

"Oh, that's only a few miles away. Not a bad commute at all. And better living here in the suburbs than in the city. You won't have any coloreds next door. Now if you go over to Southfield, you're sure to have some Jew neighbors."

Dan looked at Gavin impassively. He didn't think of himself as a bleeding heart, but the casual racism of everyday life always surprised him. That, and the assumption by the Henry Gavins of the world that Dan would not take offense.

"Better you're at Chrysler than, say, Hudson, speaking of Hudson," Gavin continued. "They claim this merger with Nash is going to turn Hudson around and make it profitable again. But I bet it will turn out to be one more company squeezed to death by the Big Three." Gavin rubbed his hands together. "So, let me tell you about the features we have here and the various options. We've sold most of the houses, but there are still some nice choices left."

Dan held up a hand to stop Gavin from plunging on. "Do you have any for rent?"

Gavin stopped his pitch. "Well, no. We're into sales, not rentals." He hesitated. "But how about this house we're standing in? It's the model home. The company hasn't been able to sell it because it's so close to Woodward Avenue."

"Not to mention the Shell gas station next door and the bar and grill across the street."

"Well, that's why we're having trouble selling it," the agent replied. "But since it's the model home, the builder actually put a little more care into its construction. If you were willing to rent it, I could try to get you a good deal. In fact, I'm sure I could get you a good deal."

"By the way, my wife and I have four children."

"Yikes!" Gavin blurted out. "Well, that doesn't make things any easier, does it? Still, we're trying to wrap this subdivision up and get on to the next project. Hard to keep up with the demand. Let me talk to the boss and see if we can't work something out. And for you Catholics, Father Coughlin's Shrine is just down the road at Twelve Mile."

"What makes you think we're Catholic?" Dan was just playing with Gavin, but he couldn't resist the opportunity to put him on the spot.

The realtor caught his breath. "Oh, I'm sorry, I just, it's just, I just assumed with the name Sheehan and four kids —"

Dan laughed. "Well, in fact, we are Catholic. And my parents and my wife's parents listened to Father Coughlin's radio program back in the thirties. My wife will be happy to hear the Shrine is so close."

After talking to Gavin, Dan tried a few more leads on rentals, none of which panned out. So, he rented the model home that wouldn't sell from Gavin's company. When he signed the rental agreement, Dan knew Margie might still be unhappy, the Shrine's proximity notwithstanding.

When the day came for the family to arrive, Dan drove the long distance out to Willow Run Airport to pick them up. He was glad Detroit was welcoming his family with a warm, sunny day.

From the gate, he watched the Northwest Orient DC-7 land and taxi toward the terminal. The ground crew pushed the rolling stairs to the plane's side. After they were locked in place, the plane's door opened. Several businessmen stepped out first and headed across the tarmac. Then came Margie, with Timmy in her arms and the other children trailing behind.

"Daddy!" the children all broke into a run when they saw him. Even two-year-old Timmy insisted on getting down and toddling over.

"Hello, my darlings!" Dan cried, wrapping his arms around as many of them as he could. He had not seen them in two months. He stood up to hug Margie. "Welcome to Detroit, dear. Welcome home!"

She briefly returned his embrace. "Please, Dan. It's been a hard day. I'm sorry we didn't take the train after all. It was a miserable flight. I have a splitting headache from the drone of the propellers." She pointed to wet spots on her jacket. "Poor little Timmy vomited every time the plane pitched up or down. I tried to clean us up a bit, but. So much for the momentous occasion of our first airplane flight! Let's just get our bags and go."

After the family collected their luggage, Dan led them out to the parking lot and loaded everybody and their bags into the station wagon. They headed east on the Detroit Industrial Freeway, Dan and Margie in the front seat with Timmy between them, Danny and the girls in the back seat, and their luggage in the cargo area.

"This is a nice car, Dan," Margie said. "A nice, brand-new car." She addressed the children. "Our family never had a car when I was growing up. We got around by bus and trolley. And since your father and I got married, we've only had second-hand cars."

Peggy sniffed. "Don't you mean third-hand? Remember that old Packard that broke down after church? There we all sat in the parking lot while everybody else went home and Daddy's suit got all dirty while he fixed it."

"None of that with this car, kids!" Dan rapped his knuckles on the hard metal of the dashboard. "This is solidly built and'll serve the Sheehans well."

"Everything's so flat here," Danny said, staring out the window. "Did God run out of hills before He made this part of the country?"

Dan laughed. "No, son. Glaciers hundreds of feet thick covered this part of the country during the Ice Age. The weight of the ice pressed the ground level down like a steamroller."

"The ice isn't coming back, is it?" Jane asked.

"No, not an ice age. But you just wait till winter. We'll

have plenty of snow and ice then!"

They turned off the freeway onto Southfield Road, a four-lane north-south road with a traffic light every mile or so. Dan pointed at a building skeleton in the middle of a field off to the right. "Look there. That's going to be Ford's new World Headquarters. It'll be all glass and steel! Just about as modern as you can get. And you can't see it from here, but on the other side of the road behind those trees are the Ford Museum and Greenfield Village, loaded with historic old buildings and cars and machinery. The kids will love it there!" He felt like Gavin, trying to sell a reluctant customer on the glories of metropolitan Detroit.

"Are we in Detroit?" Margie asked.

"No, we're in Dearborn, just west of it. Henry Ford grew up around here, and Ford's big River Rouge complex is only a couple of miles behind us. Maybe we'll take the kids on a tour there one day."

"Daddy," Jane asked, "does Mr. Ford own everything around here?"

"No, darling," he said, laughing. "It just seems that way! And actually, it's Ford the company, not Ford the man. Old Mr. Ford died about seven years ago."

"Where did the riots happen?" Margie whispered.

"We can hear you!" Danny said.

"The race riots? You mean back in the war?" Dan said.

"They were miles away from here, downtown, I think, in the colored neighborhoods. But you don't need to worry about riots. Detroit has changed a lot since then. There's no more racial tension here than there is in Philadelphia."

Margie frowned at him. "Am I supposed to find that reassuring?"

The farther north they drove, the more built up were the areas they passed. They saw block after block of new houses as they passed Six Mile Road and Seven Mile Road.

As they crossed Eight Mile Road, Dan said, "See, there to the right? That's the Northland Center."

They all looked at the collection of long, low boxy buildings surrounded by large parking lots.

"It just opened a few months ago. It has all the major Detroit stores, just like downtown but only half as far from our house! And acres and acres of parking."

Dan kept up a steady chatter of how wonderful living in Royal Oak would be, with the Detroit Zoo just a few miles down Woodward Avenue at Ten Mile and Canada just across the river and beautiful lakes everywhere.

"Somebody sure put a lot of effort into naming the streets, didn't they, with all these Mile Roads?" Peggy said.

"Well," Dan replied, "you have to admit you'll always be able to tell where you are!"

"Sure, in Detroit."

They took Southfield to Twelve Mile, and Twelve Mile east to Woodward. As they turned north on Woodward, Dan pointed at a church in front of them. "There it is, Margie! The Shrine of the Little Flower. Isn't it gorgeous?"

Margie and the children goggled. A tall limestone tower with a thirty-foot carving of Jesus on the Cross stood in front of the octagonal nave, the whole church designed in a zig-zag architectural style.

"My, it's beautiful!" Margie said. It seemed to Dan as if this were the first sight to move her. "It's like finding an old friend to greet me! Imagine all the times we listened to Father Coughlin on the radio, it was coming from right here! Is the Shrine the parish we'll be in?"

"Yes, indeed, I wouldn't have it any other way! It's only a little more than a mile from the house."

They drove north and turned right at Darby. Dan pulled the car into the driveway and the family got out. The boys ran around the front yard while the girls stood looking at the house.

Dan watched Margie as she turned slowly around to take in the scene. He had mailed her photos of the house a couple of weeks earlier, so she knew what it looked like. But she hadn't said anything about it, good or bad.

Her gaze lingered for a moment on the bar across the street and then swept past the gas station. She focused on the house, built of red brick with white clapboard gables at the ends of the shingled, dormerless roof. A third, smaller gable was positioned at a right angle over the living room, facing the street.

"It's a pretty house," Margie said. "It's nice they've got some plants in the ground. Makes it feel more lived-in."

Shouts echoed as the boys discovered the big backyard.

"Yes," Dan breathed a sigh of relief. "Since it was the model home, they did a good job landscaping the place. Shall we go in and see the inside?"

"Let's," Margie said. "When do the movers arrive?"

"Tomorrow morning."

"So just one night camping out on the floor."

Two concrete steps led up to a small concrete stoop. Inside the front door a narrow vestibule held a coat closet to the right. A half wall topped by an opaque glass partition lay straight ahead, with the entrance into the living room to the left.

"We can hang the small crucifix there," Margie said, pointing at a spot on the wall next to the front door.

The rectangular living room had a large, modern picture window facing the front yard, a coved ceiling, and a hardwood floor. A discreetly placed weeping willow shielded the picture window's view of the bar catty-corner across the street. From the living room, the dining alcove lay to the right, separated from the vestibule by the half wall.

"The dining area will be a little tight," Margie murmured to herself. "I wonder if we might try putting the dining table someplace else."

Beyond the dining alcove, at the back of the house, the large, square kitchen had a linoleum floor, an electric stove, a refrigerator, white metal cabinetry, and a sink under a window that looked into the backyard.

"Well, plenty of space for a table in here," Margie said. "Maybe we'll just plan to eat in here most of the time."

A small hall at the opposite end of the living room was dotted by doors to the two bedrooms, the bathroom, a linen closet, and the attic stairs. The larger of the two bedrooms had windows on two walls and space enough for a queen-size bed and a couple of dressers. A large double-hung window faced the side yard, and two smaller windows sat high on the wall facing the front yard. In one corner was a small closet.

"I thought the boys could have this bedroom in front," Dan said. This was an idea he had floated previously when he sent the photos, so she had had time to consider and reject the idea.

"No. It's the larger bedroom. It will be ours."

"Then put them in the other bedroom and let the girls have the upstairs?"

"We'll see." They walked up the stairs to the sloped-ceiling attic. The builder had finished it with knotty pine walls and a hardwood floor. "This is a nice, big space," she said, looking around. "There's plenty of room for all the children up here."

"But it's one big room," Dan protested. "We can't expect the girls to share it with the boys!"

"Of course not," Margie agreed. "We'll get somebody to put up a wall to divide it into two rooms. That way we can make the second bedroom downstairs the formal dining room, instead of squeezing the new dining set into that alcove in the living room."

"But, Margie, we're only renting the place!"

"I doubt the landlord will object to our making such an obvious improvement, particularly if *we* pay for it."

"You're probably right, dear," Dan said. "Whatever you say."

As they turned to go back downstairs, Margie pointed at the blank wall above the stairwell. "That's where we'll put Mama's big crucifix."

She hadn't been sure what to do with the three-foot-long crucifix her mother had given her as a going-away present. Margie preferred her bric-a-brac on a smaller scale.

"You don't think all that blood will scare the children every time they head down the stairs?" Dan teased.

"Don't be blasphemous. I could hang it in the living room, you know."

"OK! Put it here in the stairwell."

They made their way down the stairs and through the living room and kitchen. Two steps led down from the kitchen to the backdoor landing and its milk chute, and to the wooden basement stairs. The basement was an unfinished space with a washing machine and two laundry tubs to one side of the stairs and the furnace to the other. Under the front stoop was a small root cellar.

"I've never had such a big laundry area, even in my parents' house!" Margie said. "Plenty of room to hang clothes lines when the weather's bad."

"And plenty of room for Danny's train set!" Dan replied. "Let's take a look at the backyard." He led the way out the back door. "I'm going to build a brick barbecue right there." He pointed to a spot in the middle of the yard. "We'll set up a picnic table so we can eat outside in the nice weather."

"Build a barbecue?" Margie laughed. "But, Dan, we're only renting the place!"

"Touché, dear, touché."

No matter what shape your stomach's in, when it gets out
of shape, take Alka-Seltzer / Polio vaccine approved /
*Davy, Davy Crockett, king of the wild frontier* / Red Wings win
Stanley Cup for 7th time / Time now for *Lunch With Soupy
Sales* here on WXYZ-TV / Coloreds boycott city busses in
Montgomery, Alabama, following Negress's arrest / Rock-
and-roll is a musical fad leading its young devotees back to
the jungle and animalism / *Que sera, sera, whatever will be,
will be* / Will the Lions repeat their championship
performance next season? / Walt Disney brings his magic
to the TV screen! Don't miss *The Mickey Mouse Club* on
ABC-TV!

# The Sheehans Go Camping

## 1955-1958

Among Dan's happiest memories of the first few years in Michigan were those of the camping trips Up North.

Dan didn't know what to expect when he first broached the idea to Margie. "I have a week off this summer," he said as an introduction. "That's one of the benefits of not being self-employed. I was thinking we should all get out and see something of this part of the world, maybe go camping along Lake Huron or Lake Michigan. There are a bunch of state parks to choose from."

Margie looked at him for a moment. "That might be fun. The boys will love it. The girls, maybe, I don't know. Where did you say you wanted to go?"

"Well, I haven't thought that far ahead. Maybe you might call the AAA Office for some ideas?"

"How about northern Michigan?" Margie said. "I've heard it's beautiful up there."

"Yeah, sure!" Dan answered, surprised at her sudden enthusiasm.

Margie visited AAA the next day and got information and maps on the area around the Straits of Mackinac, where Lakes Huron and Michigan meet. Traverse City State Park on the eastern arm of the Grand Traverse Bay, with communal showers and toilets just a short walk away from the campsite and no electricity, became the Sheehans' summer destination for the next few years.

Dan had acquired some surplus tents in his National Guard days during World War Two. He added cots, stools, utensils, lamps, and a stove acquired at the Army Navy surplus store. He whistled as he set up the tents in the yard a week early to air them out. He made detailed shopping lists to make sure they had everything they would need: canned goods, flashlight batteries, and stove fuel. He and Margie would pack the Plymouth the night before, with an occasional assist from a couple of the children, until there was hardly room for the family. The back end of the station wagon: full. The rack on the roof: full. The small trailer: full.

They set out from Royal Oak early in the morning in order to arrive in Traverse City by nightfall. Once they got north of Saginaw, U.S. 10 narrowed to only two lanes. The Standard Oil map still called the road an "Interstate" highway, back before the country started building I-75 and the other true interstates.

This was the kind of life Dan had dreamed of as a boy growing up near the Philadelphia docks. It was wonderful to be on the open road, he and Margie and one of the children in the front seat, the other three in the back, off for a week of relaxation. Somehow the unpleasant experiences became the stories always retold. One year they had a flat tire on the road, and everything had to be unloaded to get to the spare tire under the floor of the car's cargo area. Another time the bamboo fishing poles on the roof tore loose and went hurtling into the traffic behind them.

They would stop for lunch about halfway, at a picnic ground by the side of the highway near Herrick. They'd claim an available picnic table, preferably one under a tree, and eat the sandwiches and potato salad Margie had loaded into the ice chest back in Royal Oak. Even with the traffic noise from the highway, Dan thought it a pretty spot.

He enjoyed the drive. Not even the backed-up traffic in the small towns along the way bothered him. Sometimes one or another of the kids would grow snappish; sometimes

Margie would sit for hours without speaking, lost in her thoughts. It was all just part of the experience.

When they reached the state park, the family members each had their roles for setting up camp. Danny and Timmy helped (as best they could) dig drainage ditches and raise the tents. The girls helped Margie unpack the clothes and food from the car.

They had to cross the highway to get to the bay to go swimming. Not that Margie would go in the water. This was not the Jersey shore. But the children were oblivious to the frigid cold of Grand Traverse Bay, which never warmed even on the hottest summer day. They loved the water. Sometimes Dan would join them in it.

From their base camp, the Sheehans made expeditions to places like Mackinac Island, which had no motor vehicles and people got around by horse or bicycle. The island even smelled different, with no mechanical exhaust, just the odor of horses in the air. "Please don't drop me in the horse poo, Daddy!" Timmy screamed one time as he rode in the basket on the front of Dan's rented bike. The family would stop by the island's Grand Hotel and sit on its long Front Porch and look out over the blue waters of Lake Huron.

They would visit Fort Michilimackinac to watch battle reenactments and listen to the guides talk about the colonial struggles between the French and the British. They would make an annual excursion to the Interlochen summer music camp, where students from around the world came to improve their skills. Some years they took the ferry across the Straits to St. Ignace in the Upper Peninsula, going as far as the Soo Locks linking Lake Superior and Lake Huron. Mackinac Bridge connecting Michigan's two peninsulas was still under construction, with only its two towers soaring out of the water like skyscrapers, waiting for the suspension bridge to join them together.

After a few years, Margie began to prefer trips back east to visit her family, and the girls lost what little interest they had in camping. So, the vacations stopped.

# An Interlochen Story

## 1957

Peggy hated the summer camping vacations from the very first. A week of nothing but round-the-clock family togetherness under primitive conditions. Other girls went to summer camp with their friends and got away from their families. Not Peggy. She couldn't even make friends here. If she so much as smiled at a boy on the beach, her mother came unglued. She'd quick tell Peggy to get her something or to watch Timmy.

And the day-long drive there and back! The six Sheehans crammed in that ugly station wagon for hours. Sometimes a

137

breeze might blow through the open windows. Otherwise, the car baked them like an oven. Visiting the "ladies' room" along the way was a nightmare — nothing but poorly maintained outhouses.

One day Up North, wearing a two-piece black-and-white polka dot swimsuit and sandals, Peggy went into the beach gift shop to get some suntan lotion. The shop was small and shabby and had soft drinks, candy, some magazines, local preserves, cosmetics, a swimsuit section with too many empty hangers, and cheap made-in-Japan souvenirs.

Behind the counter stood a tall, good-looking boy with curly black hair. Peggy fanned herself with her floppy yellow sun hat as she pretended to consider the various lotion choices.

"How long you here for?" the boy asked as she paid for her choice. "You with friends, or what?"

"I came with my family. We're here till Monday."

"Tell you what. There's gonna be a beach cookout Friday night, with a bonfire. Lots of kids. Maybe you'd like to come along?"

Peggy gave the boy a closer look. He had long, lovely eyelashes, a strong chin, and very kissable lips. So what if he was just a store clerk? Maybe he went to the University of Michigan or some other big school. An evening in his company — and other young people! — would beat one more

138

night around the family campfire.

"That sounds kinda fun."

"I get off work at seven that night. Why don't you meet me here?"

Just then Jane stuck her head in the door, her face hidden behind a low-slung conical hat with built-in sunglasses. "Peggy, come on! Mother says now."

Ignoring her, Peggy said, "I'll try to make it."

When Friday came, their mother decided the family would spend the afternoon at the music school in Interlochen, twenty miles away. "Ah, Ma, do we hafta?" Danny wailed.

"Why can't we go to the beach instead?" Peggy said, feeling her temper beginning to boil. Just another example of how her mother could spoil things without even trying. But they should still get back to Traverse City in time for the cookout.

As the afternoon at Interlochen dragged on, Peggy said almost nothing, giving only clipped responses when directly addressed.

"Look!" their mother exclaimed as they passed a sign. "They're giving a free concert tonight."

No one responded.

Their father eventually said, "Well, I guess we should think about hitting the road."

"No, Dan, I want to stay for the concert. They're playing Tchaikovsky's Fifth Symphony, my favorite. It will be beautiful to hear it outside under the stars."

"I'm tired!" Timmy cried.

"I'm hungry," Danny added.

"We can get something to eat at the food shack over there," their mother explained calmly. "Timmy, you can take a nap in the back of the station wagon if you want."

"It's been a long day," their father said.

"No, Dan. It's too good an opportunity. A little culture isn't going to hurt the children. What would we do back at camp? Sit around swatting at mosquitoes?"

Peggy seethed. Her mother was doing this to spite her. She wondered if Jane had overheard her plans the other day and told. Peggy had no appetite for the hamburger and fries her father bought. She just picked at them enough to keep her mother off her back.

The musicians sat under the wood and steel Interlochen Bowl at the bottom of a gently sloping hillside. People were scattered on the hillside on blankets and lawn chairs. The Sheehans found an empty spot halfway down the slope. Timmy sat between his parents. Danny lay on his back behind them, staring up at the evening stars just appearing in the waning daylight. Jane lounged to her father's right. Peggy positioned herself behind and to her mother's left, as far away as she thought she could get without the biddy barking, "Come sit here with your family!"

All through the concert Peggy imagined what the bonfire was like, what fun she was missing. She refused to let the music touch her. It was as if the whole world were against her.

The orchestra played Tchaikovsky's Fifth Symphony last in the program. When the second movement began, her mother put one hand to her breast, the other stroking Timmy's hair as he lay sleeping in her lap. Peggy watched her out of the corner of her eye. Christ, she thought, she's got tears running down her face. You'd think she was the one up there playing, the star of the whole thing. You're a frumpy housewife from a dumpy Detroit suburb. Face it. *This Is Your Life*, but nobody's going to make a TV show about it.

The Sheehans got back to their campsite about eleven that night.

## The Sheehans Have a Cookout

### 1957

Margie and Dan were only the first in their circle to move to the Detroit area. They were followed over the next two years by Dan's brother Joe and his family; Dan's long-time friend Guy Alfieri and his wife, Toni; and Cliff and Madeleine Black. All the men had worked for Chrysler at its Newark plant. They made the move to climb the corporate ladder to higher pay and executive positions.

Guy and Toni, who had no children, rented a new two-bedroom apartment only two blocks from the Sheehans. The Blacks, also childless, rented a small duplex a mile north in Birmingham. Mary and Joe bought a house half a mile away, on the other side of Woodward.

So it was that, late one Saturday afternoon, Dan and Margie were in their bedroom getting ready to go over to his brother's for a housewarming dinner.

Margie had decided years earlier that she enjoyed Joe and Mary best when they lived in another state. "Of all our relatives, why did it have to be Joe and Mary who followed us out here?" she said, struggling into her girdle. "I thought one benefit of coming to Michigan was leaving *some* people behind."

Dan was knotting his tie. "Be fair, Margie! First of all, don't forget Joe started working at Chrysler before me —"

"I mean why did you have to help him get a job *here*?" she said, putting on her slip.

"He already knew about the job openings in Highland Park. He just asked me to put in a good word for him, is all. What was I supposed to do? Tell him no?"

That would have been one possibility, Margie thought as she stepped into her dress.

Dan, finished dressing, sat on the bed to watch her. "He probably would have gotten the job anyway, with or without me. And remember, he helped me get my job at Chrysler in the first place. He's the one who told me they were hiring. You can thank him we're here in Michigan."

Margie laughed, hooking up her stockings. "Don't

worry. I haven't forgotten he's responsible for our being in Detroit! But did you have to return the favor?"

"Yes, as a matter of fact, I did."

"Have it your way." She stepped into her high heels. "Let's get a move on. The sooner we start the sooner it will be over. Come on, kids!" she shouted up the stairs. "It's time to go!"

The thundering herd descended the stairs. The family went out the back door and got into the station wagon. On the way, Margie resumed the conversation. "Why did they have to buy a house so close to ours? All of Detroit and its suburbs to pick from and they buy a house half a mile away. He's working down in Highland Park. Why don't they live down there?"

Dan winced. "Little pitchers have big ears . . ."

Margie turned to look at the four children squeezed in the back seat. "They know better than to repeat anything they hear. Don't you, dears?"

"Oh, yes, Mother," Peggy gave her mother a counterfeit smile. "We promise not to listen to anything you say!"

Margie looked at her daughter for a minute. "Peggy, don't push your luck. You can skate on thin ice only so long before you crash through."

Peggy turned and looked out the car window. Margie shifted her gaze back to her husband. "So why don't they live in Highland Park?"

Dan chuckled. "My brother live around colored people? Not likely." He pulled into his brother's driveway. The drive had taken all of five minutes, even with having to get across Woodward.

"Now, remember," Margie said to the children, "be on your best behavior. Do not embarrass your father and me. You know how particular your Aunt Mary can be."

"I think Aunt Mary is very elegant," Peggy said.

"Just because you have your nose in the air doesn't make you elegant," her mother snapped.

"That's just the English in Mary coming out," Dan said.

"Maybe so," Margie continued. "But don't you kids act like you're at home. So, you two," indicating the boys, "no rough housing, no shouting, and no feet on the furniture."

"You don't let us do that at home either!" Danny said. Margie ignored him.

"And don't ask if you can watch TV. It's a family gathering. Peggy and Janey, try to be nice to your cousin Patti. It won't kill you to be pleasant to her for a few hours."

The girls rolled their eyes. Margie had somehow gotten the idea that her daughters disliked Patti, who was a year younger than Peggy.

Joe and Mary had bought a brand-new, one-story ranch house with a low-pitched roof and large glass windows across the front and a two-car garage out back. "It looks like they ordered it out of *Better Homes and Gardens*," Margie remarked. "The model Home of Today!"

As the Sheehans got out of the Plymouth, Joe, Mary, and Patti came out to greet them. Dan and the boys were in suits and ties and Margie and the girls in swing dresses, hats, and gloves. Joe was wearing casual slacks and an open shirt, and Mary and Patti had on capri pants and open blouses.

"Welcome to our little house!" Joe said. "You didn't have to get so dressed up!"

"Of course we dressed up for our maiden visit to the residence of Joseph and Mary Sheehan!" Dan said, laughing. "Here, Joe," he handed his brother a bottle of Canadian Club, "to help warm the place."

"Well, I'll just have to whip up some old fashioneds for us to toast with! And I've got to check on the coals." Joe grinned and headed inside.

"There's a pitcher of Kool-Aid out back for the children," Mary said, ushering Margie through the front door. Patti led her two female cousins off to show them her bedroom. Danny and Timmy followed their father and uncle through the house and out the kitchen's back door to the patio.

Mary turned to Margie. "We are so happy with this house! Three bedrooms and two bathrooms. And one of them is in our bedroom. It's wonderful not to have to share with Patti! She's reaching that age where she likes to sit at the mirror for hours playing with makeup."

Margie looked at the living room, a large, square space with white wall-to-wall carpeting. A rectangular opening on the far side led into the dining room and a door to the left presumably led to the bedrooms. The furniture was all new, white upholstery, totally up to date. Even the baby grand piano. None of it like the Early American furniture Margie favored. To each her own, she thought.

At first, all Margie could focus on was the sea of plastic. Clear plastic runners covered the carpet from the front door across the living room and into the dining room. Clear plastic slipcovers protected the furniture. Even the piano had a plastic cover. She wondered whether Mary and Joe always lived like this, or had she just put the plastic down to protect her home from today's barbarian invasion?

"It was such a relief to replace all that second-hand furniture we lived with since we got married," Mary was saying. "As soon as we got to Detroit, I went right over to Northland and ordered all this furniture at Hudson's. I went downtown, though, for the Grinnell Brothers piano. It all set us back a pretty penny, but it was worth it! And with Joe's new job, we can afford it!"

"It's quite lovely," Margie said. But would Mary let anybody sit down? The place felt like a showroom.

"You must come see the kitchen!" Mary went on. "It's so very modern. I have a cooktop and two wall ovens."

"That should keep you busy. I know how much you like to entertain." Was Mary just carried away with enthusiasm for the new house, or was she intentionally contrasting it with Margie's? Maybe a little of both.

"But congratulations to you, too!" Mary interrupted Margie's thoughts. "Isn't it wonderful you'll be able to stay in the Darby house after all, now that you're buying it?"

Margie looked at her. "Yes, wonderful. When the builder decided he wanted to make another try at selling rather than keep renting it, it looked like we'd be out on the street." That would have been her preference. "But Dan insisted he was offering a good deal and we were already settled, so it made sense to buy." She would have given her right arm to get out of that house.

"So, we're going to stay neighbors after all! Let's go out back and see where Joe stands with the grilling." She piloted Margie through the dining room and out the sliding glass door.

The patio held two picnic tables and a grill. "How nice!" Margie said. "A cookout!" So, Mary wouldn't have to worry about a mess inside the house.

The coals glowed red in the grill. Joe, Dan, and the boys were now inside the garage, where they all stood admiring

Joe's new car: a 1957 Plymouth Belvedere two-door hardtop.

"It's a beauty, all right," Margie heard Dan say. "Only a few years newer than our station wagon, but boy, what a difference!"

"Uncle Joe, what do those things on the back do?"

"The fins, Danny?" Joe replied. "Nothing, really. The stylists put them on, not the engineers. They look good, is all. Kind of make the car look like a spaceship, don't you think?"

Margie called to them, "Have you both become such native Detroiters that all you can talk about is cars?" Now Mary and Joe had the new car to go with the new house full of the new furniture. The perfect American home! "Joe, I thought you were going to mix up some drinks."

"Coming right up!" He headed for the kitchen. "Dan, would you check the grill and throw on the burgers and hot dogs if the coals are hot enough?"

"Will do. Come on, boys, you can help."

"And I better get the rest of the food out," Mary said.

"May I help you?" Margie asked.

"Oh, no, dear, I wouldn't hear of it. You just make yourself comfortable." Mary turned and went inside, leaving Margie standing there. "Patti!" she heard Mary call. "Come and help me, dear."

"Can I have some Kool-Aid?" Timmy asked. He had already abandoned his father at the grill.

"May I," Margie corrected as she poured him a glass. "Be careful now, don't spill it." Cherry Kool-Aid. Its look of fresh blood disgusted her. "Danny, do you want some too?"

"Yes."

"Yes what?" Sometimes it felt like she spent half her life trying to civilize her children.

"Yes, please!" She watched as Danny poured himself a glass.

Joe came out of the house with a drink in his hand. "An old fashioned, just for you, Margie!"

"Thanks, Joe, don't mind if I do." She was a little uncomfortable having a drink at four in the afternoon, but maybe it would help relax her.

"Do you boys want to come down to the basement and see my train set?" Joe called.

"Yes, please!" Danny and Timmy both responded. Margie smiled. Maybe there was hope for them after all.

"Don't worry about me!" Dan said. "You boys go off and have fun. I'll manage on my own." He winked at Margie.

Mary and Patti came out to set the tables with plastic cloths, plastic plates, and plastic flatware.

"Why, Mary," Margie remarked, "you mean we won't be dining off the Sheehan fine china?"

Mary looked at her uneasily. "Oh, don't be silly, Margie! That would be just too much trouble to clean up afterward.

All these things can go into the garbage."

"How practical." Margie looked at Patti. "Where did you leave your cousins?"

"They're in the kitchen dishing out the beans and making salad," Mary answered for her. "You are so lucky. I often wish I had more than one daughter to help me in the kitchen."

Margie wasn't sure how to respond. She knew Mary and Joe had hoped for more children. For reasons unknown to Margie, they had never managed to do so. She decided to make light of it. "We could probably arrange something, maybe hire Peggy out for a night or two." She took a sip of her drink. Had she and Mary ever had a good relationship? Or had Joe and Dan's mother poisoned it before they ever even met?

Joe came out of the house with a tray of cocktails. "I left the boys in the basement with the trains, if that's all right," he said to Margie.

"It all depends on whether you ever hope to see your trains in one piece again."

"Would you like a freshener on your drink?"

"No, thank you. I'll nurse this for a bit." The Sheehans and the O'Sullivans had escaped the Irish curse of drink. No reason to change that now.

"Hey, Dan," Joe called. "How's the meat coming?"

"It would work better if I had a drink to quench my thirst from all this work that I'm doing by myself without any help." Margie thought he was joking, but it did seem odd that Dan had somehow wound up as the head chef.

"Coming right up, boss!" Joe said, oblivious to any implied criticism. He took his brother one of the drinks.

Peggy and Jane came out the door and set large bowls of food on the table.

"Mother, you should see Patti's room!" Jane exclaimed. "It's simply divine."

"We're lucky to have a cousin who doesn't live in a garret, like we do," Peggy added.

"It's bigger than our room," Jane said. "And she has a television all her own!"

"A television?" Margie asked.

"Yes," Mary explained. "We just bought a color TV console. It's down in the basement. So we moved the old TV into Patti's room."

"Can we get a color TV?" Jane asked. "Can we, please?"

"Absolutely not! They're too expensive and it will be years before there's more than a handful of shows broadcast in color."

Jane put her face into a pout. "Darn. We never have anything to brag about!" Then she brightened. "You know another really neat thing about Patti's room? She doesn't

152

have to go through her brothers' room to get out!"

"Well, that's good, because she doesn't have any brothers." Margie regretted the comment immediately. Mary had gone back into the kitchen. Margie hoped she had not heard it. "Patti," she said to move the conversation elsewhere, "how are your piano lessons coming along?"

"Oh, wonderfully, Aunt Margie! I have lessons three days a week and I practice every day."

"That's good, dear. Practice makes perfect, as they say!"

Mary came out of the house with a tray of condiments. "Her teacher says if she applies herself, she might be able to become a professional musician someday."

"Wouldn't that be wonderful!" Margie said. "The talent must come from your side of the family, Mary. The Sheehans seem particularly unmusical." She thought of the used piano she had insisted Dan buy so that Peggy and then Jane could take lessons. Neither girl showed any interest nor, for that matter, any aptitude. Margie had hoped for more. She had not even bothered to suggest Danny or Timmy try. Now the piano sat unused in the basement.

"I don't know where the talent comes from," Mary replied. "I'm just happy she has it and uses it."

Margie took a sip of her drink. "Patti, maybe you could play something for us later?"

"Well, maybe," she demurred. "I only know classical

pieces. It might bore everybody."

"Better be careful what you play, Patti," Peggy put in. "You might make your Aunt Margie cry."

"There's nothing wrong with appreciating good music!" Margie retorted.

As the evening went on, Margie surprised herself by how much she enjoyed it. The weather was perfect for the cookout, everyone stayed in a good mood, the boys behaved, and the conversation didn't stick too long on either sports or cars. She even accepted Joe's offer of a second old fashioned. And after the dessert of apple pie and vanilla ice cream, Margie and Mary coaxed Patti into playing a few pieces on the piano.

As she sipped her drink and listened to the music, Margie thought, Patti really did have talent. She hoped she kept at it. Just one more reason to envy her sister-in-law!

After the Sheehans left and Mary and Patti finished cleaning up, Mary allowed herself an old fashioned. She didn't like to drink when company was present — better to focus on her hostess duties. She sat at one of the picnic tables watching Joe clean the grill. It was dark now, so he worked by the light of a Coleman lantern. Patti had gone to her room to watch television.

For sixteen years Margie had puzzled Mary. Her sister-in-law had always been cool to her. Was it because Mary and

Dan had had a couple of dates before Joe entered the picture? That water had finished flowing under the bridge long before Dan met Margie. Maybe Margie knew how disappointed Mother Sheehan had been when Dan and Mary did not work out as a couple, and how thrilled she was when Joe and Mary did? And what had Margie meant by that crack about the Sheehan fine china? Mary had a very nice china set, but it came from her family, not Joe's. She didn't think his parents even had any good china.

"Joe," she said, "I always wonder about you and your two brothers, how you got along growing up."

"Got along?" He looked up from the grill with a scrub brush in his hand. "We got along, is all."

"But wasn't it odd how your parents treated Dan one way and you and Ed another?"

"Dan was the oldest, the first son. Our parents tried to act as if it didn't matter, but it did."

"But wasn't it strange, growing up like that?"

Joe looked at her. "Strange compared to what? It was the way our family was. For all I knew, all families were like ours."

Mayor Cobo died suddenly today. He was elected in 1949
campaigning against the Negro invasion of white
neighborhoods / *I said, Mr. Purple Eater, what's your line? He*
*said eating purple people, and it sure is fine* / Soviet's Sputnik
causes shock, dismay in US / The most beautiful thing that
ever happened to horsepower — the 1958 Edsel! / US
conducts nuclear test at Nevada Test Site / Senator
Thurmond filibusters Civil Rights bill for 24 hours, 27
minutes / *See the U.S.A. in your Chevrolet! America is asking*
*you to call!* / A new era in transportation, the Jet Age, began
today with the inaugural flight of Pan American's Boeing
707 *Clipper America* from New York Idlewild to Paris Orly! /
Federal troops at their side, 9 Negro students integrate
Little Rock Central High School.

## Father Hill Pays a Visit

### 1959

I'm off to Beaumont to pick up your mother," Dan Sheehan said to the children, seated in a row on the living room sofa. "When we get home, do not—I repeat—do not do anything that you and I will regret. Your mother needs quiet, and she needs rest."

"Yes, Father," Peggy answered for the group. She looked at his face. It had the tired, pained look she associated with all her mother's homecomings. An attitude of silence and deference was the best approach on these occasions. She had learned that lesson a few years earlier, that awful Christmas. Or, rather, the day after Christmas. Her mother had just gotten back from Beaumont, still looking sick and wretched, the living room decorated with the tree and the nativity set, all the presents under the tree, still unopened. Her father looked as unhappy as Peggy had ever seen him; Jane and Danny sat quiet and forlorn; and little Timmy was screaming his head off. If only twelve-year-old Peggy had had the wit to hold her tongue! Instead, she had blurted out, "You ruined our Christmas!" The attack had the desired effect. Her mother took to her bed for three days. But Peggy hadn't calculated the effect on her father. She had never seen him more furious, the rage clear on his face and in the shaking of his body. She thought he was about to beat her. Instead, he made a rushed sign of the cross and followed their mother into the bedroom.

When an hour later he called her down from the bedroom where she had taken refuge, his voice betrayed his anger. But all he said was, "Don't you ever — *ever* — speak to your mother like that again," and turned and walked away.

Here they were again, five years and several homecomings later. "Peggy, you're in charge," Mr. Sheehan continued. "I expect, with all the paperwork and such, we should be home in about an hour."

"Yes, Father."

He turned and went out through the kitchen to the driveway. None of the children moved until he had backed the car out and headed down the street.

"Can I go over to the Rouleaus' to play?" Danny asked.

"Certainly not," Peggy said. "What would the Rouleaus and everybody think if you're out playing when our dear mother is on her way home from the hospital?"

"I don't care."

"Well, I do. And so will Father. You'll stay right here. Go play with your trains in the basement if you want. But you're not leaving the house."

Danny took the offer and headed to the basement. Timmy followed him.

After making sure the boys were gone, Jane asked, "Do you think they used electroshock on her?"

Peggy looked at her sister. Well, wasn't she the little ghoul? And here they thought Peggy was the Problem Child. "I certainly hope so. I would've thrown the switch myself."

"I'm going upstairs," Jane said. "I have to finish reading *Stories of the Saints*. Sister Michael Thomas is going to give us a quiz on Monday."

When their parents arrived home, only Peggy greeted them. The other children must have heard their parents come in, but they did not emerge from the basement or the attic. "Welcome home, Mother," Peggy said.

"Thank you, Peggy. It's good to be home." Her tone did not agree with her words.

"Can I get you anything, Margie?" Mr. Sheehan asked.

"No, don't worry about me. I think I'll just go lie down for a while." Mrs. Sheehan went into the bedroom and shut the door. Mr. Sheehan went to put the car into the garage. Peggy returned to the *Look* magazine she had been leafing through.

"Dan!" She heard her mother from the bedroom. "Dan!"

"He's parking the car," Peggy called from the sofa. "What do you want?"

"Tell him I want Father Hill! I want to see Father Hill!"

"Yes, Mother," Peggy said, laying the magazine on the coffee table. Just then Mr. Sheehan entered the room.

"She wants Father Hill." Peggy looked to see her father's reaction, but no change appeared in his already bleak expression. He turned without comment and went into the kitchen to use the wall phone.

"Yes, yes," she heard him say once he got through, "we just got home a few minutes ago. She's resting now. . . But she's asking for you. . . Yes, we'll be here. . . OK, see you then." He came back into the living room.

When Father Hill arrived, dressed in his flowing black cassock, he gave them a bare greeting and went straight to the bedroom. He knocked on the door. "Margie, I'm here. May I come in?" Without waiting for a response, he entered and closed the door behind him.

160

Peggy looked at her father. He looked back at her, and winked.

Father Hill. He taught at Sacred Heart Seminary down in the city. He came to the Shrine as a substitute priest one summer (filling in for an assistant who had gone off to dry out) and suddenly he and Mother were the best of friends. Ever since then he visited the house regularly, once or twice a week, phoning ahead about nine or ten p.m., arriving an hour or so later, and staying for hours of droning conversation. By then all the children had gone to bed, after first getting Father Hill's blessing, of course. Their father gave up trying to participate in the visits. He had to get up and go to work in the morning. From what Peggy had observed, Father Hill and her mother didn't deliberately cut her father out of the conversation. They also didn't take his going off to bed as a hint to bring the evening to an end. How do you compete with a man of God? It would have been almost easier if her mother had a real affair.

Her mother and her moods. And her illnesses. If she wasn't in the hospital with another pregnancy, she was lying in bed for days at a time with some unnamed ailment. She had even had Father Hill come to the house once to give her Extreme Unction, the last rites, her parents' bedroom fetid with burning candles and incense. What a joke! All that mumbo jumbo. Whatever it was, their mother recovered, and life went on.

After an hour, Father Hill came out of the bedroom. Mr. Sheehan was sitting in his easy chair, his fingers drumming on the edge of the ashtray stand. Peggy had remained on the sofa, wanting to see what would happen. She had worked her way through *Look* and *Life* and was now pretending to be absorbed in the *Michigan Catholic*.

"Margie, haha, she's resting. Going to be all right, haha. We'll have to keep an eye. Said the rosary together. Haha, had a little chat. Dan, haha, is there anything?"

How did Mother put up with his way of talking? Peggy wondered.

"Thank you, Father," Mr. Sheehan said. "It was good of you to come on such short notice." He stood and escorted the priest to the front door. Then he turned to Peggy. "I'll go check on your mother. Will you round up the others? Let's go out for pizza tonight, maybe make a stop at Ray's Ice Cream after."

"Yes, Father!" Peggy said. "That's the best medicine for all of us!"

# Cruising Woodward

## 1961

The Saturday afternoon after she got her driver's license, Jane went down into the basement to find her father.

"Daddy, can we take the DeSoto over to Big Boy's for a hamburger? I want to get some driving practice."

Dan was bent over his bench, fiddling with some electrical wires. He peered at her over his bifocals. "Who is 'we'?"

"Patti and Anne and me."

He seemed to consider for a minute and then fished in his pocket for the keys. "OK. But be careful. If you get uncomfortable driving, have Patti take over. And remember," he added with a smile, "the D and the R stand for Drive and Reverse, not Drag and Race."

"Oh, Daddy that was silly the first time you told it! Thanks!" Jane snatched the keys out of his outstretched hand and ran up the stairs before he could reconsider.

"Come on, ladies! Let's go," she cried to her cousin and her friend as she hurried out the back door. Anne got in the back seat and Jane and Patti in the front. All three wore casual blouses and clam diggers, scarves over their hairdos and open-toed wedges on their feet—the perfect cruising outfit. They may have hated the conformity of their student uniforms, but they gave it no second thought when it came to fashion. And they were not about to let the cool spring weather dictate their attire.

In Driver's Education, Jane had learned on a stick shift, a conventional three-on-the-tree. She was glad the DeSoto had an automatic transmission with push buttons rather than a column shifter.

"I wish we had a newer car," she said as she looked in the dashboard-mounted rearview mirror and saw the DeSoto's out-of-style fins. "At least it's a hardtop and not that god-awful plain Jane station wagon we used to have."

"You've got that right," Patti said. "You couldn't pay Anne and me to go cruising with you in that old station wagon. Could she, Anne?"

"No way!" Anne agreed. "This car is so much better than the Plymouth."

As soon as they were out of the driveway, Jane took her eyeglasses off. Her driver's license said she needed them, but what girl would cruise Woodward wearing glasses? If she squinted enough, she could see where she was going.

"Are you sure you can see OK?" Patti asked.

"Don't be silly! I just need the glasses for reading," Jane lied. She drove carefully, pulling slowly onto Woodward and maneuvering from one lane to the next to make the U-turn across the median. Elias Brothers' Big Boy's was just across Woodward, barely a quarter mile from the house, but the whole point was to arrive in a car and get curbside service. Only families went into the restaurant.

Saturday afternoon and the parking lot was almost already full. Jane pulled into the last remaining empty spot. A carload of boys was in each of the adjoining spaces. When the waitress came, the girls ordered only a soda each to stretch their money. A couple of the boys talked themselves into buying them burgers and fries as well.

The girls had a good time flirting with the boys, Patti with her two extra years of cruising experience taking the lead in the conversation. Jane was happy she had come along.

The boys on the left were in a late-model Pontiac

convertible with bucket seats—obviously the driver's father's car. They tried to act cool but seemed more like earnest pupils taking a break from their studies. The boys on the right had a souped-up hot rod, 1950ish Mercury. The Merc boys were in full Brando greaser style, from slicked-back hair to pointed shoes. They peppered their conversation with "daddy-o" and "cool cat."

When the exchanges between the two male factions escalated from friendly competition to unfriendly hostility, Patti hinted that they should be getting home.

"Yeah, let's go," Jane said. "But let's drive around a little first. I need to practice my driving some more!"

"OK by me!" Anne agreed. "This is fun!"

"OK," Patti said. "But let's not take too long."

From Big Boy's, Jane headed south on Woodward as far as Nine Mile Road. She felt her driving confidence increase with each passing mile. Then they turned toward home, stopping briefly at Susie Q's and Howard Johnson's. The scene at both those places was quiet, so they quickly moved on. Patti glanced at her watch. "We've been out for quite a while now. Maybe it's time to call it a day?"

Jane resisted. "No! It's still too pretty a day to waste. I don't want to spend it at home. Let's make one last stop at Ted's Diner and get some ice cream!"

Patti held up a dissenting hand. "Not me, cousin! We're

crossing Thirteen Mile now. Ted's is way up at Sixteen Mile. Just drop me off at home."

Jane risked looking in Patti's direction so she could stick her tongue out at her. "Every party needs a pooper, that's why we invited you!"

"Party pooper! Party pooper!" Anne chorused.

"Ha ha, very funny," Patti deadpanned. "But it's still 'Home, James' for me."

"Oh, OK, be a spoilsport. What about you, Anne? Let's go to Ted's!"

Anne said, "It's your neck. My parents aren't home. If you think your parents won't mind, we'll go."

"Oh, they'll mind all right. I'll cross that bridge when I get to it."

They made the short detour to Patti's house. "You sure you won't reconsider?" Jane pleaded one last time.

"No, thanks. I enjoyed it, but I've got a million things to do. Now don't stay out too long!" Patti warned as she got out of the car.

"Yes, Mother!" Jane said theatrically.

"Bye!" they called to each other as Patti walked up the driveway.

As the two girls went on to Ted's, Woodward's suburban congestion of shops, restaurants, and gas stations gave way to a tree-lined highway.

On the way, Anne remarked, "I'm surprised Patti came along today. You and Peggy don't usually hang out with her, do you?"

Without taking her eyes off the road, Jane said, "Actually, we're kind of close, for Sheehans."

"Maybe it's your parents I'm thinking of, then. Yours and hers don't really get along, do they?"

Jane giggled. "It's very odd, really. Our parents seem to get along, but something always feels just a bit off. Like there's some history that we don't know about. So Patti and us are in league against our parents."

"You know your family is kind of strange, doncha?"

"Hey, what can I say? It's in our blood!"

"We've got a Sheehan in our family, too."

Jane glanced at Anne. "Really? I thought you were all Italians."

"Most of us, except for some great grandparents on my mother's side. Thomas and Anne Flanagan. She was a Sheehan before they married. They met in Philadelphia and came to Detroit sometime about 1880."

"Is that who you're named for?"

"Well, I guess, more or less. There've been a bunch of Annes in the family, but she's the earliest I know of. She reached over and poked Jane. "Hey, maybe we're related!"

Jane shook her head. "Not likely. Our Sheehans didn't

come from Ireland until 1910 or so, I think, not long before my father was born."

At Ted's the girls got chatting with a couple of college kids in a Thunderbird, most likely Bloomfield Hills money. Jane wished Patti had come along. She was so much better at repartee. She felt a little uneasy whenever she glanced at her Timex wristwatch, but she hoped the chitchat might lead to a date offer. In the end, it came to nothing. The boys suddenly said they had to be going and left without even asking for the girls' phone numbers.

They got back to the Sheehan house about dinnertime. As Jane pulled into the driveway, she could sense the approaching storm. Her mother came out of the back door like a shot. "Where have you been, young lady?"

"I'd better be going," Anne said, quickly moving toward her own backyard. Jane watched her go.

"I asked you a question. Where have you been?" Her father came out the door behind her. A glance at his face dispelled any hope that he would temper her mother's wrath.

"We went to Big Boy's, like I said. And it was such a nice day, we decided to drive around for a while."

"A while? I sent Danny to Big Boy's two hours ago to look for you. We called Patti's house and she was already home. We called Anne's house and Dennis had no idea where the two of you had gone."

"Jane," her father added, "we were worried sick. For all we knew you had had an accident. You said you were going to Big Boy's, so you should have gone and come back. If you wanted to go somewhere else, you should have asked us for permission first."

"We meant to go to Kroger's this afternoon," her mother said. "You had the car so we couldn't. You are grounded, young lady. You may have your driver's license now, but you need to learn responsibility."

"Jennifer and I are supposed to go to the movies tomorrow!"

"Call her and tell her you can't. Blame your Big Bad Mother if you want. You have to learn that your actions have consequences."

Some are calling new Mayor Jerry Cavanagh Detroit's answer to Jack Kennedy. The colored vote gave him his upset win over Mayor Miriani / 1,000 East Germans fleeing into West Berlin per day / Come up to the Kool taste! / Japanese automaker Toyota has given up trying to beat Detroit. Apparently Americans don't want a small, made-in-Japan car / *Everybody's doing a brand new dance now, come on, baby, do the Loco-Motion* / Joan Crawford and Bette Davis star in *What Ever Happened to Baby Jane?* / Kennedy sending 18,000 military advisors to South Vietnam / *Stay on the right track, to 9 Mile and Mack, Roy O'Brien Trucks and Cars, make your money back*!

# When Peggy Met Anthony

## 1961

B ecause Peggy waited too long before deciding to go to the Marygrove College dance, the pool of acceptable escorts had been drained of the most desirable candidates. So, she took Dennis Romano, Jane's friend Anne's brother. She and Dennis had dated off and on in high school, but they were never serious. On several occasions, such as tonight, they were happy to serve as the other's escort in the absence of other prospects.

The dance committee had decorated the college's assembly hall with fake palm trees, beach umbrellas, and fishing nets for the dance's *Blue Hawaii* theme. The four male band members on the stage wore Hawaiian shirts and flowered leis, and the female singer a colorful muumuu. The nuns had vetoed as too risqué the dance committee's proposal that the girls and their dates come in beach attire. The nuns insisted on gowns for the girls and suits for the men.

Dancing couples circled the floor under the watchful eyes of the chaperoning sisters. The girls without dates sat primly in their chairs along Wallflower Row, chatting together and occasionally giggling with hands over their mouths. Their male counterparts huddled on the other side of the room, trying to work up the courage to go ask somebody for a dance.

Peggy and Dennis were standing with Hazel Harrison and Michael Burton at the refreshment table when Irene Fiorentino entered with a tall, handsome man at her side.

"Who is that with Irene?" Peggy asked. "That's not her boyfriend." She stole a casual glance in her compact mirror at her makeup and her hairdo.

Hazel chuckled. "Matt's sick so Irene's brother, Anthony, is pulling escort duty tonight. Have you never met him?"

Peggy slipped her compact back into her purse. "No. Does he go to the University of Detroit?"

"Heavens, no, Margaret! He's twenty-five and works as a designer at General Motors. They call him a rising star there. Someday he may even head his own division!"

"I heard he's working on the team designing Oldsmobile's new sports car," Michael said as he filled punch glasses for them.

Irene spotted the two couples and hurried over to them. "Hello, Margaret! Hello, Hazel! I love your dresses! Just look who had to bring me to the dance!"

"I don't believe we've met," said Peggy, looking directly at Anthony.

"No? Margaret, this is my brother, Anthony. Anthony, Margaret Sheehan. And you know Hazel, and Michael. And you are . . .?"

"Dennis. Dennis Romano." He had to gulp a mouthful of punch before he could answer.

"Pleased to meet you."

"Margaret, how about a dance?" Anthony asked, acknowledging the others with a nod of the head.

"I'd love to," Peggy replied. She didn't want to sound too enthusiastic. The two of them joined the crowd on the dance floor, leaving the others gawking behind them.

"So, how is it we have not met before?" Anthony said. "I've heard Irene mention your name."

The band's singer began, "*Moon River, wider than a mile, I'm crossing you in style someday.*"

"Only in a good way, I hope," Margaret replied. "Maybe

174

we haven't met because you never come to a Marygrove dance? Or because you spend all your time at your drawing board?"

Anthony laughed. "Well, I do I love my job. But I also love meeting beautiful women. And how do you know I work at a drawing board?"

"Don't you? Have I been misinformed?"

"No, you haven't. Apparently, you know more about me than I do about you. I mean, I can see you are strikingly beautiful, with the most gorgeous head of the darkest black hair I've ever seen and piercing dark brown eyes."

Peggy laughed. "I bet you say that to all the girls."

Anthony laughed in turn. "Well, not to the blonds. But still, it's only fair to even the score and tell me something about yourself."

"Little old me? I'm just a simple schoolgirl who knows nothing about the great big world." She hoped she wasn't laying it on too thick.

Anthony laughed again. "No need to be coy. Just give me the straight scoop."

Margaret considered how to answer him. If she weren't interested, a flippant response would suffice, and they'd part at the end of the dance. But she didn't want to cut it short. "Well, OK, the straight scoop. I'm a junior here at Marygrove, I major in English literature, I plan to have my own career and not be a housewife, and I don't like boys who try to tell me what to do."

"Well, I won't try to tell you what to do. But what kind of a career can a woman have?"

"Good question," she answered, but the question made her bristle. "I have no interest in being a teacher or a nurse or a secretary. Why is it those are the kinds of things women are supposed to do? Why can't we do the same things men do?"

"Because you're women?"

"Wrong answer." If she didn't get him turned around soon, this would be over before it started. "My sister, Jane — she's a high school senior — wanted to become a doctor, but Sister Guidance Counselor at school told her that was out of the question and she should go to college to become a nurse. So much more ladylike, don't you know."

"Emptying bedpans and giving sponge baths is ladylike?"

Peggy laughed. "You'll have to ask the good nuns that. Why does being a woman mean Jane shouldn't try to be a doctor? Do you agree with that?"

"No, actually, I don't."

"Maybe we'll get along after all."

"You mean we weren't getting along already?"

"We've just been introduced. Let's reserve judgment. And you? What about you, Anthony?"

"I'm just a simple working stiff trying to make my mark in the world," he said with a deadpan expression. "As you apparently know, I work at GM as a designer. Car design is something I've been interested in my whole life. I still remember as a little kid the big revolution in the way cars looked in the years right after the war, when all the companies rushed to junk their prewar designs and come up with something new and completely different. Running boards were out and integrated fenders in, cars sat much lower to the ground, and they got 'longer, lower, wider,' as the advertising said. I was working on my master's in industrial design when I got a summer job at GM Styling. They liked my stuff enough that they hired me full-time, and it's been a wild ride ever since."

So, he has passion about his career, she thought. What about the rest of life? "And what is your design dream?"

"To design a sports car that people will be talking about fifty years from now."

"Maybe if Detroit wins the 1968 Olympics bid, they can add drag car racing to the events. The host country gets to propose a new sport, doesn't it?" She smiled at him.

"Maybe I'm just boring you with this car stuff." He didn't smile back.

Maybe her joke wasn't as funny as she thought it would be. "Oh, no, no, not at all. I'm just being flippant. I know nobody expects girls to be interested in cars. But living in Detroit, it's a little hard not to be. It would be like living in Washington and having no interest in politics."

In the background, the band began "Theme from *A Summer Place*."

"What about politics?" Anthony asked. "Are you interested in them?"

Good Lord, had they run out of interesting topics already? "My parents are thrilled we have a Catholic president, and an Irish Catholic one at that. I'll confess to being the stereotypical female on this subject. I'm more fascinated with Jackie Kennedy, so young and beautiful and accomplished. First Lady and she's barely thirty! What must it be like to have such a perfect life?"

He said softly, "The Kennedys have had their share of tragedy. Jackie had a miscarriage a few years ago."

Peggy stopped dancing and gave him a sharp look. "A miscarriage? Miscarriages are a dime a dozen. You should ask my mother about that."

He looked at her with a puzzled expression. "They may be a fact of life, Margaret, but that doesn't make them any less tragic."

"You're right," Peggy said as they resumed dancing. "That was harsh of me. But if one miscarriage is the worst thing that ever happens to Jackie Kennedy, she'll be one lucky lady."

Peggy spent much of the evening with Anthony. Hazel and Irene arched their eyebrows and made one or two *sotto voce* comments in her direction. Peggy didn't let any of it bother her. She made a point of staying focused on Anthony as they moved around the dance floor.

Dennis finally caught up with her as the dance ended.

"I'm sorry, Dennis," she apologized as they walked back to his car. "That was rude of me. But I didn't surprise you, did I?"

"No," he laughed. "I'm just the family chauffeur in this play, after all. He seems like a nice guy. Did you get his phone number?"

"Yes. And I gave him mine. I hope he calls. I think I'm going to marry him."

"Marry him? Shouldn't you have a date or two first before you book the church?"

"I just mean I see a possibility that we could end up together. I've never thought that before about any boy. Except you, of course," she said as she poked him in the side. "But marrying the boy-next-door is such a cliché."

"I'm not the boy-next-door," he corrected. "Our family lives behind yours."

"Boy-next-door, boy-behind-us-one-street-over. Six of one, half a dozen of the other."

# The Joyful Mysteries

### 1962

Margie knotted the scarf around her neck as she stepped into the Shrine. As her eyes adjusted to the sudden plunge from daylight to shadows, she dipped her hand in the holy water and made the sign of the cross. In midafternoon only a few parishioners were scattered here and there among the pews, some kneeling in prayer, others sitting and meditating or daydreaming.

She walked halfway down the aisle, genuflected, and knelt in a pew.

She loved this church. With its big circular nave and the

altar in the middle, it was not like any other Catholic church she had ever been in. She remembered her surprise the first time the family faced the priest while he said Mass. She had felt so exposed!

Such beautiful materials had gone into the Shrine's construction. The stone and the copper and all the statues and side chapels were wonderful. It was all so very restful. Coming here by herself when the church was empty gave her a new lease on life.

She was proud to live in the parish whose pastor was the famous Father Coughlin. Even people who by rights belonged to neighboring parishes would come to the Shrine for Sunday Mass. Of course, Roosevelt and the Bishop had forced him off the radio decades ago. But even today if you mentioned the names Father Coughlin or the Shrine, people all over the country recognized them.

Pulling out the rosary beads her brother Denis, Father Denis, had recently given her, blessed by Pope John himself, she again made the sign of the cross. "In the name of the Father, and of the Son, and of the Holy Ghost. Amen." She recited the Apostles' Creed ("I believe in God, the Father almighty"), the Our Father ("Our Father, Who art in heaven, hallowed be Thy name"), three Hail Marys ("Hail Mary, full of grace"), and a Glory Be ("Glory be to the Father").

With the preparatory prayers out of the way, she tried to

recall which Mysteries of the Rosary to reflect on as she prayed the rosary proper. It was a Thursday, so it should be the Joyful Mysteries.

"The first Joyful Mystery, the Annunciation," she murmured quietly to herself to avoid disturbing anyone else, although nobody in the church was anywhere near her. "The angel Gabriel appears to Mary and tells her she is to be the Mother of God."

She never wanted to be a mother.

She started the first decade with an Our Father ("Thy kingdom come"), ten Hail Marys ("the Lord is with thee"), and a Glory Be ("and to the Son").

She would have been fine going through life unmarried and without children.

"The second Joyful Mystery, the Visitation. Mary visits her cousin Elizabeth, who is bearing John the Baptist."

Didn't she play the mother enough the first twenty-five years of her life with her own brothers and sisters?

An Our Father ("Thy will be done on earth as it is in heaven"), ten Hail Marys ("Blessed art thou amongst women"), and a Glory Be ("and to the Holy Ghost").

But staying unmarried was something an Irish Catholic girl in Philadelphia in the 1930s could not do.

"The third Joyful Mystery, the Nativity. The birth of Jesus, come to save all men."

Well, she could have become a nun like Aunt Mary, her father's sister, Sister John Edmond.

An Our Father ("Give us this day our daily bread"), ten Hail Marys ("Blessed is the fruit of thy womb, Jesus"), and a Glory Be ("as it was in the Beginning, is now").

On her deathbed in 1938, Sister John Edmond tried to get Margie to swear to enter the convent. She was already four years out of high school with no marriage prospects, her aunt had pointed out, so why not become a bride of Christ?

"The fourth Joyful Mystery, the Presentation. The Blessed Virgin presents the Infant Jesus in the temple."

Margie thanked God she had resisted Aunt Mary.

An Our Father ("Forgive us our trespasses, as we forgive those who trespass against us"), ten Hail Marys ("Holy Mary, Mother of God, pray for us sinners"), and a Glory Be ("and ever shall be").

How she resisted, she didn't know, with her parents standing right there thinking who knew what.

"The fifth Joyful Mystery, the Finding of the Child Jesus in the Temple."

Did they hope she'd say yes?

A final Our Father ("and lead us not into temptation but deliver us from evil. Amen."), ten Hail Marys ("now and at the hour of our death. Amen."), and a Glory Be ("world without end. Amen.").

Margie put the rosary beads back into her purse and sat back on the pew, appreciating the quiet and the beauty around her. After a few minutes, she glanced at her Hamilton wristwatch. Time to get home. Everybody would start turning up from wherever they had scattered themselves, expecting dinner and waiting to criticize it.

She stepped into the aisle, genuflected, and walked to the door, stopping to dip her fingers in the holy water and make the sign of the cross. As she passed outside into the sunlight, she removed the scarf from her head and shook her hair free, her eyes shut against the sudden light.

Marilyn Monroe dead / President Kennedy says Soviet missile sites in Cuba give Reds nuclear strike capability in Western Hemisphere / *Johnny Angel, you're an angel to me* / George Romney, ex-head of American Motors, Michigan's next governor / *Flintstones, meet the Flintstones, they're the modern Stone Age family!* / Pope John XXIII, 2,000 cardinals and bishops gather in St. Peter's for 2nd Vatican Council opening / Cuban crisis ends, Russians to dismantle weapons, return them to Soviet Union.

## Dinner at the Sheehans

### 1962

Anthony Fiorentino did call Peggy, and they started dating. He was different from the college boys who were all so eager to impress, just overgrown high school seniors really, or the boys cruising Woodward Avenue who could offer a couple of hours of fun and a burger and a Coke but only had a good job on a factory floor to look forward to.

Peggy resisted the idea of bringing Anthony home for two reasons: she dreaded letting her parents get at Anthony and she dreaded letting Anthony see her home life. The longer she made excuses, the more insistent her parents became. "Look at it this way, Peggy," her father kidded her, "what kind of knight in shining armor would he be if he can't hold his own against the likes of us?" Dinner at the Sheehans was arranged.

"I promise not to embarrass you," her mother assured Peggy. "We'll give him a good meal. I just hope he's not too disappointed when we turn out not to be quite the Addams family you've painted us."

"Don't worry. I haven't exaggerated anything," Peggy answered. "The truth is frightening enough."

When Anthony arrived at the front door and rang the bell, Peggy rushed to answer it. "Hello, Anthony," she said, holding out her hand for a shake to avoid a kiss in front of the family. Her action seemed to startle him a bit, but he quickly recovered.

Once the introductions were out of the way, Danny and Timmy wandered off to watch *The Rocky and Bullwinkle Show*. Mr. Sheehan and Anthony had a good conversation before dinner about engineering and electronics. It irritated Peggy to see them get along so well. They actually had something in common besides her? Jane played the bashful schoolgirl, tittering at odd moments. Peggy wanted to slap her. Her mother kept herself busy with the dinner in the kitchen.

Mrs. Sheehan had set the dining room table with her best china and silver and Waterford crystal, all on the starched Irish linen tablecloth. Peggy couldn't decide whether she was happy her mother had made this a special occasion.

At last her mother called them all to the table. The others followed suit as their father folded his hands and bowed his head. "Bless us, O Lord, and these Thy gifts which we are about to receive from Thy bounty, through Christ our Lord. Amen."

"Amen," everyone answered. Peggy thought Anthony seemed caught off-guard by the Grace. She hoped her mother hadn't noticed.

As the meal got underway, Mr. Sheehan turned to Anthony. "So, how long have you been at General Motors?"

"Five years, sir."

"It must be quite a job trying to stay one step ahead of the competition when it comes to styling."

"Absolutely. There's always a trade-off between coming up with a design that makes your product look more up to date than the competition's and getting too far ahead of the public and producing something so avant-garde it hurts sales. Chrysler carried it off with its 'Forward Look' cars in the late fifties. But everyone in the industry is still talking about the Edsel fiasco. I really enjoy the process. We've got a good team at the GM Tech Center. We start off with far-out designs, what cars might look like in twenty years, really, and then bit by bit we dial it back to something upper management will live with."

"My daddy's an engineer!" Timmy piped up. "When I was little, I thought that meant he drove railroad trains. Are you an engineer?"

Peggy wanted to tell her little brother to shut up. Anthony regarded the boy sympathetically. "No, I'm a stylist, not an engineer. The engineers do the hard work. They make sure the cars work the way they should. You know, go when you put your foot on the accelerator, turn when you turn the steering wheel, and stop when you hit the brakes. We stylists have the fun side of the job. It's all about turning the nuts and bolts into a piece of art. We wrap those machines in flowing sheet metal, with sculpted lines and angled fenders. We want to make them look fast even when they're standing still."

"Where do you live, Anthony?" Mrs. Sheehan asked abruptly.

"I have a place over at Somerset Park Apartments in Troy."

Jane giggled.

"What's so funny?" Peggy asked, glaring at her.

Jane looked down at her plate. "Well, it's just that – don't they – I heard they call Somerset 'Sin City,' is all."

"Where do you hear talk like that, young lady?" their mother demanded.

"Jane's got her mind in the gutter!" Danny said with a

snort.

"Quiet, Danny!" their father said. "Eat your food."

Anthony laughed. "Well, it does tend to be a lot of single people and couples in their twenties without children. But I think 'Sin City' takes it a bit far."

"It's a lovely apartment complex," Peggy said. Her mother frowned at her. Peggy couldn't remember whether she had ever let it slip she had been to his place.

Surprisingly, Mrs. Sheehan did not pursue the subject. Instead, she asked, "What parish is that?"

Anthony looked at her blankly. Peggy gave a theatrical sigh. "It's St. Alan's, Mother. As you well know. Don't worry. Anthony is a good Catholic boy."

Mr. Sheehan intervened as his wife opened her mouth to speak. "But not a good Irish Catholic boy!" Everyone looked at him. "A joke," he added, when he saw the looks on their faces. "It's a joke. We're not your grandparents' generation. I can tell you stories about the run-ins I had with my parents over non-Irish girlfriends."

Their mother laughed. "I can, too. In the end, our parents each got what they wanted, an Irish son-in-law and an Irish daughter-in-law. Both families were still disappointed!" She looked at her husband and they both laughed.

Timmy gaped. "Mommy, you had boyfriends before Daddy?"

Amid the laughter, Mr. Sheehan said, "Son, don't you know your mother was a famous beauty in her time? Why, after high school, she was part of an all-girl band called Six Sizzling Beauties! I was lucky she chose me."

"No!" Danny and Timmy shouted while Jane sniggered and Peggy rolled her eyes.

"You better believe it," their mother said lightheartedly, "or no dessert for either of you."

"What did you play, Mommy?" Timmy asked.

"The cello."

"What's that?"

"A fiddle bigger than you are."

"Wow! How did you hold it on your neck?"

The dinner conversation went on in a similar vein. Anthony seemed to enjoy himself. Peggy nervously waited for some unseen bomb to go off.

Finally, Mr. Sheehan led the closing Grace. "We give Thee thanks for all Thy benefits, O Almighty God, Who livest and reignest world without end. Amen. May the souls of the faithful departed, through the mercy of God, rest in peace. Amen."

"Amen," they all replied.

"Well, we'd better be going, Anthony," Peggy said as they stood up from the table.

"Where are you two off to?" her father asked.

"A movie," Peggy replied evasively.

"Which movie?" her mother asked.

"*Jules and Jim*," Anthony said.

"*Jules and Jim*?" Mrs. Sheehan sputtered. "You can't see that! The Legion of Decency condemned it!"

"Oh, Mother, what does the Legion of Decency know about films?" Peggy asked. "The movie has great reviews. It's already called a classic of the French New Wave. I'm not going to let a bunch of frustrated old spinsters pick what movies I can see."

Her mother was about to respond, but Mr. Sheehan cut her off. "Let it go, Margie. She's old enough to decide for herself. If she thinks a movie is worth risking the loss of Heaven and the pains of Hell, it's up to her."

"Dan, that's not funny."

"It wasn't meant to be. You two go and have a good time. If you reconsider, I think *The Music Man* is still showing at the Oak Drive In."

"I enjoyed dinner with your family," Anthony said as he walked Peggy to his car.

"I didn't."

He laughed. "Well, I did have the feeling I was at a job interview. But you have to admit, the first dinner with your girlfriend's family is always going to be a little stressful."

"You've had a lot of practice in that department?"

"No, not really. You know what I mean. I enjoyed talking to your father. And your mother was nice."

"Wait till she slips the switchblade in."

"Well, anyway, she didn't do it tonight. I think you underestimate my charms and their ability to win your mother over."

"Good luck with that."

In the end Peggy hated *Jules and Jim*, the whole story a tedious bore. Falling in love with a woman because she reminds you of a Greek statue? Telling your best friend to sleep with your wife while you all three live together? And then the woman kills herself and her lover in front of her husband? How melodramatic!

When she got home, Peggy found her father in his easy chair with his pipe on the ashtray stand, giving the room a pleasantly acrid aroma, and her mother on the sofa knitting.

"How was the movie?" her father asked.

"Excellent! It deserves all the rave reviews."

"Well, I'm glad you had a good time. We enjoyed meeting Anthony. I hope we didn't scare him too much."

"He said he had a good time."

"So, what's next with you two?" her mother asked, her eyes focused on her knitting.

"What's next?" She didn't really know. But Anthony wasn't seeing anybody else, or so she thought, and she certainly wasn't. "I think we're starting to get serious. Don't you think he'd be a wonderful catch?"

"Don't you think he's a little too old for you?" Her mother set her knitting aside and looked directly at her.

"Too old for me? He's five years older than me! That's the same age difference between the two of you!"

"Yes," her father agreed, "but we were thirty and twenty-five when we got married. You're not even twenty. You're still in school."

"I graduate next year."

"We don't dislike Anthony," her mother said. "It's just that girls who spend too much time with one boy get a reputation."

"Only if they get knocked up."

"Peggy, there's no need to get vulgar," her father warned.

Her mother continued, "I think if he takes you to a dirty movie like the one he did tonight, it shows he has no respect for you. Maybe he has expectations."

Peggy laughed. "Expectations? Expectations of what? That I'll go all the way with him? No. He's a gentleman. People can see a movie with mature themes and still be moral."

Her father jumped in. "Anyway, we thought you liked the Shaughnessy boy."

"Kevin? A sweet kid, but much too immature for me."

"Well," her father replied, "as I said, we enjoyed meeting and talking with Anthony. We just ask that you take it one step at a time."

"I'm tired," Peggy answered. "I'm going to go upstairs and get to bed."

Her parents' comments caused Peggy to take a fresh look at Anthony, but not with the result they might have hoped for. Their reluctance strengthened her interest in him. But she became more guarded in mentioning him. They knew she still saw him; they just didn't know how often. They didn't know how many times "I'm going for a soda with Judy!" or "I'm going to the library to study!" really meant "I have a date with Anthony."

# Family Roots

## 1963

D an sat up and looked at the clock on the hotel nightstand. Four in the morning. He cursed under his breath as he picked up the receiver. "Hello?"

"Dan, it's Margie."

"Honey, do you know what time it is in San Francisco? Is there something wrong?"

"Dan, Ed just called. I'm sorry to have to tell you this. Your father died during the night."

"Dad? Dad is dead? Not Mother?"

"Yes, Dan, your father, not your mother."

He looked around the hotel room, all laminated wood and plastic Danish furniture. Dad dead at eighty-three. "What happened?"

"Ed said he died in his sleep. A stroke, apparently."

"And Mother? How is she?"

"Ed says she's all right—well, as all right as she ever is these days. He's moving her to a nursing home as soon as he can make the arrangements."

Dan and his brothers had had any number of conversations about their parents in the previous months. Their mother was in declining health and increasingly senile, but their father though feeble had been doing well. The Sheehan brothers assumed their mother would go first. They had even discussed putting her in a nursing home and moving Dad in with one of them. The grandchildren were keener on that idea than the daughters-in-law. Well, now Dad's situation had resolved itself and they would have to move their mother out of the house after all.

Dan cut short his business trip and caught a flight back to Detroit and then, with Margie, to Philadelphia. Brother Joe and his wife Mary arrived in Philadelphia a day ahead of them. Joe and Ed had already made the funeral arrangements.

Dan and Margie went to visit his mother in the old folks' home. The building looked a hundred years old. Its dingy grey façade was broken by rows of tall, narrow windows marching across each level. Once inside the massive oak front doors, Dan and Margie found themselves in a long, high-ceilinged corridor lined with doors topped with transom windows. The paint was peeling off the walls and there was a faint scent of urine.

"Holy Mother of God!" Margie said. "Is this the best Ed could do for your mother?"

Dan sighed. "There's no money. We don't have any to spare, and neither do my brothers. Our parents had enough to get by, but they could only live comfortably as long as they stayed healthy. I don't know what's going to happen now. I don't know what my parents have at this point."

"This place will kill her within a year," Margie predicted.

"It would kill me faster than that," Dan said.

"As hard as it was, I'm glad Mama died quickly last year, just like your father, and not have to face living like this."

Dan's mother sat slumped in a wheelchair in the middle of a large common room, a large space with a wall of unwashed windows at one end and a mix of unmatched old chairs and sofas scattered about. Most of the room's occupants sat quietly, lost in their thoughts or maybe just lost. Two men played checkers at a table by the windows. A few sat watching a television — *The Guiding Light*, Margie thought.

It had been two years since Dan had last seen his mother and he was taken aback. Her uncombed white hair half hid a face full of wrinkles and eyes full of nothing except the occasional stab of terror.

Margie took her hand, "Mother Sheehan, it is so good to see you! It's Daniel and Margaret. We are just heartbroken with Father Sheehan's death. At least he went painlessly. I hope you are comfortable here."

The old woman's expression gave no hint of understanding, the mutters under her breath barely approximating speech.

Margie turned to Dan. "Dan? Say something!"

Dan shook his head as if he were trying to awake from a dream. He bent close over his mother. "Mother, we've come a long way together. You and Dad have done so much for Joe, Ed, and me. And we are forever thankful and grateful. We will take care of everything." After a moment's hesitation, he added, "I love you."

His mother did not respond. A trail of spittle formed on her chin. Margie wiped it away. "Don't you worry about a thing. Everything will be all right."

They did not stay long.

That night at dinner with Joe and Ed and their wives they heard more about Daniel Sheehan's last weeks. "I stopped by every day," Ed said. "It was so, so depressing, the two of them trying to pretend as if nothing had changed, as if they weren't both in their eighties and unable to fend for themselves. Dad would not discuss leaving the house or allowing Mother to be taken from him. 'We've been married more than fifty years,' he told me. 'We have never spent a night apart. We never will.' Mother would sit there, nodding. But it had been months since she last participated in a conversation in any meaningful way. And Dad, it took all his energy to take care of her. He barely had enough in him to take care of himself. I'd go home crying."

"Yes," agreed Ed's wife, Patricia. "I'd visit with Ed a couple of times a week, go by myself during the day once in a while. It took everything I had to pretend with them that things were going to be OK. It was heartbreaking. Father Sheehan just could not accept that Mother Sheehan needed more than he could give her."

"Is this the fate we all face?" Dan pondered. "We go from youth where everything is possible to old age where even the simple tasks are too much to handle."

"When they got married all those years ago, do you think they could have imagined us now?" Joe asked. "Me a chemical engineer, Dan a rocket scientist, and Ed—what exactly do you do, Ed? I always forget."

Everyone laughed politely. "I'm a babysitter for our parents, of course," Ed replied, "since the two of you ran off to Michigan. In my spare time, I'm an airline mechanic."

"That's my point!" Joe said. "Back then, how could they even have imagined the kinds of things we'd all be doing today?"

Margie interrupted. "Let's remember why we're here. We're burying your father tomorrow. Let's talk about him and your mother. In all these years, I've never heard much of their story, except that they each came from Ireland, met here, got married, and had you three darling children. There must be more to it than that."

"They never really talked about Ireland, either one of them, did they?" Dan said. "I guess they must both have had it really rough just to up and come over here, leaving their families and everything behind. I remember Margie's father once telling me — in fact, I think it was the first time I ever met him — he asked about our family and I didn't know much and he told me I should ask our parents about their history. I never did. I guess I just figured I wouldn't get anywhere with it."

Ed reminisced. "Remember that school project I had that time? All us kids had to prepare reports on our families' backgrounds. Being a typical Catholic school, we had the usual mix of paddies, polaks, dagoes, krauts, and even one or two ukies."

"Dear," Patricia said, "sometimes I think you say things

like that just to get a rise out of people. It's the 1960s. You shouldn't use terms like that in polite company."

"Polite company? We're a pack of paddies!"

"Excuse me," Mary held up a dissenting hand. "My grandparents came from England."

"And for that we forgive you!" Ed nodded in her direction. "We don't hold you personally responsible for seven hundred years of English oppression of our native land!"

"I can't tell you how thankful I am for that," Mary answered.

Ed ignored her. "Anyhoo, as I was saying, I had this school project on family history. I was maybe ten or twelve, don't quite remember, so this must've been the late twenties."

"We remember that," Dan and Joe said.

"Yeah, I tried to get our parents to open up about their families, and they both shot me down, said it was ancient history and to leave it in the past. Thanks, folks, I thought, that's a big help. I'm sure Sister Brigid will be very impressed."

"How strange!" Margie exclaimed.

"So, what *did* happen with your school report?" Joe asked. "I don't remember."

"I made up a family history, about how our parents had

been driven off the land by the evil English landlord who burned down their pathetic little cottage. They barely escaped to America with their lives and the rags on their backs. Sister Brigid loved it. Her people came over during the Famine."

Everyone laughed.

"Still, why should the past be so mysterious?" Dan wondered.

The conversation returned to an earlier discussion Joe and Ed had had about what to do with their parents' house and the things in it. If he felt slighted by his brothers' making decisions without his participation, Dan said nothing.

Margie spoke up, "Dan is the oldest son. Don't you think he should have some say in this?"

Ed looked at her. "Well, Dan may be oldest, and I may be youngest," he responded with a smile, "but the fact is I live here and I've had to worry about this stuff nonstop. I just shared my ideas with Joe. After all, he got here yesterday. He seems OK with my plans. It's not like there's any big estate to break up. There's just the furniture and stuff in the house, and the house itself. They had no real money."

"That's true," said Joe agreeably.

"But the stuff in the house includes things of sentimental value to each of you," Margie pressed. "They lived in that house for decades. Why, the three of you grew up in that house. I'd just hope you don't get rid of things until you know who wants what."

"No quarrel from me," Ed replied.

"What will you do with the stuff nobody wants to keep?" Patricia asked. "The clothes and the furniture and the kitchen stuff, for example."

"I think Mother would want us to give it to St. Vincent de Paul," Joe proposed.

"I told you!" Ed exclaimed. "We can't do that! We need the money to pay for her nursing home. With luck, she'll be dead before the money runs out."

"That's a cheery thought," Patricia said.

"You know what I mean," Ed huffed. "I'm assuming none of us wants the big stuff and we're just each expecting to keep little mementoes of the past. Everything else, we have to sell. We can't give it away."

"Agreed," Dan said.

"Agreed," Joe said.

The wake took place the following afternoon at O'Kelly's Funeral Parlor on Wayne Avenue. Coming in from the cold and drizzle, Dan and Margie passed through the front doors into a reception hall, off of which opened three viewing rooms and offices. A wooden placard outside one room read "Daniel Joseph Sheehan." A shelf below it held a condolence book and a stack of funeral prayer cards. The front of the prayer cards had an image of Jesus Christ holding in His left hand His Sacred Heart encircled with a crown of thorns and surmounted by a cross. The back of the card read: "My Jesus, have mercy on the soul of Daniel J. Sheehan, Sr.," and a prayer for the dead.

Daniel J. Sheehan Sr. lay in an open casket at the far end of the viewing room. He was dressed in a dark suit, a white shirt, and a green tie with a shamrock pattern. His hands lay folded across his chest holding a small crucifix. From somewhere came the low sound of organ music.

Dan and Margie stepped up to the kneeler in front of the casket. "Oh, my," Margie whispered, "he looks so lifelike. And younger. It's like the mortician took the pain and the age away."

"Yes," Dan agreed, scarcely able to accept that this lifeless corpse was his father. "It's quite remarkable."

They knelt, bowed their heads, and made the sign of the cross. "Well, Dad," Dan murmured to himself, "this is it. Time to say goodbye. It's hard to imagine you not being in this world with us. Thank you for all you did for me. Thank you for being good to Margie. Thank you for being a good grandfather to Peggy, Jane, Danny, and Timmy. Joe and Ed and I will take care of Mother for you. Rest in peace. I love you."

Dan made the sign of the cross and stood up. Margie had

finished before him and was talking to her sisters-in-law. He looked around the room. Flower wreaths and bouquets stood like sentinels along the wall. The funeral home had set up four rows of folding chairs.

Ed had placed an obituary and funeral notices in the *Inquirer* and the *Bulletin*. Their parents' old friends and neighbors were dead, so they did not expect a large turnout for the wake. But there were a few surprises. A young couple who had recently moved in across the street from their parents and developed a pleasant relationship with Daniel Sheehan came to pay their respects. One or two old-timers from their father's job turned up. Even a couple of Dan's Central High classmates came. He had had no contact with them for more than thirty years. They had seen the obituary and come to pay their respects to a man they once knew almost as well as their own fathers.

Toward the end of the wake another elderly man entered the room. He looked around uncertainly and then shuffled up to the casket. He peered in at Daniel Sheehan and sighed deeply. He knelt, made the sign of the cross, and prayed silently.

"Who do you suppose that is?" Ed asked.

"Never saw him before in my life," Joe said. They moved over to the casket.

"Good evening," Dan said to the man as he rose from the

kneeler. "Thank you for coming. My brothers and I appreciate it."

The man looked from Dan to Ed to Joe.

"It's a sad day," he said after a moment. "I never imagined years ago when we were children that this was the way it would be at the end."

"None of us ever does, I guess," Joe offered. "Did you know our father well?"

The man looked at each in turn. "You are his sons?"

"I'm Daniel Sheehan, the oldest," Dan said. "And these are my brothers Joseph and Edward."

"I am Patrick Sheehan. I am your father's brother."

"What?" All three reacted.

"We didn't know our father had any family in this country," Dan explained. "We thought he came over by himself."

The man gave them a quizzical look. "Came over?" he repeated. "You mean came over from Ireland? Is that what he told you?" He looked around. "Your mother, might she be here?"

"No," Ed answered. "She's not. She's not well."

"Ah, I had hoped to see her. It's been so many years. She was a beautiful woman, your mother, when she was young. Your father would do anything for her."

"Please," said Joe, "won't you come over here and sit

with us? You seem to know things about our family that we obviously don't."

The four of them sat in some of the easy chairs at the side of the room. Dan saw Margie begin to move toward them. He waved her away.

"So, what is our story?" Ed asked. "Our father didn't come over by himself from Ireland 1905 or so?"

"Well, no. Your father was born and grew up in Gloucester City, just across the river in New Jersey. All of us were. It was our father, John, who immigrated about 1870 or so."

"All of us?" Dan said, dismayed. "Who is all of us?"

"Well, besides your father and me, there were Lizzie, John, Ellen, Charlie, and Mary. Your father was the third oldest."

"And our mother? Was she born in Jersey too?"

"Oh, no, she was an immigrant. She and her family came over in the 1880s."

"Wait—she came with her family? We thought she came alone."

Patrick Sheehan gave them a troubled look. "I didn't mean to stir up things that have lain quiet for fifty years. I just came to say goodbye to Daniel Sheehan. With his passing, I'm the last of Jack and Meg Sheehan's children."

"You're not stirring up anything. We want to know. We

have the right to know."

Patrick Sheehan considered for a moment. "All right. I will tell you about our family. I make no judgments and I hope you make none. As I said, my father, your grandfather, landed in Gloucester City from Ireland about 1870. By himself, I believe, but who knows? Within a few years he met Margaret Kelly, another recent immigrant. They married and we started to arrive one by one, although Lizzie may have already been on the way when they married.

"Your mother, Margaret Danaher, came with her family, she the baby with about a half dozen older brothers and sisters. Our two families lived on the same block in Gloucester City, almost directly underneath where the Walt Whitman Bridge is now. It was a poor neighborhood, full of immigrant families scraping by.

"As we got older, my brother Daniel took a fancy to young Margaret. And why not? She was just about the prettiest and most charming colleen in Gloucester City. And such a sad life, what with her mother, Johanna, and half her brothers and sisters dead of tuberculosis in their first years here and her father, Liam, working himself to death by the time she was twenty. She had a dark streak, too, and Heaven help you if you crossed her. Of course, that's not unknown among us Irish. I don't mean to speak ill of her."

"We know exactly what you mean," Dan interjected.

"We grew up with her." He cast a look in Margie's direction. She was talking to a pair of mourners but watching the brothers.

"She had a way of taking to heart almost any slight and not letting it go. My wife, Katherine (God rest her soul), said it was almost as if she cherished the hurt. So as time went on she pretty much stopped talking to her family.

"Well, Daniel and Margaret got married, oh, about nineteen aught eight or so. I was one of the witnesses."

"That's right," Joe agreed. "It was June 1908."

"Once she was married, your mother wanted out of Gloucester City. 'I'll not be raising my children in a place like this!' she said more than once. We thought it was all talk, but she did have a point. We were a bunch of mick stereotypes: barkeeps, dockworkers, common laborers. Even our parents had met in the saloon our mother's father ran. Not a lot of schooling in the whole lot of us. We had jobs, but we weren't high society. She wanted more for her children. I tried to tell her to get over herself. 'You're no better than the rest of us, Maggie Mae,' I'd tell her. 'I know you started out crawling in the dirt of a potato farm in Tipperary. Don't be giving yourself airs.' Not that I had any influence with her. And she and my mother, oh, they would go at it like wildcats. They never got along. My mother was already a widow then, and I will confess she did have a way of involving herself in other

210

people's affairs. All her daughters-in-law resented it, your mother most of all. Well, then, one day leaving Gloucester City wasn't just talk. Daniel and she announced they were going up to Rahway near New York City."

"Rahway is where I was born," Dan said.

"Well, after the move we heard from Daniel on occasion and from Margaret not at all. Strange when you think it's usually the women who hold families together. But it being Margaret, none of us was all that surprised. Then, after a couple of years the cards and letters stopped arriving and mail we sent their way came back marked 'unknown at this address.' So that was the last we knew of your parents. And now after all these years I find my brother and his family living just this side of the river in Philadelphia all this time."

"What about our grandparents?" Dan asked. "What became of them?"

"My father died in 1905, and my mother, Margaret, in 1926."

"1926!" Joe exclaimed. "And the three of us alive at the time and our grandmother just the other side of the river!"

"Well, no, actually," the older man corrected. "She was living with my sister Lizzie and her family when she died, on Dauphin Street here in Philadelphia."

"Just a few miles from us," Ed murmured, "and we never knew her."

Their uncle sighed deeply. "Well, families can be strange, can't they?" With help from Dan, he rose from the chair.

"Will you come to the funeral tomorrow?" Ed asked. "There's so much we would like to know."

"No, I think not. I came to say goodbye to Daniel and now I have. It's all very tiring. I am sorry to have caused you any trouble. Please tell your mother Pat Sheehan sends his regards and wishes her good health and long life."

"Please call if we can do anything for you. Or if you just want to talk," Dan handed Patrick Sheehan his business card as the three brothers walked with him to the door. "There is still so much we would love to learn about the family."

When they returned to the wake, Margie stopped Dan. "Who was the old man you were talking to all this time? The three of you have been ignoring people!"

Dan shrugged his shoulders. "Who was he? Believe it or not, that's my Uncle Patrick."

"Your Uncle Patrick? I didn't know you had any uncles."

"Neither did we."

Later, Dan preferred not to dwell on the memories of that week: the funeral itself on a cold, rainy day; the last goodbye with his mother at the nursing home; the last visit to his parents' house.

Margie called it the house he grew up in, but that wasn't

really true. The house he grew up in was the one down on Gladstone Street by the docks. The house Dan's parents had lived in for the past twenty-five years stood in northeast Philadelphia on Longshore Avenue. A row house too, like the Gladstone house, but on a pretty street with a small front yard, a living room, dining room, and kitchen on the first floor, three bedrooms and a bath upstairs, and a garage in the basement facing the back alley. Dan was already twenty-five when the family moved there, already finished with school and out in the workforce.

The brothers agreed to meet at their parents' house the morning after the funeral — the day before Dan and Margie planned to return to Detroit — to see who wanted what. Dan and Margie arrived in a taxi and walked up to the front door. Ed let them in. They stepped into the living room to find Joe and Mary already there.

Dan had not visited the house in several years. Everything still looked as it always had: a chesterfield sofa with a large oval mirror over it, a couple of easy chairs, some side tables with lamps on them, a china cabinet full of knickknacks, and the old RCA Radiola. The only "new" thing in the room was the Magnavox television that their father had bought just a few years earlier. It felt so strange to be in this place with neither parent present. He could not remember such an occurrence in all the years they had lived here.

"So, how are we going to divide the spoils?" Joe asked.

"Don't be morbid, Joe," Mary chided.

"Why don't you fellows just wander around the house and leave a slip of paper with your name on it with anything you want for yourself?" Margie suggested. "If nobody else wants it, it's yours. If somebody else is interested, you can discuss."

"Sounds like a plan," Ed said.

"I really don't want much of anything," Dan put in. "Too much trouble to cart stuff onto the plane!"

"Don't worry about that," Ed said. "I can always box stuff up and ship it to you in Michigan."

Joe said, "I'll start upstairs."

"I'll start in the basement and work my way up," Dan said. He and Margie walked into the dining room. Margie ran her finger along the dining room table as they passed, leaving a finger trail in the dust.

"I wonder when this place was last cleaned," she said.

"I imagine cleaning was low on my parents' list of priorities the last few months," Dan answered. "With their eyesight, they probably couldn't see the dirt anyway."

They went into the kitchen. Dirty plates and dishes covered the counter and sat in the sink. Dan thought the sight was almost worse than seeing his father lying in the coffin.

"Holy Mother of God," Margie exclaimed. "It breaks my heart to see this. Your mother was always so meticulous in her house cleaning."

They went down the stairs into the basement. Off to one side in the garage stood Dad's decade-old navy-blue Studebaker, undriven for years but, except for a layer of dust, still looking factory-new.

"Dad was so proud of that car," Dan said wistfully. "The first time he ever bought a brand-new car. A long way from his first used Model T!" The way of the world: you spend your life trying to get ahead and then you die.

His mother's old washing machine stood in a corner. Shelves along one wall held unmarked boxes and mildewed books. Other boxes sat scattered randomly on the floor.

Dan made his way across the floor to his father's workbench. It and the rusting tools lying on top of it brought a flood of memories. "Margie, do you remember that Christmas a few years back when we had no money and I glued some Currier and Ives pictures to wood blocks and cut them into jigsaw puzzles as presents for the children?"

"Yes, dear. I do. That was very sweet. The children loved them."

"Well, yes, they were happy to get them, but they couldn't hide their disappointment when we didn't bring out more presents."

"Yes, it hurt that we couldn't give them more."

"It hurt that they demanded more. Anyway, this bench reminds me of that Christmas. I learned that trick of making a jigsaw puzzle from Dad, in his work shed at the old house, decades ago. Just me and my dad. That was in the old house, but it's the same bench." Dan stood looking at it.

Margie cocked her head. "Do you want to take the bench to Detroit?"

"No, of course not," he answered, startled out of his musing. "It's just an old bench, and not a very good one at that. But it takes me back. I always smile when I think of those days." He balanced a level on his finger. "I wonder if Danny and Timmy will say stuff like that about me forty years from now."

"Of course they will, dear!" Margie assured him.

A few weeks after Dan's father's funeral, the phone on the wall in the kitchen rang.

"I have a person-to-person call for Mr. Daniel Sheehan," the long-distance operator's voice droned.

"I'm Daniel Sheehan."

"Go ahead, please. Your party is on the line," the operator said.

"Mr. Sheehan? This is Patrick Sheehan."

Dan was pleased to hear the voice. "Yes. It's good to hear from you."

"No, I'm sorry, I'm Pat Sheehan, Junior. It was my father who spoke to you at your father's funeral."

"I see. So, you're my cousin Pat."

"I just found your business card in my father's wallet."

"I gave it to him when we talked."

"I wanted to let you know my father died."

Dan sagged into a kitchen chair. "I'm very sorry to hear that. When's the funeral?"

"It was yesterday morning. It was only after we got back home afterward that I went through his wallet. I don't know why I didn't think to do that sooner. He told me about his visit with you, but I didn't realize he had your phone number."

"I'm very sorry. I wish we had known him and your family long ago."

"Yes." An indifferent sound to the voice. "I have to go. I just wanted to pass on the news."

"I understand. Please accept my condolences. Goodbye."

In the end, despite promises to box things up and ship them to Detroit, Dan got nothing of his parents'. He tried not to let it bother him, until dinner at Joe and Mary's one night. Joe and Dan and their wives were at the dining room table with the three daughters, with the two boys at the table in the kitchen.

The Sheehans were discussing Patti's recent first-place

finish at the Detroit Symphony Orchestra's Young Musicians Competition.

"That's so exciting!" Margie said. "We're all so proud of you!"

Dan's look happened to linger on Mary's china cabinet. His eyes suddenly focused on the little sterling silver bowl Dan—not Joe, not Ed—had given their parents on their twenty-fifth wedding anniversary in 1933 and the gold wine goblets the three brothers gave them on their fiftieth in 1958. Dan said nothing until they got home.

"What?" Margie exclaimed. "That's just crazy. Ask your brother what he's doing with them. Ask your other brother where all the other items are he promised to send. Better yet, ask your sister-in-law. I special ordered those goblets from Wanamaker's! If she has them out in full view, I wonder what else they have hidden in the rest of their house."

"Margie, let it go," Dan said. "I don't understand, but I'm going to let it go."

# Margaret Says Goodbye to Her Mother

### 1963

Margaret Sheehan sat slumped in her wheelchair. Who visited her? Daniel and Margaret. But Daniel was dead. Eddie had told her so. And she was Margaret. One of them, anyway. She, young Daniel's wife, their daughter.

She looked around the common room. All these old people. Half dead. She supposed she looked the same way to them. She squinted at the unwashed windows. Why does no one wash those windows? She tried to think. Where was she? Such a large room. Had she ever sat in such a large room? Her thoughts drifted.

"Where is Maggie? Let me see my Maggie." Deep coughs

219

punctuated the request. Little nine-year-old Margaret stepped to her mother's side. Her mother cupped her face in her hands. "A stór, you are our little treasure. I think — I pray that when we are all gone you will still live." She turned aside as another cough overwhelmed her. Blood dripped on the rag in her hand. "Mairead, you must live for me. You must live for all of us." The girl looked at her in horror. "Do not be afraid, my little one. I know that you will have a long life. That thought is what makes me happy now, what makes me think my life has been worthwhile. Promise me you will have a happy life."

"That I will, Mamaí," Margaret answered quietly.

Her mother smiled and lay back on the mattress. She pointed at Margaret's father. "Remember, your dadaí will take care of you, even when I am gone." Another wracking cough. "Today is a New Year. It means better things to come." Her mother had to give in to the pain in her chest. She coughed even harder than before, the exploding blood escaping around the rag with which she sought to contain it. "Now I think I need to rest a bit. You had better go and call the others so I can bid them all slán."

"Yes, Mamaí." Margaret ran off in search of her siblings.

Early one morning six months their father's death, Dan answered the phone to hear Ed say, "The nursing home just called. Mother is dead."

Dan hung his head. "Well, that's not much of a surprise. Did she ever have any moments of lucidity since Dad's passing?"

"Not that we ever saw. Once in a while one of the nursing aides would claim she had said something coherent, but if she did, it passed quickly. I got to tell you, I feel almost nothing. It's like she died months ago, with Dad."

"I feel the same way."

"We should plan a family gathering sometime that doesn't involve a funeral."

Dan chuckled. "Now that's an idea."

"Should I bother with a death notice in the paper?"

"I don't think so. What would be the point? Everybody she knew is dead."

George Wallace, Alabama's new governor, promises 'segregation now, segregation tomorrow, and segregation forever' / Chevy Corvair Monza: mated to the road like it's married to it! / *He's a rebel and he'll never ever be any good* / Post Office speeding up mail delivery with introduction of new 'Zone Improvement Plan' / Lots of ladies are snapping up Betty Friedan's *The Feminine Mystique*. Let's hope it doesn't go to their heads / Tune in today at 1 p.m. for ABC's new daytime serial, *General Hospital*, brought to you by Proctor and Gamble! / Al Kaline remains highest paid Tiger at $55,000 / Does she or doesn't she? Only her hairdresser knows for sure! / And now, that hit song from Japan, 'Sukiyaki!'

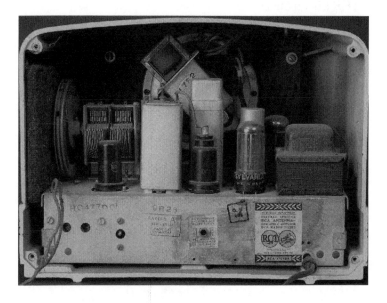

# Dan Fixes a Radio

## 1963

An April Sunday in the late afternoon, Dan sat in his basement workshop repairing an old Bakelite radio he'd had since the 1930s. He peered at its wiring through his bifocals. The radio lay on the bench, a patient on an operating table, Dan poking and prodding its innards. A fluorescent lamp humming in the ceiling and an old metal desk lamp on the bench made up for the weak sunshine leaking in through the small window at the top of the basement wall. Over against the far wall, Timmy played quietly with his trains.

Dan heard Margie come down the steps humming a

classical tune. "Are you down here, dear?" she called.

"Yes, over here in my cave. What're you humming?"

She hesitated a second and laughed. "I actually had to think about it. It's 'Addio del passato' from *La Traviata*."

He heard her go into the laundry area and drop a pile of clothes on the floor. "It's a lovely melody, isn't it, but it sounds kind of sad."

"Yes. Quite sad. The heroine is singing her heart out as she dies of tuberculosis. It starts out, 'Farewell, happy dreams of the past,' and ends, "God pardon and accept me, all is finished.'"

Dan replaced one of the radio's vacuum tubes. "So, not exactly a light-hearted comedy?"

"That's for sure."

Margie's knowledge of classical music always surprised Dan. He enjoyed it when she put a record on the phonograph or listened to the classical music station, but he had never shared her enthusiasm. And it had never occurred to him she would know the words. They'd been married more than twenty years, he thought, and there was still so much they didn't know about one another.

"Timmy, enough of your railroading," he heard her say. "Time to go upstairs and get cleaned up for dinner."

"Yes, Mommy." Dan heard the boy leave the basement.

"Margie, did you ever picture us this way twenty years

ago?" he asked

"Whatever are you talking about?" She sounded more engaged with the laundry than with the conversation.

"I mean, when we got married. Did you ever imagine us twenty years later, here in this house, four kids, another one on the way, the whole works?"

"Ha! Lucky for you I didn't, or you might have gotten a different answer that night at Pasquale's."

Dan's hand slipped, dislodging a radio wire. "But I mean, think how much the world has changed, how much we've all changed. What if we could have known then what all would follow?"

"Thank God we didn't." She started the washing machine. "Dan, I think this is the kind of conversation that works better after an old fashioned. Which reminds me," she called as she headed up the steps. "Guy and Toni Alfieri are coming over tonight after dinner to play bridge. So be sure to wash up, and don't forget to mix the old fashioneds. Oh, my back hurts! And where is Peggy? She's been gone for hours. I swear that girl tries my patience. Just wait till she gets home!"

"Be up in a minute," he called. "I just need to replace one last tube in this radio."

# Peggy's Good News

## 1963

Peggy ran up the stairs. She stepped quickly through the boys' bedroom into her own and slammed the door.

She swore to God, if Mother pulled this stunt one more time, she was going to smack her back. She dropped on the bed. "Don't give me any back talk!" her mother always said. "You better show me some respect!" she said. Respect? Fat chance. Here she was in college, and Mother still treated her like a child. Between the nuns at school and Mother at home, she couldn't breathe. Going steady was no big deal. It was the sixties, after all, not the thirties. Peggy didn't drink, she didn't smoke, she brought home good grades. And besides, sooner or later, she would marry Anthony. What did her mother want from her?

Peggy closed her eyes, thinking of her childhood fantasy, she the kidnapped princess whose captors kept her as unpaid help. Someday a prince would come and rescue her and give her the life she deserved. Someday.

Shouldn't she have some connection to these people who were her parents? To Jane? Her brothers? She felt out of place, wrong, in the Sheehan household.

Peggy hated her parents' attempts to do things as a family. She wanted nothing to do with family togetherness. The Sunday drives in the DeSoto, for example. Sightseeing around Detroit or across the river in Windsor might be fun with her friends—but it was decidedly *not* fun with her family.

Worse still was the religious stuff. Mass every Sunday, evening Benediction every Thursday, tuna casserole on Fridays, confession on Saturdays, all the Holy Days of Obligation, and the rosary after dinner almost every night. God help you if you said the prayers too quickly or miscounted the ten Hail Marys in any of its five decades. You'd think the family lived in a goddamn convent the way they had a crucifix or a saint's statue in every room!

Peggy preferred anywhere to home. She enjoyed her

time at Marygrove with the friends she had made there and the activities they did together, whether in the school drama club or at parties at one of their houses (never at the Sheehans'!). Her friends came from nice places like Birmingham and Bloomfield Hills and Grosse Pointe. They had wonderful homes and refined mothers. Some even had colored maids.

Peggy hated this house, this neighborhood. She looked around at the knotty pine walls. She lived in an attic! She looked out the window at a stack of wrecked autos next door at the gas station. She lived in an attic next to a junkyard!

Her friends called her Margaret. Margaret sounded distinguished, elegant, even if it were her mother's name. Peggy might as well have been the Irish washerwoman. That's what she was around here. God forbid the boys ever did anything. They were boys.

Peggy considered sneaking out to the drug store to call Anthony. More than five minutes on the phone at home and her mother would whine, "Other people live in this house, too. What if somebody's trying to call us?"

When Peggy appeared at home tonight with Anthony's GM Tech Center pin fastened to her sweater, her parents were caught off guard.

Dan and Margie were sitting at a folding card table in the living room playing bridge with the Alfieris. The boys, just out of sight around the corner in their parents' bedroom, lay on the bed watching *Bonanza* on the portable Zenith television they had wheeled in from the kitchen. The announcer declared, "The following program is brought to you in living color on NBC," as the NBC color peacock flickered in various shades of grey on the black-and-white screen. Peggy announced, "Anthony and I are going steady! We're going to get married!"

The four people at the card table turned to look at her. Her mother slowly lay her cards down. "You are what?" she asked.

"Margie." Dan cautioned her.

"I'm getting married. Aren't you happy for me?"

"No," Margie responded. "It's out of the question."

"You hate Anthony, don't you? That's it."

"No, we don't hate him. He is a fine, young man. That's not the problem and you know it."

"Maybe we should go?" Toni said to Guy.

"No," Margie said. "Stay. This won't take long."

"Peggy," Dan interjected, "all we've asked is that you wait. You graduate soon enough."

Ignoring him, Peggy faced her mother. "Yes, I know the problem. You hate me. You just have to stand against anything that might make me happy."

Toni laid a hand on Peggy's arm. "Dear, please let's not

do this." Peggy shrugged the hand away.

"Peggy, that's not true," her father said. "That's not true and you know it."

Margie sat with her head down, idly flicking her cards on the table. "Peggy," she said in a low voice, "I do not hate you. I have tried for twenty years to do my best for you. It has not been easy. You have not made it easy."

"That's right, blame me. As if I'm the one with all the problems."

"Peggy, please. Stop it," Dan said.

"I'm not the one—" Margie began.

"Why did you even have children? You never wanted us. You never wanted me."

Her mother gasped and put her hand to her mouth.

"I'm done. I'm going upstairs," Peggy said. She turned to open the stair door. Margie jumped from her seat and crossed the short space between them. Peggy, her hand on the doorknob, turned and looked at her. Without a word, her mother slapped her across the face, hard, and Peggy fell to the floor.

The Alfieris sat with their heads down, looking at the cards in their hands. The boys lay motionless, facing the TV screen, not seeing the gunfight it displayed. Dan stared at his wife. Margie covered her face with her hands and sobbed. Rubbing her cheek, Peggy jumped up and ran up the stairs.

Footsteps on the stairs. A knock on the bedroom door.

"Come in," Peggy said more sharply than she intended. Her father entered and sat next to her on the bed.

"Your mother didn't mean it, Peggy," he said. "You just took us by surprise, and she didn't know what she was doing. Now she's crying her eyes out."

"Let her cry. It's not the first time."

Dan exhaled. "She does her best, we both do our best, to be good parents. We know we're not perfect. But we love you. We love all four of you."

Peggy stared at him. "Love? Love? I feel no love in this house. All she wants to do is make my life miserable, and you do nothing to stop her." She turned to face him. "Why do you have to judge everything I do? Why can't you just be happy for me, for once in my life?"

He sighed again. "Sometimes being a good parent means making your life miserable. It's not all sweetness and light. If I don't interfere, it's because I agree with your mother. Can't you hold off on Anthony until you graduate? You're young. Your whole life lies ahead of you. Anthony's a fine man in many ways. You have plenty of time to get to know him without all this talk about going steady and getting married." He hesitated a second. "You know, you and your mother are very much alike."

Peggy bristled. "We are not at all alike."

231

Dan laughed. "Yes, yes, you are. And you both remind me of my own mother. Maybe there's something in the name Margaret? But you are each very strong-willed, very black-and-white, very unbending. I could tell you about some of the run-ins I had with my mother growing up."

"That was different. You were a boy. Things are different for me. For Jane, even."

"Maybe so. But we all have to live together. We all have to get along."

She considered his statement a moment. Then she said, "Do we? I'm not sure we can. Or that we should even try pretending."

US conducts underground nuclear test in Nevada /
Winston tastes good like a cigarette should! / Detroit
Council for Human Rights plans June 'Walk to Freedom'
down Woodward to Cobo Hall. Marchers to include Martin
Luther King, Mayor Cavanagh, UAW President Reuther /
*It's my party and I'll cry if I want to* / Wayne State University
report: Detroit to lose quarter of population by 1970 / Flash:
Birmingham police use dogs, cattle prods on demonstrators
/ Avanti from Studebaker, America's only 4-passenger
high-performance personal car! / This is a test. For the next
60 seconds, this station will conduct a test of the Emergency
Broadcast System. This is only a test.

# Timmy at Play

## 1963

Timmy sat on a stool in the basement observing his own private world: the four-foot by eight-foot green plywood platform with his model trains.

Through the small window at the far end of the basement, he saw a car pull into the driveway. A car door opened and closed, and the car left. Someone came in the back door and up into the kitchen. Probably Jane, he thought. He kept quiet, hoping she didn't call down to see if he were there. No reason to spoil the afternoon by risking a run-in with her. He returned to his trains.

At least nobody shamed him for playing with them. They were an okay outlet for a boy's imagination. But his family of stuffed animals collected over the years had been a different story. On his last birthday, his tenth, Timmy had finally given in to his parents and gathered his stuffed animal friends together. What a group they made: one little boy among a bunch of stuffed old folks. Truly, they had aged. Their fur was faded and discolored, a few eyes and even one or two mouths were missing, and none had enough muscle tone to sit up by himself. Even poor Boo Boo oozed clumps of his insides out of the holes in his armpits. Timmy took them outside. Without hesitating, he dumped them into the round metal garbage can and dragged it out to the street next to the other one Danny had put out.

Another car in the driveway. A door opened and closed. This time the car stayed. Someone else came in the back door. Timmy heard Jane say, "You're home early," and Peggy answer, "I skipped my last class. Anthony picked me up and brought me home."

"Blah blah blah," he mouthed, and paid them no more attention.

He stood at the curb as the garbage truck pulled up. Two men jumped off to empty the cans, one a bald-headed, old man with a pot belly and yellow teeth, the second, a tall, young man in jeans with wavy blond hair, a dirty T-shirt with holes in the armpits, a crushed pack of cigarettes in a rolled-up sleeve, and tattoos on both his muscled arms. Timmy had only ever seen tattoos in Popeye cartoons before.

The young man grabbed the can with Timmy's friends. It took all Timmy's willpower to remain still, not to run over and grab the can from the man, to rescue his friends from the trash and hide them in the attic from the big people.

The young man smiled at Timmy. "You look like you just lost your best bud, squirt," he said as he lifted the trash can and emptied the stuffed animals and the rest of the garbage into the back of the truck.

"No, sir," Timmy said.

"Do you wanna be a garbage man like me when you grow up?"

I just wanna go home with you, Timmy thought. "No, sir." He pointed at the gas station. "I wanna work there so I can live at home."

The older man laughed. "That's a plan."

The younger man said, "But think of all the adventures you'll miss sticking so close to home. What will your folks think, you staying at home when you're all growed up?"

Timmy didn't answer. The man put the empty trash can back at the curb and paused for a second as if he were waiting to see if Timmy had anything else to say.

"Come on! Let's get a move on!" the truck's driver called out from the cab.

"Well, see ya, kid," the garbage man said. "Go play with your friends. Don't hang around here."

They jumped back up on the truck as it pulled away.

The memory made Timmy think of the family camping trips Up North. Brushing his teeth in the shower building, he would watch in the mirror as the men came in and undressed. He would watch them stand under the shower heads in the gang shower, soaping themselves, water splashing everywhere. He wondered whether he would ever be so muscular, so hairy, so big. And then his father or Danny would tell him to hurry up and finish and he hoped they hadn't noticed his stares.

The nuns had told him the importance of making a good confession. "Bless me, Father, for I have sinned," he would say when the priest slipped back the panel separating them. "It has been one week since my last confession. I lied three times, I was disobedient to my parents two times, and I got mad and pushed Lucy in the playground." What about looking at men undressing? Or thinking about that garbage man? Was that a sin? The nuns had talked about impure thoughts. What were impure thoughts?

Timmy heard steps overhead move from the living room through the kitchen. The back door slammed twice. He wondered what his sisters were up to.

Things had been so strange since the other night. Peggy flat on her back, their mother towering over her. Not the first screaming match between the two of them, but the first time their mother had socked her. One minute, their mother would be all sweetness and light, and then somebody would say something wrong and it was like an A-bomb went off. Timmy usually managed not to light the fuse, but Peggy and the others did it often enough.

Someone came back into the house. Jane? He decided to go upstairs.

# Sheehan Field

## 1963

Standing in the middle of the backyard on a cool and sunny afternoon in spring, Danny surveyed the open space. The yard sloped gently away from the house, with one large oak tree out behind the garage, two pine trees in another corner, and a crab apple tree off to one side. A metal mesh fence with wooden posts lined the boundary with the neighbors' yards and along the alleyway.

Yes, Danny thought, the yard would make a great baseball field. The biggest backyard on the street was something to brag about. Let the other kids go over to Memorial Park and try to find an open diamond. Sheehan

Field would be available whenever he and his friends wanted.

When he grew up, he thought, he would be a manager or maybe even a team owner. Wouldn't it be something to watch the Tigers from the owner's box at Briggs Stadium? They had recently renamed it Tiger Stadium, but both the Tigers and the Lions played there, so what was the point? He would change it back, or maybe even name it Sheehan Stadium!

Danny heard a car pull into the driveway. Jane came around the corner of the house and walked toward the back door. She looked in his direction, but he pretended not to see her, and she didn't say anything. The car left.

He examined his planned home base, a round patch already stripped of grass from all the times he had stood on it, throwing a ball against the back of the house. He saw a clear shot from home to first, and from first to second, but second to third might be a problem. The crab apple tree sat just off its line. Some stupid kid not paying attention might run into it, Danny thought. Maybe Timmy could smack into it and smash his face. Assuming he could ever hit a ball and get himself on base in the first place. Timmy was so clumsy with the bat. He couldn't even decide whether he wanted to swing right- or left-handed. As if it mattered. He could strike out in both directions. He had to be dragged into a ball game,

WILLIAM J. DUFFY

only giving in to the other boys' jeers. If they had more neighborhood kids, they'd never have to ask him again.

Danny heard another car in the driveway. This time Peggy swept past on her way to the back door, oblivious to everything around her, including Danny.

He wandered over to the driveway. Anthony sat there in a convertible, a car Danny had never seen.

"Hiya, sport," Anthony said. "Like the new wheels?"

"Neato! What is it?"

"It's the prototype for the 1965 Oldsmobile. I'm just giving it a little test drive."

"Cool! Say, watcha doin' here, anyway? Off on a date?"

Anthony looked uneasy. "I'll let Margaret tell you."

"OK. Well, see ya!"

"See ya, kid!"

Danny went back to work on his ball field. He started to unravel a string to mark out the baseline between home and first.

He thought about his bout with rheumatic fever back in 1958, the worst time of his life. He spent months downtown in Henry Ford Hospital, wondering whether he'd ever walk again, or whether he'd die like Jimmy Kaminski in the bed next to him. And he still had a bum heart. What was the point of all that bed rest and time in the hospital and everything if he never got well? The stupid disease might as well have

241

killed him. Nine years old and his life was over. Now every time he tried to do something fun, his mother said, "Danny, be careful! Remember what the doctors said!" The stupid doctors. What did they know? They should have fixed his heart.

He planted the string where first base would be.

If life was fair, Timmy's the one who should've got the fever. He would've loved just sitting around doing nothing and reading. What did he need a healthy heart for, anyway?

Peggy came out the back door, dragging a suitcase behind her. Jane quickly followed. Danny heard them say something to each other but couldn't make it out. Then Jane went back into the house and the car drove off.

A few minutes later, Timmy ran out the door and started across to the Romanos' backyard. "Hey, Timmy," Danny called, "what's up? Did the Wicked Witch lock us out again?"

Timmy paused briefly. "Nah. I'm jus' goin' over to the Rouleaus' to play." He started running again.

"Don't be late for supper," Danny called after him, and resumed his work on Sheehan Field.

A few more minutes and Jane came out the back door, heading for the garage. Who did she think she was fooling, smoking in the garage?

He decided to follow her.

# Say an Extra Hail Mary

### 1963

Jane got out of Jennifer's Falcon. She was the last of the girls to get dropped off at home from school. She walked up the driveway in her plaid skirt and white blouse uniform and turned the corner at the back of the house. Danny was out in the middle of the backyard doing some weird practice involving taking giant steps. He didn't notice her, and she didn't call to him.

She went inside. Nobody home. Their father was still at the plant. Their mother was scheduled to work the afternoon shift at her part-time job at the R&B Dress Shop. Peggy never got home from Marygrove this early. Timmy might be in the basement. It was hard to tell; he was always so quiet.

She put her schoolbooks down on the kitchen table and

poured herself a glass of papaya juice out of the refrigerator. As she sipped it, she thought about the blow-up between her mother and Peggy. Jane came home that night and quickly realized the best course was to lie low. Peggy had not said a single word to their mother since Sunday. She looked right past her as if she were invisible. Their mother acted as if life were going on as usual. Their poor father looked like a lost soul.

She heard a car pull into the driveway. A few minutes later Peggy came through the back door, in a hurry. "You're home early," Jane said, alarmed by her sister's demeanor.

Peggy came to a stop in front of her. "I skipped my last class. Anthony picked me up and brought me home."

Jane looked out the kitchen window and saw Anthony sitting in a convertible in the driveway. "So, what's up?" she asked.

"You'll find out soon enough," Peggy answered, brushing past her and heading upstairs. Jane followed her to their bedroom. Peggy got a suitcase out of the closet and put it on her bed. She started pulling clothes haphazardly out of the dresser drawers and laying them next to the suitcase.

"What're you doing, Peggy?"

Peggy glowered at her. "What does it look like I'm doing? I'm packing up and clearing out of here before she and I kill each other."

244

Peggy had often muttered threats about leaving home, but until now it had been just words. "Where will you go? Do Mother and Daddy know?"

"They'll find out soon enough."

"I think you should wait for them."

"I think you should mind your own business."

Jane started to cry. "This isn't right, this isn't good. There has to be some way to work this out. It's wrong. You can't just leave like this, without talking to them first."

Peggy looked at her in disbelief. "Oh, yes, I can. Look on the bright side, sis. You'll have this crummy room to yourself from now on." She forced the suitcase shut and started down the stairs, using both hands to drag it. Jane followed her out to Anthony's waiting car.

"Tell Danny and Timmy goodbye for me, sis," Peggy said. "Maybe say an extra Hail Mary for me when you do the rosary tonight." She started to get into the car, but turned around. "You might want to say a prayer for yourself too while you're at it. From now on, you're the only daughter Mother will have to kick around. Go ahead — be sure and tell her I said that."

Jane watched Anthony and Peggy drive off.

Crap, she thought. She wiped her tears away. There'd be hell to pay when their mother got home. And Jane would pay it.

She went back into the house. Their mother could be such a pain. But Peggy always pushed it one step too far. Jane decided to go outside and have a smoke.

Timmy came up the stairs into the kitchen. "Hiding in the basement again, I see," Jane remarked. He looked at her vacantly. "What do you want, anyway?"

"Wutter you and Peggy upta?"

Jane glared at him. "None of your business. Why don't you get lost?"

"Can I go over to the Rouleaus' to play?"

"Sure. Just be back in time for supper. And don't make me have to call over there looking for you."

She watched Timmy run out the back door. She fished in her pocketbook for her cigarettes and headed out to the garage. No sneaking a smoke in the house, even if their father smoked there. The only place to escape their mother's keen nose was the garage, where the smells of old paint and oil and garbage masked the nicotine. She pulled a sawhorse out from the wall and perched herself on it. She lit a cigarette and drew a deep breath, idly looking out the open garage door down the driveway to the street.

Why couldn't they get along with their mother? When did they start to picture her as a monster? Jane guessed when they became teenagers. Well, in her case, anyway. Peggy probably always thought of their mother as the enemy. Jane wanted to hate her mother too, she did hate her, but . . .

She exhaled a cloud of smoke as Danny walked through the open garage door. "What do you want?" she asked, flicking some ash on the floor. "Come to spy on your nicotine sister?"

"Nah. Just wond'rin' what you and Peggy were upta."

She stared at him. "Jesus, you sound like Timmy. Do you two practice your lines together? We weren't up to anything. Well, I wasn't. Peggy, though, she took off with Anthony."

"Whaddaya mean 'took off'? On a date or sumthin'?"

"You know, sometimes you're as dumb as a rock. No, not a date. She's packed her bags and *hit the road, Jack.* Or so she says. I guess Mother knocking her down the other night was the final straw."

"Jeez Louise! That was sumthin' all right. There was a second there when Peggy first jumped back up I thought she was gonna punch her back."

"I almost wish I'd been there to see it. But all in all, I'm glad I missed that episode of *The Fight of the Week*."

"And now Peggy's gone? Won't tonight be a barrel of monkeys in the Sheehan house! Say, do you think we'll still have to say the rosary after dinner?"

Jane snorted. "Mother'll probably add a few more decades to it. Praying for Peggy's soul and all that."

"Do ya think Peggy will come back? Maybe have second

thoughts and come home? I mean, the fight was serious and scary and all, but leaving for good? Aren't people supposed to talk things over? Even the Russians talk to us."

Jane tried to imagine their mother and Peggy sitting around a conference table, a mediator between them. "I don't know. I don't think so. She seemed pretty determined."

"Are other families like ours? Or are we in a league by ourselves?"

"Oh, I think the likes of us are one of a kind," she replied, taking another puff.

"I know Ma can be a bitch—"

"Where did a good Catholic boy like you learn such a word?"

"From you, for one. Ma can be a bitch, but she sure does seem to have it in for Peggy more than any of the rest of us."

Jane took a long, deep drag on her cigarette. "I've got a theory about that. My theory is that Mother started out wanting perfect Catholic children, just like she and all our uncles and aunts supposedly were. So she did her best to mold Peggy into that, and Peggy being Peggy started resisting, probably as soon as she could walk. I wonder what her first word was. Probably 'No!' Then I came along and Mother had the two of us to deal with, with Peggy having already started to wear her down. And with you and finally Timmy—plus you were boys—Mother didn't have the energy anymore to keep us all in line. You and Timmy can get away with almost anything. But Mother never gave up on Peggy. Too many years of practice, I guess. So, Peggy is still her Project. And anyway, I do a better job of not resisting everything Mother says or wants. I prefer to pick my battles. Peggy wants to fight them all."

She stubbed out the butt of the cigarette on the trash can lid. Lighting another one, she continued, "But you'd think Mother with all her experience helping to raise our uncles and aunts would have come to marriage and motherhood a little more prepared."

"Or maybe she's just nuts?" Danny suggested.

They both looked up as a car pulled into the driveway.

"Christ on a stick, it's Mother!" Jane hurriedly put out her barely lit cigarette. "I hope she didn't see me. I want to keep the focus on Bad Girl Peggy." She stood up and smoothed her school uniform skirt. "Well, fasten your seatbelts. It's going to be a bumpy night."

Aren't you glad you use Dial? Don't you wish everyone did? / Project Mercury ends with Cooper's splashdown after 22 orbits / *I will follow him, follow him wherever he may go* / Patrick Bouvier Kennedy, 2 days old, has died / Compact cars sure were a good idea. Plymouth Valiant still is! / Buddhist monk sets self on fire, burns to death, protesting South Vietnam's anti-Buddhist policies / *You can trust your car to the man who wears the star, the big, bright Texaco star!* / This concludes this test of the Emergency Broadcast System. If this had been an actual emergency, you would have been instructed to tune to one of the Civil Defense stations in your area.

# Laundry Day

## 1963

Saturday. Grocery day. Errand day. Laundry day. Everything-you-didn't-get-to-the-rest-of-the-week day.

Margie dropped the basket of dirty clothes on the floor and started to sort them. She felt like she had been doing laundry all her life. Maybe she had. That's what came from being the oldest of eight children. Maybe she had spent more time in the basement with the washing machine, in her parents' home, here in her own house, than anyplace else. One thing she knew for sure: only the people who did the wash cared anything about taking care of their clothes.

It didn't help to have another baby on the way. Margie's back hurt so much she could just never get comfortable. Each

251

pregnancy took a further toll on her figure, leaving her just a little thicker around the waist. She hadn't needed to wear a girdle before she got married.

Maybe this baby would survive. Margie's mother never had a miscarriage and had all her children with about as little effort as a person could hope for. Margie knew. She had been there to help with half of the births.

Margie's pregnancies were never as easy as her mother's. After Timmy came Denis and Michael and Eileen. None of them survived the nine months. None of them. Michael almost fooled Margie. He waited till he was almost full term before miscarrying. Denis miscarried so early the doctor did not know if he were really a boy or a girl. But she thought of him as Denis, with a personality as big as her brother Denis's.

People said, "Oh, you've got four healthy ones. You're blessed." Or, "Don't worry. There'll be another baby. Just you wait. You'll see." Every time Margie heard something like that, she wanted to scream. Each time she lost a baby, she felt so low, so crushed down by such an immense weight that she could scarcely breathe. Part of her despair was the realization that she almost felt relief that the baby had died. How could she think that? How could she admit that? What kind of a person was she?

Margie wondered whether Dan, like she, didn't feel some relief about the three children they had lost. He didn't have the same big family experience Margie did. But he knew how expensive raising children was, particularly since they sent them all to Catholic schools. Margie and Dan never discussed not trying to have children. That wouldn't be right. They left it in God's hands. Who knew why God did what He did? They had made do, she thought, as she finished sorting the dirty clothes.

Of the four children, Peggy was the one they both worried about the most. She had moved out the other day in a huff. She shouldn't have hit her, Margie admitted to herself as she pulled the clean sheets out of the washer. She didn't know why she did it. The proverbial straw breaking the camel's back, maybe. She'd be back. Margie would ask Father Hill what he thought next time he visited.

Without consciously deciding to do so, she started to hum an opera aria. How she loved music! When she was growing up, the O'Sullivans did not have much music around the house, only the radio and some John McCormack records. Her mother arranged for her to take piano lessons, paying for it out of her pin money without telling her father. But it was only when she went to Hallahan Catholic Girls' High School that she truly discovered music.

Margaret's first week at Hallahan, in the fall of 1930, Sister Frumentia concluded the first freshman student assembly by urging the girls to participate in extracurricular activities of interest to them. As they filed out, Margaret's friend Rose asked, "Gee, Peggy, what do you think? What should we join?"

"I don't know. Maybe the Legion of Mary?"

"Oh, Peggy, you don't want to be with those holier-than-thou prisses! I have a better idea. I would kinda like to see about the orchestra. I've got the clarinet, and you've got the piano. So howz about we give it a go?"

"Alright," Margaret said without enthusiasm.

They found their way to a large, shabby room buried in the school's basement. Faded opera posters for *La Traviata*, *Carmen*, and *Madama Butterfly* decorated the beige walls, well-used instrument cases stacked below them. A jumble of music books sat on a desk just inside the door. An older man with flowing white hair sitting at a desk looked up.

"We were thinking about joining," Rose said.

"Excellent. Now, who are you and do you have any musical experience?"

"Rose Smith. I play the B flat clarinet."

"Excellent! You will be a welcome addition."

"Margaret O'Sullivan. I play piano."

"Piano? Not in the orchestra." He tapped his nose with his finger. "But if you already know music, Miss O'Sullivan, perhaps we can find another instrument for you. I need another cello. Shall we try you there?"

In no time at all Margaret was at home with the cello. It came to her easily. Her fingers and the bow moved across the strings faster than she could think where to place them. She let them do the work. Thinking too closely about what she was playing only led to mistakes.

Throughout her high school years, the basement band room was Margaret's second home. A few weeks before her graduation, Maestro did one last thing for her. "Miss O'Sullivan, I have some news for you," he said, sitting at his desk, surrounded by music books. He hesitated.

"Yes, Maestro?"

"Miss O'Sullivan, your musical development has been exceptional. That first day, I did not expect more from you than a body to fill a seat. Tell me, what do you plan to do after graduation?"

Margaret considered her answer. "Well, Maestro, I expect to do what most girls do. I'll get a job, help out at home, and eventually get married and start a family."

"And your music? You will give it up?"

She shrugged. "I love the music. But how can I keep it up? I can't get a job as a musician. I'm not good enough."

"That is true, Miss O'Sullivan. You would need to continue your music studies to become a professional."

She scoffed. "That's not possible, my family doesn't have money for that sort of thing."

"I understand. Which is why I've taken some initiative. Do you remember last winter when you and I and some of the other young ladies made our little expedition to the recording studio down on Broad Street, and I made gramophone recordings of each of you?"

Margaret laughed. "I'm not likely to forget lugging that cello all the way downtown on the trolley."

"Well, I sent your recording with an application off to a number of summer music schools. And one of them responded! Interlochen."

"Interlochen? What's that?"

"Interlochen, in Michigan. The National Music Camp. It's a relatively new place, just founded a few years ago. The school was so impressed with your recording and, I might add, my glowing testimonial that it has accepted you for its summer program, with a full scholarship."

Margaret began to read the acceptance letter the Maestro handed her. Very quickly her eyes blurred, and tears began to flow. "I—I can't believe this. It's like a fairy tale. How can I thank you?"

Mr. D'Amelio sat back with a dismissive gesture. "You can thank me by going to Interlochen and showing them I was not wrong in my assessment. A successful summer there could lead to other musical opportunities. Even if not, you will still have had an amazing experience, one that will stay with you the rest of your life. Such memories you will have!" For a moment he was lost in his thoughts, as if he were going to music school. "Then you can come home and get your job and find your husband. I would hate to see you give up music now."

Margaret waited impatiently until dinnertime to tell her family. She had barely finished when her father spoke. "We will be having no more of this talk, Margaret Marian. It is time for you to give up your books and your music. You have had your fun with the fiddle. It is over and done. Off on a summer's lark whilst Mama needs your help here around the house? I think not. And who is to be paying for it all? A scholarship, is it? But I hear no mention of train fare nor board nor pin money. From where might that money be coming? The thought of a girl your age travelling hundreds of miles alone! It is almost indecent to think of. Putting ideas in your head that will come to nothing! That teacher should be ashamed of himself. He should have minded his own business!"

Her mother sat with her head down and her hands folded in her lap. Her brothers and sisters stirred uneasily in their chairs. "Yes, Papa," Margaret whispered.

After the meal was finished, Margaret and her mother cleared the table as usual. Laughter came from the living room where her father and the children clustered around the radio, listening to *Amos 'n' Andy*. Without a word she and her mother did the washing and drying.

At last her mother turned to her. "I think it breaks Papa's heart to speak like that, Margaret. Maybe he believes what he says. Maybe he is a wee bit frightened and ashamed. I think he fears he hasn't done enough for us. Were he to find some way to pay for this trip of yours, what then? There are all your brothers behind you, not to mention your sisters. You are a woman now, Margaret. You must put these childish things behind you. Some day you will marry, and all this will be forgotten."

Margaret nodded at her mother. She could not bring herself to answer.

"But I didn't forget, Mama," Margie murmured to herself. She started to stretch the clean sheets along the basement line and clip them with the pins. And now she was pregnant for the eighth time. This child would be ten years younger than Timmy, twenty years younger than Peggy. Margie would be forty-six when this baby came.

"Tonight, when the family says the rosary after dinner, I'll say a special prayer for the baby. We'll call him Patrick."

We interrupt this program for the following news bulletin. In Dallas, Texas, three shots were fired at President Kennedy's motorcade in downtown Dallas. The first reports say that President Kennedy has been seriously wounded by this shooting / From Dallas, Texas, the flash — apparently official — President Kennedy died at 1:00 p.m. Central Standard Time, 2:00 o'clock Eastern Standard Time, some 38 minutes ago.

# Jane Has a Date

## 1964

"Jane, Frank's here!" Mrs. Sheehan called up the stairs. Frank had taken Jane out a few times, come to dinner and met the family, made a good impression, and even felt comfortable enough to spend an afternoon at the house when his car was in the shop.

Jane looked at her Timex. Seven o'clock. Right on time. She checked her face in the mirror. Thank heaven for the new contact lenses! Now she could go on a date and see what she was doing. She had her hair up in a beehive, first time ever, using a fall hairpiece and Aqua Net hair spray to pile it even higher. She patted it to make sure it was holding in place. She smooshed her lips together to even out the lipstick and pinched her cheeks to put some color into them. She wore a new lemon-yellow sheath dress with a matching bolero jacket and a pair of too-tight high heels. Everything in readiness, she took one look around the room—her room, now that Peggy was gone—to see if she had overlooked anything. She grabbed her clutch handbag and headed downstairs.

Her mother turned to look at her. "You look nice, Jane. I like your hair like that. Very modern, very Jackie Kennedy."

"You do look very pretty tonight," Frank said. "Definitely a Mrs. Kennedy, not a Lady Bird." He was shorter than her previous boyfriends, shorter than her father, his flattop haircut emphasizing the square shape of his head.

"OK, let's get out of here before the compliments get me blushing!"

"Where are you two headed?" Mrs. Sheehan asked.

"First dinner at Machus Red Fox and then maybe meet up with some friends," Frank said.

"Have a good time! Be home by midnight!"

Frank escorted Jane out to his Rambler and opened the passenger door for her. She got in, being careful with her hairdo. He shut the door and ran around to the driver's side.

"What were you and Mother talking about before I came downstairs?" Jane asked as they backed out of the driveway.

"Oh, nothing. The weather, school, chitchat."

Jane laughed. "My sister Peggy would've told you to watch out. With Mother chitchat can turn into a minefield."

"Really? I don't get that impression."

"Maybe that's why her method works. Anyway, I'm with Peggy — I get nervous when someone I'm seeing talks to my parents. Too much could go wrong."

"That's kind of immature, don't you think?" He turned north on Woodward.

"Maybe. So, you wouldn't mind it if I had a quiet chat with your father?"

"OK. Good point. But like I said, your mother and I were just making small talk, very small."

"So enough of that. Let's talk about something more important."

"Like what?"

"Like, what're we going to do after dinner?"

"Some of the guys suggested we might meet up at Ted's or Big Boy's to hang out for a while."

Jane scrunched her nose as if a bad odor had filled the car. That did not sound much like the romantic evening she was hoping for. "Will Bobby Mitchell be there?"

"Sure. Why?"

"I just think he's a jerk, is all."

"Bobby's one of my best friends! He's the life of the party! He's the class clown!'

262

That was pretty much her theme. "Nobody enjoys his jokes more than he does."

"You don't think very much of my friends."

She couldn't disagree with that. She tried to defuse the conversation. "I only mentioned Bobby."

"You get snide about the other guys too."

"What of it? I'm dating you, not them."

"You know, you can be a real bitch, sometimes," Frank said.

Jane looked at him in surprise. "Where did that come from?"

"Just a statement of fact."

"Well, as long as we're stating facts, you might try making friends with people a little more mature than that gang you hang around with." In for a dime, in for a dollar.

"Shut up, Jane," Frank said quietly.

Jane looked at him. "Shut up? You're telling me to shut up? I'm not allowed to express an opinion?"

"I said shut up!"

"No, I will not shut up. I'm entitled to my opinion."

Frank turned and slapped her hard across the face, the slap dislodging one of her contacts.

"Stop the car," she said.

Frank ignored her.

"Stop the car!" she screamed.

"What are you going to do if I don't? Climb onto the trunk like Jackie in Dallas?" He suddenly pulled into a parking lot and slammed on the brakes. He turned to her, his face a rictus of hostility. "No bitch gets away with insulting my friends. Take it back or get the fucking the hell out."

She jumped out of the car, slammed the door, and started to run. Frank put the car in gear and drove off.

He had left her on Woodward in front of Barry's Drugstore, half a mile from home, cars rushing by in both directions. With only one contact, she could hardly focus on her surroundings. She ran as fast as she could, her high heels pinching her feet. She got off Woodward and took Cooper, one street over, in case Frank followed. She crossed Normandy and ran down the alley behind the Woodward businesses. She turned on Hunter and cut through the Romanos' yard to get to her own house.

It was not until she got in the back door and sat down on the two steps leading up to the darkened kitchen that she finally felt safe to sob uncontrollably. Mrs. Sheehan came in from the living room.

"Janey, honey, sweetheart! What's wrong?" Her mother sat next to her and took her in her arms and rocked her. "Oh, my darling daughter!" She turned her head toward the living room and called, "Dan! Dan, get out here!"

Her father came running. "Jesus! What's going on?"

264

"I don't know. Jane, won't you tell us? Please tell us what's wrong!"

"I lost one of my contacts," she sobbed.

Margie looked at her husband, befuddled. "What? That's nothing to be so upset about," she said. "What's wrong, really?"

"Frank. Frank hit me."

"Oh, sweet Mother of God!" her mother moaned.

"Jesus Christ! Is he outside now?" Mr. Sheehan asked.

"No. I walked home."

"What!?" her mother said. "He didn't bring you home?"

"That son of a bitch!" her father screamed. "Danny, get your baseball bat! We're going out!"

"Dan, wait. Shouldn't we call the police?"

Dan looked at her in amazement. "The police? What are they going to do about it? They're not interested in lovers' quarrels."

"But he hit her!"

"Men hit girls all the time. The police aren't going to care. Maybe if he broke something . . ."

"I can't believe this," Mrs. Sheehan said, rocking Jane.

"Where'd he leave you, Janey?" her father asked.

"In front of Barry's." Jane held on tighter to her mother. "But he's long gone by now."

"I don't care. Danny, where the hell are you? Get your

265

baseball bat!"

Her mother looked up at her father. "You won't call the police about Frank and I'll just have to wait for them to arrest *you* when you've beaten his head to a pulp?"

"It won't get to that. The bat's just to let him know I mean business."

So, Mr. Sheehan and Danny went looking for Frank. They didn't find him. The Sheehans never heard from Frank again.

Khrushchev out, Brezhnev in as Communist Party head /
Martin Luther King receives Nobel Peace Prize / *Baby's*
*good to me, you know, she's happy as can be, you know, she said*
*so* / Red China now 5th member of nuclear club / Today!
Gas War prices, 23 cents per gallon / U of M clobbers
Oregon State in Rose Bowl, 34-7 / LBJ outlines vision for
"Great Society" / A new choice for viewers: WKBD,
Channel 50, joins WXYZ, WWJ, WJBK, and CKLW in
Detroit's TV line-up.

## The Sheehans Lose a Daughter

### 1965

The *ring ring ring* of the phone. Dan glanced at the luminescent dial of the Bulova clock next to the bed. Four in the morning. Nobody called at four in the morning with good news.

Margie said with a yawn, "I'll get it." She shrugged her robe on and went into the bedroom-turned-dining room where the Princess phone sat.

"Hello?" She listened quietly for a few minutes. Dan wanted her to say something so he would have an idea what was going on. She started to cry, "No! No! No! . . . Sweet

Mother of God, no! . . Yes . . . Yes, we'll be right there." She came back into the bedroom, her face ashen.

"What? What is it?"

"At least she got the priest!" Margie wailed.

"Peggy and Anthony? Married?"

"That was Joe. Patti is dead."

Dan leapt out of bed and moved to his wife. "Oh my God, no, that can't be!" He put his arms around her. "What happened?"

Margie was breathing heavily, almost to the point of sobbing. "An accident. A car accident. She was coming home from the late shift. A drunk driver hit her Corvair and totaled it."

"Where are they now?"

"They're still at the Beaumont E.R., but they're going home. I said we'd come right over."

"Let's get dressed then. Will the kids be all right by themselves?"

"I'll tell Jane to make sure the boys get off to school on time. They can have some of those new Pop-Tarts I bought for breakfast. That should make them happy."

It snowed the night before the funeral. The white of the landscape contrasted with the black hearse carrying the casket and the black limousines carrying the family.

Joe and Mary had a reception for the mourners back at

their house. The Shrine Ladies Guild prepared the food.

Throughout the reception, Mary sat upright in a dining chair to one side of the living room. She was dressed in black from head to toe, including the veil screening her face. She did not initiate conversation with anyone. She responded quietly to those who pulled up a chair and sat next to her.

People moved around the living room and the dining room. With Jane helping, the Guild women went from guest to guest to offer hors d'oeuvres. Father Coughlin, who had done the family the honor of saying the Mass, came and stayed a short while. Joe insisted on playing the bartender. For the most part he kept up a fragile air of geniality. Dan stepped into his place whenever Joe disappeared into the bedroom and shut the door.

Margie shunted the boys (they had served as altar boys at the funeral Mass) and the other children off to the basement to watch television. "Don't touch anything down there! And don't make any noise. I'll not have one of your Aunt Mary's memories of the day she buried her daughter being my sons causing a ruckus in her house."

Peggy was there. Mary and Joe had invited her to live with them after she left home. In theory, Peggy had reconciled with her family. In practice, she and her mother simply chose silence over argument. In the days after Patti's death, Margie and Peggy refrained from any discussion not related to funeral arrangements. Margie knew that General Motors had recently transferred Anthony to Australia, and that Peggy would fly out in a month or so to get married.

Margie had only spoken to Mary a few times since they got the news about Patti. That first morning, Mary had been in shock and gone to bed as soon as Dan and Margie reached the house. When Mary's sisters arrived from Philadelphia to take charge of things, Margie deferred to them. Were they shutting her out deliberately? She didn't know Mary's family well enough to judge.

Now, here in the living room with Mary momentarily sitting alone, Margie decided to make more of an effort.

"Mary, can I get you something?" she asked.

"No, thank you," Mary answered without looking up.

Margie pulled up an empty chair and sat down next to her. "How are you doing, Mary?" She asked. No response. She tried again. "People always say, 'There are no words.' It's true. There are no words. My heart is so full of emotion and I have no way to express it, other than to say I am so, so sorry and I am so, so sad for Patti's loss."

"Thank you, Margie." Mary scarcely moved as she spoke. Not knowing what else to say, Margie decided just to sit. Indistinct conversations went on around them.

For a quarter of a century Margie had resented Mary. She thought her sister-in-law looked down on all the Sheehans (even her own husband). She felt like the two of them were in some unspoken competition. Those thoughts vanished as she looked at her sister-in-law now. She wondered whether she should wrap her arms around her.

Suddenly Mary started to speak very softly. "All my life, I always accepted that, at some level, it was part of the natural order for children to bury their parents. And yet when the time came and first Father and then Mother died, I found myself totally unprepared to face it. My head said, yes, of course, they have gone, but my heart cried out, how can this be?"

"Yes, I know what you mean, dear," Margie said, shifting to look directly at her.

"But this. This. I cannot accept this."

"No, of course not." How else could she respond? No, no, no, a thousand times no. No one can accept a child's death.

"I know how hard it must have been for you when Margaret left home. But I'm glad she came to stay with us. She's almost like a second daughter to us. And now that Patti's gone—"

Where was Mary going with that thought? If this were a soap opera, Margie thought, this would be her cue to stand up and shout, "You're not going to steal my daughter!" But she could hardly accuse Mary of stealing something Margie had thrown away. She decided not to explore Mary's meaning. "I will miss Patti very much. I will miss her music. She had a great gift."

Was it just a month earlier that Patti had celebrated her twenty-first birthday? Joe had splurged on dinner for the two Sheehan families at the Top of the Flame Restaurant downtown. The spectacular winter views of the Detroit skyscrapers, the Detroit River, and Windsor on the other side compensated for the pretentious but bland food and indifferent service.

Patti had taken Margie aside. "Aunt Margie, I wanted you to be the first to know! Well, other than my parents, that is. We're not just celebrating my birthday! I have a scholarship to Interlochen Arts Academy! For piano! I'll be going this summer!"

Margie had embraced her niece. "Oh, my goodness, Patti! I am so happy for you! I couldn't be happier if I were going myself!"

Margie looked at Mary. "We will all miss Patti very much. She was a wonderful woman. You raised a wonderful daughter. Her music made me very happy."

*You know that it would be untrue, you know that I would be a liar, if I was to say to you, girl, we couldn't get much higher /* Detroit mobs burn and loot 800 stores / LBJ approves all-out drive to end strife / Troopers seal off nests of snipers / *When we're older things may change but for now this is the way they must remain /* Martin Luther King murdered, Negro leader shot at motel in Memphis / *It's a beautiful morning, I think I'll go outside a while an' just smile /* Robert Kennedy dies, succumbs to assassin's bullet / *What's the news across the nation? We have got the information in a way we hope will amuse youse: ladies and gents, Laugh In looks at the news!*

# On the Alpine Slopes

## 1969

M argareta Fiorentino!" the ski instructor called. None of the tourist students moved.

"He means you, honey," Anthony whispered, his breath steaming in the frigid air. "He just said your name the way it should be said."

Margaret stepped forward. The instructor's pronunciation had such a rich Italian intonation she had hardly recognized her own name. And yet it sounded so right that way, every syllable tripping off his tongue. She felt a thrill go through her. The Matterhorn loomed over them like an Egyptian pyramid, they were surrounded by beautiful mountains covered in the most dazzlingly white snow, and this man mistook her for a European.

When she reached his side, the instructor — Margaret's dark black hair confirming his assumption — began to pour out a stream of Italian.

"Mi dispiace, ma non parlo italiano," she said with her American accent.

The instructor did a double take. "Scusi. But I thought — your name, your look. I make mistake. You are then — ?"

"American."

"Then we speak English together, no? Today I show you the basics to ski. Maybe tomorrow you ski Cervino on your own." He laughed good-naturedly.

After four years in Australia at GM Holden, she and Anthony were en route back to the United States, on the tour of a lifetime. From Australia they had flown to Kenya, where they took a weeklong safari, the days spent stalking animals and the nights in open tents under a sky full of stars. From Kenya they went to Greece, visiting Athens and Olympia and sailing among Mykonos, Lesbos, and Santorini. Now — after Rome, Venice, and Florence — they were at the end of their visit to Italy. Soon they would go on to Paris, and then London. This was the life she had always hoped for. Unfortunately — and of course — their final destination was Detroit, a return to the Motor City so Anthony could rejoin Oldsmobile. For Margaret all roads led to Detroit. She took consolation in the fact that, if Detroit had royalty, it was in the upper levels of the auto companies' management. As the wife of a major GM designer, she would stake her claim.

Margaret found herself less interested in the ski lesson than in the ski instructor, Giovanni. She told herself that there was nothing wrong with a married woman recognizing that he was a very handsome man, with his curly black hair framing his face half-hidden by sunglasses, perhaps even more handsome than Anthony. No one would criticize her for a little flirting, and in any event the Fiorentinos would leave Italy in two days.

After her lesson finished, Margaret watched Giovanni with her husband. Anthony had previous skiing experience, so his was less a lesson than a review. She enjoyed watching the two men working together, Anthony anticipating Giovanni's suggestions and Giovanni applauding Anthony's quickness.

The Fiorentinos returned to their chalet in the late afternoon to get out of their ski gear and get ready for the evening. Then they headed to the lodge for cocktails and dinner. As they were sitting at the bar sipping Cinzano, Anthony asked, "So, Margaret, as our Great Expedition draws to an end, do you have any regrets of the past few years?"

She looked at him in amazement. "I should think not!

277

Living in Melbourne was an experience I will cherish forever. We met so many wonderful people there, and living in a foreign country was like an entire college education all its own. And this trip home—I never imagined such an adventure! Thank you so much for it!"

"Not just me. Thank General Motors. They're picking up a big chunk of it in exchange for a few visits to auto plants here and there along the way. Anyway, I wanted to take the edge off having to go back to Detroit."

Margaret swirled the ice cube in her glass. "I'm trying not to think about that." She knew he did not find living in Detroit as distasteful as she did.

"That's the price of working in the auto industry. But at least we'll be able to take trips like this one, maybe only a week or two at a time, but we'll get out of Detroit often enough."

Margaret laughed. "Getting out of Detroit has been my dream ever since I got in."

Anthony's glance moved behind her. "Look, there's Giovanni. Shall we have him join us?"

"Yes, why not? He seems very —"

"Giovanni!" Anthony called. "Over here!"

Margaret turned to see the Italian's face break into a smile as he headed toward them. Sunglasses no longer hid his eyes. She had always thought "piercing blue eyes" was a cliché, but not in his case. It was as if he were looking right through her.

"Buona sera!" he said. "How are my favorite Americans who could pass as Italianos if only they kept their mouths shut?"

Margaret was surprised how much more fluent his English seemed tonight. Had the broken English this afternoon been an act?

"Won't you join us for a drink?" Anthony said.

"Si, whatever you are having."

"Tre piú, per favore," Anthony said to the barista.

"How are you enjoying Italy?" Giovanni asked as he accepted the glass of Cinzano.

"We're having the time of our life!" Margaret said.

Giovanni smiled at her and turned to Anthony. "I felt like I was stealing your money today. You paid for the basic lesson but clearly you didn't need it."

Anthony laughed. "Well, we're on vacation. It didn't matter. I wanted to stay with Margaret. And if I had taken a more advanced class, I wouldn't have met you."

Giovanni smiled and held his glass up for a toast. "Salute."

"Salute."

"Well, I hate to drink and run, but I must be going," Giovanni said, putting his glass down.

"You couldn't join us for dinner?" Anthony asked.

"Oh, yes, please do!" Margaret said. It would be a shame not to spend the evening with such a handsome representative of Italy.

Giovanni looked from one to the other. "No, grazie. Maybe another time." He paused a second and laughed. "But I guess there won't be another time. We're—what is the expression? —two ships passing in the night. Or three, in our case," as he nodded to Margaret.

"Well, good night, then," Anthony said. "Maybe we'll see you on the slopes tomorrow?"

"Si, forse. Buonanotte." Giovanni kissed each of them on both cheeks and left the room.

Margaret turned back to face the bar. "I rather enjoyed his company. Didn't you?"

"Yes," Anthony agreed, still looking toward the exit. "I hope we didn't offend him somehow?"

"I don't think so. Why would you think so?"

"Well, he came and he went, just like that." He snapped his fingers to demonstrate. "Maybe I should go make sure?"

"Make sure of what?" She waved her empty glass toward the barista. "I'm sure he's used to Ugly Americans."

Anthony laughed. "I thought we were trying not to be Ugly Americans." He downed the rest of his drink. "You wait here—I'll be right back."

"But, Anthony—" she began, even as he headed to the door. The barista put another Cinzano in front of her.

It was so pleasant, so elegant, Margaret thought, sitting here at a bar in a mountain lodge in northern Italy. If only all of life were like this!

She took her time sipping her drink, but even so the glass was soon empty, and Anthony had not returned. How long could it take to apologize or whatever to Giovanni and either bring the man back or have them go their separate ways? Or, if he hadn't caught up to Giovanni, why didn't Anthony just come back?

Margaret started to feel uncomfortable. She wanted to believe sitting at the bar by herself was very cosmopolitan. But instead she heard the whispers in her head from the Marygrove nuns suggesting another adjective than "cosmopolitan" for a woman alone at a bar.

She decided to follow Anthony. "Il conto, per favore." As she considered the bill, she tried to remember whether she should tip or not. Which way would make her the Ugly American? Opting for the American way, she left a ten percent tip and signed her name and chalet number.

As she stood up from the bar stool, she felt slightly light-headed. How many Cinzanos had she had? Well, once she was outside the bracing air would wake her up. She pulled the sweater around her as she stepped through the door and made her way down the pathway, dimly lit by a series of ground-level lanterns. Seeing neither Anthony nor Giovanni, she decided to wait in the room for her husband to reappear for dinner.

She turned the corner of the lodge in the direction of their chalet. Before she realized what she was seeing, she became aware of two figures in the dark under the lodge's overhang. There they were! She was about to call to them—unaware of her presence—but instead she stepped quickly back into the shadows herself. She looked more closely, letting her eyes adjust to the dark. Anthony and Giovanni were kissing, their arms wrapped tightly around each other. She stood watching, feeling like a voyeur stalking two lovers. Then she turned and ran back to the lodge, slowing down to a fast walk to avoid drawing attention as she passed through the bar to the other exit, and took another path to their chalet.

She sat numbly on the bed. She felt so alone. She had to talk to someone! But there was no one within thousands of miles she could confide in. Until now, that wasn't true. Until now, she could have confided in Anthony. She felt keyed for action, but she had no idea what action to take.

She did not know how long she sat there. A key turned in the lock. Anthony entered. "There you are!" he said jovially. "I thought I had lost you when I went back to the bar and you weren't there."

"I finished my drink and felt uncomfortable sitting there by myself."

"Yes, the barista said you had left." He hesitated. "Did you come straight back to the room?"

No, she thought, I didn't come straight back to the room. I watched you and Giovanni kissing and then I took the long way around so you wouldn't see me seeing you. "It was such a beautiful night. I took the long way around." She decided a little boldness was in order. "Everything OK with Giovanni?"

"Oh, yes, he's fine."

She looked at him, his face smiling genially at her. Her lips formed a reflexive smile. How could he be so calm? So relaxed? How is it she wanted to scream, and he acted as if nothing had changed? Or maybe from his perspective nothing had changed?

"Shall we go to dinner?" Anthony extended his hand to her.

"Yes, let's."

New York police raid queer bar, homos riot / Man walks on moon / 500,000 hippies camp out in Woodstock, New York, biggest rock concert ever / *This is the dawning of the Age of Aquarius* / Pinto, the new little carefree car from Ford! / Local girl off to Vietnam! Lieutenant Jane Sheehan, daughter of Mr. and Mrs. Daniel Sheehan of Royal Oak, is on her way to South Vietnam for a year's assignment / Cavanagh out, Wayne County Sheriff Gribbs in as Detroit mayor / Ohio National Guardsmen shoot, kill four Kent State University students / *Like a bridge over troubled water, I will lay me down* / Massive demonstration in Washington against Vietnam War / Pan Am introduces the Boeing 747 Superjet, the plane that's a ship, the ship that's a plane!

# Jane Calls Home

## 1970

Jane stepped into the MARS Office — the Military Affiliate Radio Service — and shivered. It was always a jolt to move from the steaming Vietnam heat into an air-conditioned building.

"Good evening, Lieutenant," the clerk at the counter said. He didn't hesitate to check her out, even if she were an officer. "You wanna schedule a call home? I'll need your name, the person you're calling, and the phone number." He pulled a paper pad toward him and picked up a pen.

"I'm Lieutenant Jane Sheehan. I'll be calling Mrs. Daniel Sheehan, Margaret Sheehan, in Royal Oak, Michigan. The area code is 313, and the number is Liberty 9-4400. It's Beaumont Hospital. She works there in the personnel department." Their mother had gotten a full-time job a couple of years earlier, after Timmy — Tim, now — had entered high school.

"It has to go as a collect call once the radio operator back in the world picks it up. Will that be a problem?"

"No, no, I'm sure it'll be OK. I'll have better luck catching her at the hospital than at home."

"Is this your first time calling home, Lieutenant?"

"Yes."

"So, what we do is schedule a call date and have the serviceman write home to alert the family to stand by."

Her mother had been a regular writer ever since Jane had joined the Air Force a year and a half earlier, her letters full of innocuous news about neighbors and friends and ramblings about the weather and happenings at church. The family had once even sent a cassette tape letter, borrowing a recorder from one of Jane's friends. Jane had been in Vietnam for six months. At first the flow of letters had continued, even if she did not always answer each one. And then for the last six weeks — silence. Every day Jane waited for mail call to bring a letter, a postcard, something. Every day, nothing.

286

"But I can't wait that long," she said. "I'm afraid something's wrong with my family. I haven't heard from them in weeks. Isn't there any way I could call now?" She gave the clerk a pleading look. She was not beyond using her sex to advance her cause in an environment where round-eyed women were in short supply.

The clerk looked at Jane and then at the men sitting behind her, waiting to make their calls. He clucked his tongue. "Let me see what I can do," he said, disappearing into another room. She waited nervously until he returned.

"OK, Lieutenant, we're going to squeeze you in," he said quietly. "Don't tell anybody we're doing this, or we'll get all kinds of special requests. Please take a seat until we call you."

Jane gave him a sweet smile and sat down. She glanced at her Seiko wristwatch. Eight in the evening Vietnam time. If she calculated correctly, it should be about eleven this morning in Detroit.

Jane thought about the road that had brought her to Cam Ranh Bay. She had signed up with the Air Force to do her duty, and her duty was nursing. Whether the war made sense or not was irrelevant. The final impetus to enlist came with the news of Dennis Romano's death in Vietnam.

She had spent her first year at Reese Air Force Base in Texas. The wounded young men arriving at Reese broke her heart, with their missing limbs, their disfigured bodies, and

287

their haunted minds. She decided she should do more by being closer to where the action was, so she volunteered to work in the hospital emergency room at Cam Ranh. Her mother had insisted on a Christmas-in-September celebration before her departure, duly reported in the *Michigan Catholic*.

Reese proved insufficient preparation for the daily horror of Vietnam. At Reese, the men she took care of — no matter how bad off they were — had already been stabilized and survived the transpacific flight. At Cam Ranh, the wounded men arriving by helicopter were as little as only thirty minutes from their firefight or battle. They arrived with only the most basic care a field medic could give them under fire. Some died on the way. Working twelve-hour shifts, six days a week, she and her fellow nurses could not keep up.

She had tried to assure her parents that she was safe and nowhere near the fighting. She didn't mention the routine Viet Cong mortar attacks or the occasional sniper making his way through the base's Agent Orange-denuded defense perimeter.

"Lieutenant Sheehan," the clerk broke into her reverie. "Through that door. Booth number three. Please remember, it's an unsecured line. Don't discuss casualties, troop movements, or anything about the base. And no profanity, please. Also, only one of you can talk at a time, so you'll need to say 'over' for the radio operator to switch the conversation. You have five minutes."

Jane went into the next room. A bank of telephone booths lined the far wall, just like in an airport or a bus station. She entered the one marked "3" and sat down. She closed the folding door behind her and picked up the receiver. "Hello?"

"Lieutenant Sheehan? I have your call. They've accepted the charges. Go ahead, please."

"Hello?" Jane said. "Hello? Mother? Over."

"Jane? Jane? Is that you? It's wonderful to hear your voice! Over!" Jane froze. It was a man's voice.

"Daddy? Daddy?" Why was he answering the phone? "Are you in Mother's office?" Nothing. "Over," she remembered.

A cough at the other end. "Well, no, actually. Although if I had known you'd be calling I would have made a point of being there! Over."

"Then, why? What? I don't understand. Over."

"It's like this, Janey. I'm not exactly back in my old room, but I'm back in the hospital. Ever since my heart attack last year the old ticker hasn't been the same. I haven't been feeling up to snuff. So Dr. Weiner wanted me back in here to do some more tests."

"Tests? What tests?" Her father hadn't said "Over" and

289

he couldn't hear her.

"I don't know, exactly," he answered her anyway. "This and that. I can't keep them all straight."

Please say "Over," she urged in her mind.

"Over."

"When will you go home? Over." Static. "What? What did you say, Daddy? I didn't hear that! Over."

"That I don't know. Over."

"Daddy, are you all right? Over."

"Well, now that I'm talking to you, I am. Will you be coming home soon? Over."

"I do so much want to, but I have six months to go before the end of my tour. Over."

"Couldn't you come home sooner? Over."

"Daddy, I'd really like to, but I don't see how. Over." This was getting frustrating.

"I hope they're treating you all right out there. Over."

"Yes, yes, everything's fine here. How's everyone there? Mother and the boys? Over."

"They're fine, fine. We really miss you." A brief silence, and then he started to cry. "Janey, I think I need to see you."

"Daddy, Daddy! Don't cry! What's wrong?" But without the magic word he couldn't hear her. A woman's faint voice in the background at the other end said, "Mr. Sheehan, please stay calm."

"Who's there, Daddy? Who's there? Operator!" She practically screamed. "Over! Over! Over! Please switch it back to me! Who's there, Daddy?"

"The nurse," he answered between sobs. "A nurse just came into the room."

The nurse interrupted, "Miss Sheehan, I think we need to stop now. This is too much for your father."

Another voice came on the line, a male voice. "Your time is almost up. You'll need to end your conversation."

"Nurse! Nurse!" she heard her father cry. "Nurse, I want my daughter to come home!"

"Daddy! I'm coming home," she shouted, not knowing if he could hear. "I'll manage it. I love you!"

The male voice again. "I'm sorry. Time's up."

# Dan Has a Visitor

## 1970

We've seen quite a bit in our lives, haven't we?" Joe said, sitting in one of the visitor's chairs in Dan's hospital room. Dan had the room to himself, the second bed without a patient. The hospital noises of beeps, conversation, and announcements came through the doorway from the hall.

Dan was lying back against the pillows, the top half of the bed raised at an angle. He pulled himself up, trying to make himself more comfortable. He thought his brother at fifty-three acted more like an old man than their father had in his eighties, and here he was off on another one of his ramblings.

"The Depression, the war, the Korean War, now the Vietnam War, men on the moon, riots in the streets, drugs, crime, assassinations. Do you think the next generation will have a quieter history?"

"Maybe. If World War III doesn't blow us all to kingdom come." Dan wished Joe would stop talking. The drone of his brother's voice made his head ache.

"The last few years, it's like the whole country is having a nervous breakdown, with the hippies, the drugs, the riots, protestors protesting everything. Has the country ever been this mixed up?"

"I think Lincoln and those folks back in the Civil War might think they faced a tougher time than we do." Dan's headache was getting worse, and he had a pain in his side.

"OK, but in our lifetime, then. Even in the Depression I never thought the country was coming apart. The Germans and the Japs were pretty scary customers, but we were pretty sure we wouldn't have German or Jap bombers in the skies over our cities."

"Except for Honolulu."

"That was a one-time thing, a sneak attack. No way could they repeat it. But now, what's the country coming to? Every summer we wait to see what cities will go up in flames. We gave the coloreds civil rights. What more do they want?"

"For one thing," Dan replied, "I don't think they want to be called 'coloreds.' It's Negro now, or Afro-American. And there's still plenty of segregation and discrimination."

"Have you been down where the riots were? A couple of years later, and it still looks like Berlin 1945! Pretty soon there won't be any whites left south of Eight Mile Road. And all these rich white kids who should be in classes shutting the universities down because of the war. I just want to scream at them, 'Get a haircut! Take a bath!' All this 'turn on, tune in, drop out' crap."

Dan really would prefer not to hear any more of this. "You sound like an old fogey. And that's putting it politely."

"Well, I feel like one. Not even thirty years ago, you, I, and Ed were all still living at home, our whole lives ahead of us. And now what are we? We're as old as our parents were then. We've become responsible adults, looking forward to retirement!" They both laughed.

The pain in Dan's side stabbed at him. After a pause to catch his breath, he said, "I think you focus too much on what's gone wrong with the world. All in all, it's not been a bad life, has it? For one thing, we've got some good kids, you and I." Even as he uttered the words, he didn't need to look at his brother's pained face to recognize his mistake. "Oh, Jesus, Joe, please forgive me. After five years, I just can't believe Patti is gone."

Joe squeezed his eyes shut. "Every morning, I wake up thinking, what is Patti going to be up to today? And then reality sinks in. They say time heals all wounds. It doesn't. Mary can't even talk about her. Except when we go out to visit her at Holy Sepulchre. We still go every month. For some reason sitting next to her grave is the only time we can talk about Patti." Joe looked at Dan. "I have no clearer memory in my life than getting that call in the middle of the night and being told Patti was here in the emergency room and the priest had already given her the last rites. I don't know how Mary and I got over here without having an accident ourselves."

Dan tried to imagine how he would feel to lose his only child. Margie's miscarriages seemed almost inconsequential by comparison. "Patti was a beautiful child, Joe," he said. He remembered that morning, too, the half-sleep turning to full awareness as the meaning of Margie's words sank in. He remembered thinking, "Dear God, No! Not Patti. Don't do this to Joe. Leave them Patti. Take one of ours instead."

His brother smiled. "With all the time one or another of us Sheehans spends here in Beaumont, maybe they should keep a room reserved for us!"

"Maybe." Dan could not shake the dark mood so easily. "And nobody more than my Margie. The miscarriages, and those other times. Each one just a kick in the teeth. We were

295

so hopeful with that last little guy. She was going to call him Patrick. But in the end, it wasn't meant to be. I thought losing Patrick was going to be the last straw for Margie, that I was going to lose her for good and she would just go off the deep end. It didn't help that it happened so soon after Peggy left."

"No, that was a hard time all right."

Dan glanced at his brother. He hoped Joe didn't think he was trying to compare family tragedies. "Joe, I don't think I've ever thanked you and Mary properly for taking Peggy in when she left home. Margie was furious about it, as I'm sure you know, but it sure beat some of the alternatives." Dan had been furious, too, but in retrospect he saw it as the best solution.

"Margaret has always been like a second daughter to us."

"I guess in the end it all worked out. Going off to Australia with Anthony was a blessing. Putting half the world between mother and daughter for a few years seems to have helped. Have you seen them since they got back?"

"Yes, Mary and I had them over for dinner the other night. Anthony seems happy back at Oldsmobile, still trying to come up with the next hit car."

"We had them over to dinner too. I'll bet your evening was more relaxed than ours. Margie and Peggy are civil to each other, but there'll always be some tension there. They seem to have had a great trip home, between African safaris and Italian skiing excursions."

Joe laughed. "Margaret told us when they were in Italy the skiing instructor said her name with such a thick intonation, she hardly recognized it. And when she stepped up, her name and her black hair made him assume she was Italian."

"I bet that was a dream come true," Dan said ruefully. "Something she's dreamed about her whole life, not being like the likes of us." He paused. "Do you think Peggy and Anthony are happy?"

"I don't see why not. They sure act like they are. They've got that nice new house in Bloomfield Hills, fully air conditioned. Although I wonder what the neighbors think of having an ultra-modern shoebox house next door."

"Yeah, I can't get quite as enthusiastic as Peggy and Anthony do when they go on and on about the house's architectural significance."

"I think it's just flat ugly."

Dan laughed despite his pain. "I'm guessing neither of us will ever tell them what we really think about the place."

"That's for sure."

It certainly seemed like the life Peggy had always aspired to, Dan thought. But sometimes it was almost as if she and Anthony tried too hard to be happy. "It doesn't look like they're planning on having any kids." Dan had always looked forward to grandchildren.

"Still plenty of time for that. Speaking of daughters, what about Jane? We haven't seen her since she got home."

"Jane? Oh, she should get here any minute. She promised she'd sneak me in a chocolate milkshake. She understands the horrors of hospital food."

"We're so proud of her, serving her country, unlike so many people who don't seem to care if Southeast Asia goes Red or not. Wasn't one Munich in our lifetimes enough?"

Dan sighed. "She's proud of her service, and so are we, but when you see her don't get her started on the right or wrong of the war. It makes her furious. Even after eighteen months with the Air Force, she says she still can't get used to taking care of all these young men with their horrific wounds. She wonders whether it's worth it. Jane told Margie, if Dan or Tim gets a draft notice, they should just jump in the car and drive across the bridge to Windsor and not come back."

"I'm not sure that's the right thing to do."

"I'm not saying it is either, Joe. But that's the way she's thinking." Dan took a sip of water. "By the way, she's getting married, did you hear? To a fighter pilot!"

"Yes, Mary told me. That's great!"

"I'm not sure whether they met in Texas or Vietnam. She

had a boyfriend in Texas who went to Vietnam, but I'm not sure this is the same guy. Kind of odd, isn't it, after all the to-do about Peggy and Anthony, and now Jane just shows up and says she's getting married to a guy we don't know from Adam, and we just say, 'That's nice.'"

"Well, after all, she's a bit older and has a bit more world experience than Peggy did at the time."

"But there are other differences too. Jack—I think his name is Jack—isn't Catholic."

Joe gave a low whistle. "How did Margie take that?"

"Another 'That's nice.' But here's the kicker: he's divorced."

"Is there no end to this nightmare?" Joe chuckled. "It's lucky both our parents are dead, or this news would surely kill them!"

"I mean, it's not that his religion and previous marriage don't give us pause. But it's not like it would have been five or six years ago, when we would have definitely put our foot—feet?—down and said no way."

"Five or six years ago? You mean about the time you were dead set against Margaret's marrying a Catholic boy with no questionable marital history?"

"Well, when you put it like that, it does sound, I don't know . . ."

"Hypocritical?"

"No, it was a different time. A lot of water under the bridge since then." Dan tried to think how best to phrase it. "For one thing, Margie's a lot less Catholic than she used to be. Of course, we do confession on Saturday and Mass on Sunday, but not so many rosaries or benedictions. Her heart's not in it the way it used to be. I'm not saying that she's lost her faith. It just isn't quite the same center of our universe. Sometimes I think Margie thought all that praying and stuff would hold the family together."

"I always had the impression the O'Sullivans were a lot more involved in their faith than any of us Sheehans were. I'm not certain our parents would have been terribly thrilled if any one of us had come home and said we wanted to become a priest like Margie's brothers."

"Yeah, you're probably right." After a moment, Dan continued, "You know, before Jane called me last week, I was fine with the fact that she was in Vietnam and I wouldn't see her again until November. Well, maybe not fine. I woke up every morning half sick with worry. And I know she'll have to go back and finish her tour. But thank God the hospital operator misrouted her call to me. If she had gotten through to her mother like she planned, Margie might have just told her everything was A-OK. Suddenly as I was talking to her I knew I had to see her now. I got so upset the nurse threatened to give me a sedative. I had this premonition I won't be here come November. I don't know what Dr. Weiner put in that letter to get her compassionate leave. Maybe I won't be."

"Don't be morbid, Dan! Only the good die young. Both our parents lived into their eighties. You're not even sixty! You'll live a long life."

Dan shook his head. "Forget the happy talk. Neither of them had a bad heart. This last year and a half since my heart attack has been hard, really hard. Even on a good day, I feel so weak. I don't think I can face a life in and out of the hospital like this. And no cigarettes or cigars!" The heart attack had shaken him. Suddenly at age fifty-eight, he had had to face his mortality.

Dan paused to drink some water. "The one I worry about is Tim. He's just so turned in on himself. He and I used to be very close, the way little boys will be with their fathers. Once he hit his teen years, he just kind of shut down, stopped talking to me or Margie. It's as if he has something to say but is afraid to say it. Since he gets good grades and all I guess I shouldn't worry about it too much. Maybe he'll grow out of it. There's that old saying, something about 'When I was fourteen, my father was the most ignorant man around, and when I turned twenty-one, I was amazed how much he had learned in the meantime.' Tim came to visit me the other day, all on his own. It took me by surprise. It was almost like old times. We actually had a good conversation."

"Tim's a good kid. Both your boys are good kids."

"Yeah, Dan was difficult as a teenager, but he's turned out all right. He was never the handful Peggy and Jane were, and he never got all withdrawn and morose like Tim."

"I guess all people can do for their kids is just try to be there for them. Is Dan coming home from school to see you?"

"No. He'll be home next month, after the semester ends. No need for him to come now."

Dan felt a sharp pang in his gut and started to get out of the bed. "I gotta use the john."

"You need some help?"

"No, no, I'm good." He slowly stood up and started to shuffle across the floor. He stopped halfway and turned to Joe. "You know, one thing I've always regretted is, we weren't closer growing up. I mean you and I. And Ed for that matter."

"What? Well, we were always just your obnoxious little brothers."

"The age difference doesn't stop some people. I look at Margie's family, with the kids strung out over fifteen years and now scattered all over the place. They've always been a pretty close bunch."

"We'll just rack it up to our genes, then. Maybe we're just following in our parents' footsteps, the way they were with their families. Anyway, we're here together now, right?"

"Yeah, right." Dan went into the bathroom and shut the door.

Joe looked out the window. They were on the hospital's sixth floor, so he had a good view of the surrounding neighborhood, Woodward Avenue cutting a diagonal slash across the landscape. If it weren't for all the trees, he thought, he could see both their houses from here.

He heard a noise from the bathroom. "Dan, are you OK?" A muffled response could have been yes or no. "Dan?" Then, a hard thump against the door. "Dan?" Joe got up and moved toward it.

Jane entered the room, smiling, with the promised chocolate shake in her hand. "Hi, Uncle Joe!" she said. "Where's Daddy?"

Joe tried to push open the bathroom door, but something blocked it. "Jane," he said, trying to remain calm, "we need help. Get some help!"

Jane turned and ran to the nurse's station, the dropped milkshake splattering in all directions.

## Moving Day

### 1971

Margie sat in Dan's easy chair, her chin resting on her fist, her elbow on the chair's arm, a cup of coffee on the table next to her. She looked at the moving boxes surrounding her, some closed and taped, their contents listed in Magic Marker on the lids, some still open and ready for more. Early morning, such a grey day outside, rain drizzling against the window. The movers would arrive shortly, and still the packing wasn't finished. The radio tuned to WQRS played a Beethoven sonata.

Fifty-three and a widow. It was bad enough when her father died when her mother was only fifty-nine. Even after

304

Dan had had that first heart attack, Margie still assumed they'd both live till retirement. Everyone should get to live to retirement. The autopsy showed his heart was in such bad shape he was lucky he hadn't keeled over ten years sooner.

She sipped her coffee. Dan had had a lovely funeral. So many people visited, so many called to express their condolences. Even friends from back East who Margie hadn't heard from in years wrote letters. It was very moving.

Now she had to decide. Should she stick with "Margie," or go back to being "Margaret"? Dan had insisted on calling her Margie from the time they first met. He said it was because he liked the song "My Little Margie." She hated the song. She hated the name. But she lived with it. She always thought Dan wanted to create a distinction between his mother and his wife. Well, what's in a name, after all? "A rose is a rose is a rose."

She guessed she should count her blessings. At least now Tim was off to college and all four kids were out the door. Boy, were they out the door! No sooner did Jane get back from finishing her tour in Vietnam than she took off to England, following Jack Oldman to his next assignment. While still in Vietnam, she had told her parents they were engaged, but there had been no more mention of that. Still no wedding date and Margie hadn't asked, but she assumed they were living together. Right now, she didn't care. Well, just so long as she didn't get herself pregnant before they got married. That would bother Margie.

She walked out to the kitchen to refill her cup. Why hadn't Jane gotten pregnant? Everybody knew kids these days thought nothing about having sex before marriage, and if they were having sex and she wasn't pregnant — they were using contraception! Why hadn't she thought of that before? It's the kind of thing she'd assume about other people's children, but not about her own. Mote in your neighbor's eye, but what about the beam in her own?

So, from a Catholic point of view, which would be worse, using contraception (that's wrong) or having an illegitimate baby (also wrong)? She'd have to talk it over with Father Hill.

She returned to the living room and resumed her seat. She had relied on Father Hill for years. She hadn't always liked the advice he'd given her. Sometimes she thought the Sheehans would all have been better off if she had listened to him more often. He had urged them not to go so hard on Peggy over Anthony. If only they had — but, no, Margie knew full well there was no way she would ever have behaved any differently than she did.

All water under the bridge. She had worried too much about Peggy then. She refused to worry too much about Jane now. She just would not care. If Jane was happy, she was happy. That year in Vietnam gave her lots of bonus points to run her life anyway she wanted. Holy Mother of God, how Margie had hated that year!

Jane told the Sheehans how safe she was, but Margie knew from the nightly news that "safe" had little meaning in that hellhole. She kept wondering when the phone would ring in the middle of the night — or did they send military personnel to the front door? She didn't know and she was glad she had never found out. She almost died with agony both times Jane got on the plane to go over there, and she almost died with joy when Jane came home at last. And then she was off again. Better England than Vietnam.

Dan got out of school and off to Europe, gallivanting around with pretty much just the clothes on his back and that *Europe on 5 Dollars a Day* book. He said in his last letter he wanted to join the Peace Corps when he got home. Didn't kids nowadays ever have to grow up? Margie had stayed at home after school, working. Working at home, working at Lit Brothers, working until she got married. Then she kept on working. No, she wouldn't be jealous that her own children had more options than she had.

And Peggy. Could Margie ever put that right? She had shattered that beautiful vase. She tried to glue it back together, but it was no good. It would always be just a broken vase. Peggy was more distant from her just up the road in Bloomfield Hills than Tim was at school in Milwaukee or the other two in Europe.

How curious that now Margie was living alone for the first time in her life. She had always been surrounded by others—her parents and her siblings in Germantown, then marriage and her own children. This was her house now. Well, this *would* be her house now, if she hadn't sold it.

This house. In some ways a dream house, a lovely brick Cape Cod, brand new when the Sheehans moved in. She hated it.

She took a sip of coffee. Would the Sheehans' lives have turned out differently if they had stayed in Philadelphia? She dismissed the thought even as she formulated it. Their fate did not depend on where they lived. They were who they were, wherever they were. She had lost Dan and one way or another she had lost her children. They died, or they moved out and got on with their own lives.

She was leaving this house at last, just taking her clothes, enough furniture for a one-bedroom apartment—in Somerset Park of all places!—and the pots and pans. Everything else she had given away: Dan's clothes and tools to St. Vincent de Paul, the furniture she didn't need to Father Cunningham's Focus HOPE, Tim's trains and all the stuff that went with them to the orphanage where Father Hill was the chaplain, and the piano that had sat unused in the basement all those years to the Little Sisters of the Poor. Oh, and the encyclopedia. To the trash. Who needed a 1940's encyclopedia? Good riddance to all of it!

Through the picture window she saw the moving van pull into the driveway. She took a final sip of coffee and rose from the chair to open the front door.

Thousands die in Haiphong bombing / Maxi dresses or miniskirts? There's a fashion to fit any girl! / George Wallace wins Michigan's Democratic primary / Everyone's playing PONG, the exciting new electronic video game! / British troops open fire on peaceful civil rights march in Northern Ireland / Break-in at Democratic headquarters, 5 men arrested / *The first time ever I saw your face, your face, your face* / No Nobel Peace Prize awarded this year.

## Splitsville in Bloomfield Hills

### 1972

Margaret Fiorentino ran her hand caressingly along the back of the white velvet sofa. She looked around the living room of the ultra-modern Bloomfield Hills house she and Anthony had bought when they had returned from Australia. The house's award-winning architecture was all right angles of wide glass panes divided by narrow steel strips, trees filling the view through the windows in every direction, as few walls as possible dividing the rooms, all of them grouped around a greenhouse atrium bursting with exotic plants that would never survive outside in the harsh Michigan winter. This was the dream house Margaret had always wanted, the dream house she had filled with Bauhaus-inspired furniture, its utilitarian beauty overriding any bourgeoisie consideration of comfort. She loved the cocktail parties and formal dinners she had held here for auto industry executives and their wives, all of whom eagerly accepted the invitations to the home of a rising General Motors star. Royal Oak, only a few miles down Woodward Avenue, lay a world away.

This was the house she would leave today. Her packed bags sat on the floor beside her.

Margaret had never talked to Anthony about the incident with Giovanni three years earlier, but ever since she had observed the world with different eyes. There were the little things which to an unsuspecting wife would not look suspect, to an unaware wife would look merely odd. For Margaret, her observations made her begin to wonder whether all men, or at least many men, were not like Anthony. Because now she knew her husband was queer.

Homosexuality was not a subject that had ever arisen in the Sheehan household or her years of Catholic schooling. Margaret still wasn't entirely clear on what it meant, other than that she knew she was not the center of Anthony's life. Other wives joked about their husbands' close male friendships. Margaret had come to assume the worst about such relationships. Anthony had not one but two "good friends" with whom he liked to spend time apart from her. Neither man was married, but each was young enough for that not to cause suspicion on its own. She had grown tired of the weekends Anthony spent with one or the other. She automatically chose to believe that Anthony's business trips to New York with Jack (yes, they both worked at Oldsmobile, but still) were just too convenient an excuse.

And then she found the photograph of Anthony and Mike (the other one). She found it in the back of Anthony's underwear drawer because—yes—she was snooping. An unaware person might assume the photo simply depicted two close buddies, the way they looked at each other as they embraced, shirtless. To Margaret's informed eyes—and why hide the picture in the underwear drawer?—it represented proof positive. She wanted to scream at her women friends, "Wake up! They're all doing each other!"

Now she sat and waited. Anthony should be home soon (if he hadn't stopped for a drink with a friend). She didn't know what direction the conversation would take, but at the end of it she would go out the door.

She heard the key in the lock. Anthony came into the small foyer, a puzzled expression coming over his face when he saw her sitting there. "Hello, dear. What's up? What's with the luggage? Are you going somewhere?"

She looked at him, standing tall and handsome in his

tailored suit, his hair already beginning to gray around the temples. She rose to her feet and smoothed the pleats on her skirt. "Anthony, I'm leaving you." She wanted to keep her voice steady.

He goggled at her. "You're what?"

"I said, I'm leaving you."

"Leaving me? Where the hell did that come from? How do we go from having no marriage problems to you walking out?"

She wanted to choose her words carefully. She didn't want to hurt him, but how could she avoid that? "Anthony, you're homosexual. That's a marriage problem."

He took a step in her direction, a look of anger on his face. "I am not queer!"

She pinched the bridge of her nose. "Please, Anthony, this conversation will be difficult enough without us lying to each other and ourselves."

He looked at her, the realization his protests were futile showing on his face. "I never meant to hurt you."

Margaret looked at him. "But why? Why? I don't understand. If you were interested in men and not women, why did you marry me?"

Anthony collapsed into one of the Wassily chairs. "I thought we could have a happy life together. I loved—I do love you. What choice did I have? Even as a boy, I knew I was different, but I didn't realize that what made me different had anything to do with whether I would get married or not. And how could I not get married? How is it possible to stay unmarried? Who wants to be a 'confirmed bachelor' or an 'old spinster'? You don't get ahead in this life without a wife, in Detroit or anyplace else."

Margaret kept her tone neutral. "Well, I'm glad I could be of use."

"But that's not why I married you. I wouldn't marry just anybody. I married *you*. I wanted *you*."

She refused to let the pain on his face touch her. "Except when you wanted someone other than me."

"I can't help who I am. I fight it every day. But sometimes I fail."

"Was Giovanni the ski instructor the first? Or just one of many?"

"Oh my God, what do you mean? Did you see us?"

"Yes, I saw you. I've known ever since. I've known what to look for ever since."

"Oh, Jesus. I never knew."

She could see him running through a calculation of the past three years. "So, what do you suggest? Do we go on pretending we're Mr. and Mrs. Middle America, or do we accept the fact that our marriage is based on a lie?"

As he sat there in misery, part of her still wanted to

pretend they could make it work, part of her wanted to rush over to him and put her arms around him, part of her wanted to keep this perfect Bloomfield Hills life. But she would not.

"It's not a lie. I told you—I love you."

"Our marriage is based on the lie that each of us is supposed to be sexually excited by the other."

"But it's true. You do excite me."

"Until a man comes along to excite you more." What was the point of continuing this conversation?

"What do you want from me? I give you all that I can. I'm sorry if I can't give you more. Don't I deserve some credit for making the effort that comes so naturally to other men?"

She felt her heart harden. He was almost too pathetic. "Well, that's the way to a woman's heart!"

"Please don't be cruel. I wish I were different, but I'm not."

Her patience was gone, his protestations degrading. "I wish you were different, but you're not. And I can't live the rest of my life like—this, whatever 'this' is."

"So, there's no hope for us?" His face reflected defeat.

"I don't see any. I want a divorce."

He stood up. "All right. I won't fight it. I can't tell you how sorry I am that I cannot be the husband you deserve."

Suddenly they were both businesslike, impersonal. "We'll sell the house, of course," Margaret said. "I've already looked into renting an apartment at Somerset Park. It will feel like home. I'll even be closer to my mother. You know, it may have been Sin City when you lived there but now it's kind of an unofficial retirement community. I'll fit right in." She picked up her bags and headed to the door.

"Goodbye, Margaret." He looked like he might make one last plea to her.

"Goodbye, Anthony." Unintentionally, she slammed the door behind her as she left. As she got into her Firebird, she thought, I won't take anything with me from this marriage. Except the name. I'll hold on to Fiorentino. I'm not going to be Peggy Sheehan again.

# Jane Comes Home, and Leaves

## 1971-1973

After her father's death, Jane returned to Vietnam. If anything, life grew even more dreary and depressing as her final departure date drew nearer. By now she had turned completely against the war, aghast with every new casualty who came into her care, who came to her to die. She found consolation with Jack Oldman, the Air Force Captain she had told her parents about, even said they planned to get married, to let them think Vietnam had one redeeming feature. She wasn't sure exactly what their relationship was. When he wasn't off on missions over Haiphong and Hanoi, he might or might not be available to her. But she cherished their times together. Whether it was sex or romance, it was at least a relief, a crutch, a way to get through the nightmare.

She said goodbye to Jack the day she left Cam Ranh Bay, thinking it was for good, not expecting to see him again. She went home to Detroit, adrift, twenty-five years old with no idea what her future held. Getting a job as a nurse posed no problem. But how could she readjust to normal American life after Vietnam? It seemed so empty, so meaningless, so superficial. She felt disordered, lost. She knew her mother wondered what was going on as she sat around aimlessly day after day in the house. Yes, she was back home on Darby, in the room she and Peggy had shared for a decade before it became Jane's alone. With Dan off to Europe and Tim off to school, Jane and her mother were alone together. As if Vietnam weren't frightening enough, she thought. Jane did nothing, made no effort to connect with old friends, reacted almost hysterically to any loud noise. Her mother's expressions of concern were as annoying as her flares of temper.

Then one day as she sat there alone, the phone rang. "It's Jack. I'm in Illinois at my parents. How are you doing?" She felt the emptiness of her life drain away. As they talked, suddenly the affair in Vietnam became more than a desperate escape from reality. "I'm being transferred to Lakenheath Air Base. In England," he said. "Why don't you come with me? It'll be the life we deserve after what we've been through!"

By the end of the call, she agreed to join him. Two weeks later — leaving her bewildered mother behind — she was on the BOAC flight from Detroit to London. As she watched the oh-so-polite stewardesses go about their work and the other passengers on their way for holiday or business settle in for the night, she thought of her flights to and from Vietnam. Those planes had looked like normal commercial aircraft — they were normal planes, Pan Am and TWA charters. But the mood was very different, the chipper stewardesses doing their best to act as if they weren't carrying these young men (they were almost all men, of course) off to a war, the quiet rows of passengers sitting in grim resignation, a few here and there engaging in bravado about the grand adventure to come. Her two flights home from Vietnam had presented only a little more joy, the young men (again, they were almost all men) too exhausted and dazed from their experiences to celebrate their liberation or — like Jane — wondering what awaited them back in the world.

As the hours in the overnight flight to England passed and she smoked one cigarette after another, Jane found herself as scared and nervous as she had been the first time she flew to Vietnam. Who was this person she was going to? Why had she agreed to run off with a man who hadn't even asked her to marry him? Before Vietnam, the whole idea would have been absurd. Now –

After circling Heathrow over an unbroken cloud cover for an hour in the early morning, the flight diverted to Manchester. "We are most sorry, ladies and gentlemen," the pilot said in a clipped English accent. "We regret that London is too fogged in for us to attempt a landing."

In Manchester, the BOAC staff were very efficient about making arrangement for the passengers to get to London or wherever their destination was. "I'm headed to Cambridge," Jane told the BOAC agent. "Can I get a direct train from here to Cambridge?" Well, no, all the trains in England ran to and from London. She would have to go to London's Euston Station and transfer from there to King's Cross for the Cambridge train.

The trip from Manchester to London gave her her first glimpse of England, long stretches of gritty industrial neighborhoods full of ancient buildings and rundown tenements, with an occasional glimpse of the pretty countryside in the breaks between the towns.

Jack met her at Euston, smiling from ear to ear, his face as handsome as she remembered it, a bouquet of roses in his arms. How did he know she would arrive in Euston rather than at Heathrow, as scheduled? "I have connections."

They hopped a cab to King's Cross Station and got on the

train to Cambridge. On the way, surrounded by English passengers, he suddenly interrupted the torrent of their conversation and knelt in the aisle before her. "Jane Anne Sheehan, will you marry me?"

She put her hand to her mouth in amazement. Could he be serious? Already it had been such a long day — by now she had hoped to be comfortably asleep. Suddenly she found herself saying, "Yes, Jack, yes, I will." The other passengers cheered and passed around a bottle of gin in celebration. Having long since used up her own cigarettes, she bummed some off their fellow passengers to calm her nerves.

Jack and Jane settled into a small house in Thetford near the Air Base in Lakenheath. What Thetford lacked in amenities it made up for in quaintness, a picture postcard of a small English town. Jane quickly grew to love the daily ritual of visiting the shops for groceries (those they didn't buy at the base commissary) and visiting the tearoom for a daily cuppa. Such a long way from the dreary life of trips to Kroger in Royal Oak! The shopkeepers embraced her as one of the Americans who actually stopped and talked to them, unlike the majority who rushed by in their "Yank tank" American cars and acted as if England were an alien planet, if they deigned to stop at all.

Jack of course was busy with his new duties, training other pilots. Unavoidably they did a lot of socializing with

WILLIAM J. DUFFY

their fellow Americans, most of whom lived on base in a simulacrum of American suburbia. Jane found these encounters tedious, even when she liked the individual Americans involved. Somehow the larger the gathering, the smaller the talk.

Jack and Jane got married at St. Cuthbert's Church, eliding the fact neither of them was Anglican. They "forgot" to report the marriage to their respective families for months.

"What was that, Jane?" her mother said when she called to tell her. "I didn't quite catch that. The connection keeps breaking up."

"I'm married, Mother!" she almost screamed into the phone. "Jack and I are married."

"Oh, Jane, I am so happy to hear that!"

By the time her mother arrived on a visit with Aunt Madeleine and two of the uncles (Denis and Michael, the priests), Jane was pregnant. The four O'Sullivans had made a trip to Ireland, the first for all of them, including a visit to their father's family's farm. They all insisted on adding England to the itinerary so they could visit Jane and her husband. Jane had hesitated when her mother had proposed the visit. Jack after all had yet to meet any of her relatives, and she had given him only a bare outline of Sheehan and O'Sullivan history. But she was fond of her aunt and uncles and figured they were as good a first delegation of the family

323

as she could hope for.

As soon as the group got home from the train station, Jack presented his mother-in-law with a toy stove holding a biscuit. "We've got a bun in the oven!" he announced triumphantly. Margie Sheehan, who had watched in puzzlement as Jack went and got the toy stove out of the corner, burst into laughter. The other O'Sullivans applauded.

Jane was relieved Jack took an affectionate interest in his mother-in-law. He got along very well with Margie's siblings, particularly her uncles. Jane again experienced the bafflement that apparently her mother did not display to others the shortcomings that were so obvious to her own children.

She was also intrigued to discover a subtle role reversal. For the first time, her mother was in her house, not she in her mother's. Even her mother seemed to sense the difference, passing up obvious opportunities to weigh in on something Jane did or said that would have not gone unremarked in the Darby house. Her mother's reticence had a salutary effect on the entire visit.

It surprised Jane how sad she was when it came time for the visitors to leave.

The pregnancy passed uneventfully, and then Anne Eileen arrived. Afterwards, Jane remembered little of the pain of the labor. But she would never forget when the hospital sister first put little Anne into her arms, such a perfect little creature. All her life had led to this moment. Nothing that had come before would take away from it.

She stroked Anne's face. "Where's my husband?"

"He's not here, Mrs. Oldman," the sister answered as she fluffed the pillows.

Jane learned later that, after dropping her off at the hospital, Jack had spent the day bowling. He explained that the whole birth process so distressed him he could only calm down by bowling. She snorted. "You found it distressing? What about me? I wish I could have gone bowling with you and let somebody else have the kid!"

After two years in England, the time came for Jack to separate from the Air Force. He had an idea of opening an American-style pizza parlor in Thetford. Many Air Force pilots went to work as commercial pilots, so it surprised Jane that his plan seemed so prosaic. But he said the economy was slow and the airlines weren't hiring pilots. She wasn't too keen about the idea of being a pizza shop owner's wife, but she couldn't deny that Thetford (or anyplace in England!) could do with a good one, and she did very much like the idea of continuing to live in the United Kingdom. They decided to go home to America, visit their families, have Jack complete his service separation, and buy the equipment needed.

Now Jane looked out the window as the BOAC VC-10 began to circle for its landing at Metropolitan Airport, bringing her home to Detroit from London. Jack had stayed on in England and would join her in another ten days. The flat midwestern landscape looked as it always had. She laughed as she thought about Danny's question on that long-ago day when the family first arrived in Detroit, whether God had run out of hills before making this part of the country.

Once the plane landed, she waited until the other passengers had deplaned before she made her way up the jetway. Her mother and Tim were waiting as she exited Customs, beaming at her. "Welcome home, Jane!" her mother said.

"Mother, I'd like you to meet your granddaughter, Anne Eileen Oldman."

"Oh, she's beautiful, Jane!" her mother said as she wrapped them both in an embrace. "She looks just like you did at that age!"

"Don't all babies look like that at that age?" Tim asked.

# Jane Comes Home, Again

### 1974

Jane watched passively as Peggy turned off Coolidge Highway into the Somerset Park Apartments. She had somehow resisted the urge to ask Peggy let her have a smoke on the ride from the airport. Her sister probably would have said yes, but Peggy frowned on smoking in front of the baby and smoking in her prized Firebird—maybe not in that order.

"Here we are, sis," Peggy said as she parked in a snow-free space in front of their mother's apartment. "Do you need help getting out with the baby?"

Help? God, did she need help! Jane thought. "No, I can manage." She opened the passenger door and slid out with Anne in her arms. She made sure the blanket was wrapped tightly around the little body in her arms.

"Careful!" Peggy called from the back of the car. "It's a little slippery in spots." She opened the trunk and pulled Jane's two suitcases out.

Jane looked toward her mother's apartment building, with its eight apartments, four upstairs and four down, like all its Somerset Park counterparts. Not as pretty in the dead of winter as it was the previous summer when she first came home. "Ready for the family reunion?" Peggy asked, coming up to her side. The two women walked up the pavement to the building's entrance. Before they could ring the bell, the buzzer signaled the door's opening. They entered the overheated hallway. Tim stood in the hallway in front of their mother's apartment. The last time Jane had seen him look like that was the day their father died.

"Hello, Jane." It was almost a question.

"Hello, Tim." Hers was almost a question too.

"Peggy, let me help with the bags." He grabbed one and led the group into the apartment.

Their mother waited just inside the door. For two days, Jane had looked forward to this moment. For two days, she had dreaded it. "Jane, welcome home, dear," her mother said, awkwardly trying to embrace her without crushing Anne.

"Hello, Mother."

"Thank you for picking her up, Peggy."

"Of course," Peggy answered. "We talked a bit on the way. Jane's really worn out — aren't you, sis?"

"Yes, yes, I am. I'm just exhausted from the trip — and everything."

"Mother, where shall I put her bags?" Tim asked.

"Put them in my room. Not much choice at the moment. She can have your room when you go back to school."

"I think I'll just go to bed," Jane said. "Or at least lie down for now. I'm really feeling the jet lag." She followed Tim to her mother's bedroom.

"Do you need anything?" Tim asked as he put the bags down.

"No, I'm fine."

Jane closed the door behind him as he left the room. After taking off her coat and sweater, she undressed Anne, changed her diaper, put her in a clean nighty, and laid her in the bassinet which still stood in the corner. She washed her own face in the bathroom sink.

She lit a cigarette and sat in the chair. Had it only been four days since she was last here? It felt like years. How could so much happen in such a short time? How could so much change so quickly?

They had had a wonderful summer and fall in the United States, she and Jack and Anne, visiting family and friends and planning their return to Britain. Jack had left in early October to go make the final arrangements for the Thetford pizza parlor. Jane still thought the idea was pretty crazy, but she had confidence that if anyone could pull it off Jack could. When the Yom Kippur War happened, she was concerned how it and the Arab oil embargo would affect their plans, how the grand pageantry of world history would conspire to crush the hopes of two Americans in a small English town. Jack assured her there was nothing to worry about.

After several frustrating delays and at best random communication with Jack, she and Anne finally got on a flight to London just after the New Year. Because of an airline schedule change, it left a day earlier than she had told Jack to expect her. She didn't know whether her Western Union telegram with the correct information would arrive in time. So, it did not surprise her not to find him at Heathrow Airport, not even at Thetford Station. She was just happy to experience another mild English winter, to escape Michigan's deep cold.

She had left Detroit the night before, flown all night to get to London, and spent several hours on the train to

Cambridge and then to Thetford. With a shrug of resignation, she got a taxicab to take her and the baby to the new home Jack had rented. She hoped he was home. She was exhausted — thank God Anne was a cooperative baby, but a transatlantic flight was a tiring experience no matter what — and she didn't have a key to the new house.

It was a sunny, cool afternoon in Thetford. The sight of the familiar streets gladdened her. The taxi stopped with a screech of brakes in front of the address she had given the driver. "Please wait till I make sure my husband is home."

"Yes, love."

Jane opened the metal street gate and passed through the small front yard to the front door of the small stone cottage. How pretty! she thought. How unbearably English! There was no doorbell, so she banged the door knocker a couple of times. A few minutes passed without a response, so she banged again.

"Just a minute!" She heard Jack's voice from somewhere inside. In a few seconds more the door opened, her husband in boxer shorts and a tee shirt, looking like he had just tumbled out of bed. His face showed disbelief. "Jane! Honey! You're here! I didn't expect you till tomorrow!"

Jane stepped through the door, holding Anne to one side so Jack could kiss her. "The airline changed the schedule. I sent a telegram, which I guess you didn't get. So here we are!"

"Who is it, dear?" A woman's voice inside.

Jane froze. "Am I intruding?" she asked, stepping away from Jack.

He looked over his shoulder. "I can explain."

"I'm sure you can," she said. "Anyone I know? Wait— don't answer that." She turned and walked back to the taxi. "Please take me back to the station," she said to the puzzled driver. "I seem to have made a mistake."

She could hardly remember the next forty-eight hours. She stayed in a bed and breakfast next to the station that night. "Good to have you back, dear! And such a beautiful baby!" the proprietress said, remembering Jane from her previous Thetford incarnation. "Staying long?"

For a long time, she sat in the second-floor room's window, Anne in her arms, idly watching the street. She didn't know whether she was angry or relieved that Jack did not come find her.

The next day she made her way to Heathrow Airport. She bought tickets (thank God she had Jack's American Express card, not to mention a couple of thousand dollars in cash for the pizza parlor) and sent her mother a telegram. "ARRIVING DETROIT 7:30 PM WEDNESDAY BOAC STOP PLEASE MEET JANE." It was the hardest thing she had ever done.

On the flight, she sat in a daze, alert only to Anne's needs and resistant to the stewardesses' goodwill. She almost collapsed with relief to find Peggy waiting for her at Metro Airport.

"Even our dear mother could guess from your telegram that something was really wrong," Peggy said as she wrapped her arms around her sister and her niece. "She thought maybe with my history I should be the one to meet you."

"Thank you, Peggy," Jane said and started to cry. "Every once in a while, Mother manages to make the right choice."

"If you want to talk, we can talk. If you just want to go straight to Mother's, we can go straight to Mother's. If you want to go someplace else, I'll take you there."

"I'm too tired to think. Take me to Mother's, please."

They collected her bags and made their way through the Detroit winter to Peggy's Firebird. Jane settled into the passenger seat and sang softly to Anne. Peggy waited until they were headed east on I-94 before trying at conversation. "So what is going on? Or would you rather not talk about it?"

Jane continued to pet Anne's hair. "Oh, no, I'll talk."

Peggy cast a glance in her direction. "Obviously something happened as soon as you got to England that sent you scurrying back here, and it must have been big."

Jane laughed. "Well, yes, you could say it was big. And surprising. What wife expects her husband to greet her at the door and then hear a woman call 'Who is it, dear?' from somewhere inside the house?"

"Holy Jesus!" Peggy unconsciously tapped the accelerator.

"Did you ever have one of those moments that suddenly clarified a lot of questions that have been nagging at you?"

Peggy snickered. "Someday I'll answer that. But right now, let's stick to your situation."

"I mean, I never thought to doubt Jack before, but now I can see there were all sorts of warning lights in our relationship. I just didn't know they were flashing. There were all the things on the 'good' column side, and a few on the 'bad' column side — when aren't there? — but suddenly a whole bunch moved to the 'bad' side. I just didn't want to put them there before."

"Like what?"

Jane glanced at Peggy. "Jack never told me he was married before."

"But Mother told me long ago he was divorced."

Jane laughed. "I just told Mother that to shock her and get her off my back. But I didn't know it then. Turns out the joke was on me."

"So was his divorce good or bad?"

Jane thought Peggy's tone suggested she thought it bad. She considered her answer. "I thought it was good, that he was trying to spare me. His mother happened to mention it while we were talking last summer."

"And now it's bad?"

"Yes, I think it is. How do you not mention a fact like that to your wife? But that's not all."

"What? He has more than one ex-wife?" Peggy asked in a neutral tone as she turned the car north on Southfield Freeway.

"He has a son I never knew about. That's how his mother happened to mention the ex-wife. She and Jack's father were going off to see their grandson after they visited us. I tried to act as if none of this was news to me — I don't know whether she noticed how flustered I was — but it really set me back. And at the time I tried to justify it — that he was protecting me."

"Does Jack know you know about the ex and the kid?"

"No, I don't think so. I thought we'd discuss it later. Now I guess there won't be a later."

Peggy laughed. "You know, either one of us would have been better off marrying Dennis Romano."

"Dennis? Dennis got killed in Vietnam."

"I don't mean we'd be better off with a dead husband. I mean Dennis was a good man."

Jane thought about the years Dennis and his family had lived behind the Sheehans. "Yes, yes, he was. I don't know what I would have done if he had come into the ER at Cam Ranh when I was there. Not knowing any of those boys I took care of made it a lot more bearable."

Jane put out her cigarette and looked over at Anne's bassinet. "Oh, my little baby, I have one wish for you in this life. I wish that you do not make the mistakes your mother made. I promise you this. I will do my damnedest to help make sure of that." She lay down on the bed and turned out the light.

Scientists identify cause of Legionnaires' disease /
President Carter pardons Vietnam War draft dodgers /
Chevy Chevette: it'll drive you happy / *Rhiannon rings like a
bell through the night and wouldn't you love to love her?* / 2
Boeing 747s collide in Tenerife, Spain, hundreds dead /
Alex Haley wins Pulitzer for *Roots* / US, Panama sign treaty
to return Panama Canal in 1999 / The FORCE is with you at
these theaters / *You light up my life, you give me hope to carry
on* / Smallpox eradicated / Air France begins supersonic
Paris-New York flights.

# Wear Some Flowers in Your Hair

## 1970-1977

Margie Sheehan arranged a birthday party for Dan's twenty-first birthday, just Dan and his girlfriend Maria and a few buddies and their girlfriends. Five months after Daniel Sheehan's death, the Sheehans were still adjusting to Life Without Father. Peggy couldn't make Dan's party because of some fancy dinner she was giving, Jane was still in Vietnam, and Tim had gone off to college a few weeks earlier.

As Dan leaned forward to blow out the candles, everyone urged, "Make a wish!" He thought a second and expelled a gust of air from his throat. *Get me out of Detroit!* He knew wishing wouldn't make it so. But it was a step in the right direction.

When he graduated from college the following June (a degree in social work), he packed a bag and headed off to Europe. He wandered around from country to country, from historic site to archeological dig, from museum to cathedral, and from pub to beer hall. Not a care in the world – until his mother forwarded him the notice ordering him to report for a draft physical. His draft board had at last realized his student deferment had lapsed.

He considered whether to obey the notice or to ignore it. Staying in Europe was not an unattractive option. Lots of other men in the same situation had chosen to leave the United States for Canada or other destinations to avoid Vietnam. But he decided to go home.

When he came back to his mother's apartment, he couldn't tell whether she welcomed his return or not. By then Jane had already moved to England, leaving behind a trail of very strong anti-war views. That might have had something to do with Margie Sheehan's attitude.

He had drawn 115, a low number in the draft lottery, making his chances of getting called up very good. But when he appeared at the Veterans' Administration Hospital in Allen Park for his physical, his rheumatic fever paid off at last. His heart disqualified him from military service. 4-F.

Until the moment he read the official notification, he hadn't realized how heavily the prospect of the draft had weighed on him. When he told his mother, she broke down and cried.

That left the question: What to do now?

He joined the Peace Corps. They sent him off to live with a family in Puerto Rico to learn Spanish on a diet of rice and beans. After that, he headed off to the mountains of Bolivia to teach farmers about hydrology, a word he didn't even know until six months before he arrived. The altitude and his heart conspired to curtail his adventure after only one year. "I guess they should've never cleared you medically for Bolivia," the Country Director said as he bid Dan farewell at El Alto Airport.

He returned to Detroit with a good command of Spanish and a passing acquaintance with hydrology. On a whim, he and his new girlfriend Carolyn packed all their belongings into a VW Beetle and headed to San Francisco, the Beetle barely robust enough to lift them over the Rocky Mountains. Once in California, he became involved with immigrant rights issues, working in a rundown storefront law firm in the Tenderloin. He enjoyed the work, but not the low pay. After a few months he found a job with the Transamerica Corporation that paid actual money.

Working for Transamerica proved financially satisfying and intellectually mind-numbing. But that didn't matter. On the twenty-fourth floor of the Transamerica Building he met Jennifer Gehl, secretary to an executive vice president. Tall, thin, blond, older than him, divorced, with a little boy — she was wonderful.

Of course, there was Carolyn, the now-superfluous girlfriend. He debated what to do and decided to do nothing, including not telling Carolyn about Jennifer or Jennifer about Carolyn. That worked for a couple of months, even as it kept his calendar complicated.

Then one day he came home from work to the apartment he and Carolyn shared, one of several carved out of an old mansion. "When were you going to tell me you're seeing somebody else?" she asked. He hadn't even finished shutting the door.

How could he respond? "Never" was his first choice. "I can explain" sprang to mind, but without an accompanying explanation presenting itself. He settled on, "I am so sorry. I fucked up. I didn't mean to hurt you."

Carolyn and he went their separate ways, both moving out of the apartment neither could afford alone.

A flower child from the sixties who resisted joining the seventies, Carolyn forgave him. A couple of months after their breakup, she met a mandolin-maker from Oregon in

San Francisco on vacation. He dropped in one night at the restaurant where she waited tables and ended up jamming with the house band. She was smitten. When he headed home to Medford a week later, she rode shotgun in his VW Bus.

Jennifer, whose knowledge of the situation did not go much beyond understanding that Dan suddenly needed a place to live, invited him to move in with her and her son Ryan in their small Sausalito apartment. She did so reluctantly, not wanting to rush into a relationship after the experience of her marriage to Ryan's father. She wondered what impact a strange man in the house would have on Ryan. But the eight-year-old boy had already gotten to know and love Dan over the previous months, and Dan found himself relishing the role of stand-in dad.

One Sunday the three of them made a trip to Mount Tamalpais State Park. As Dan and Jennifer walked hand-in-hand among the redwoods, Ryan darted back and forth, astonished by everything he encountered.

"Are you happy, Dan?" Jennifer asked.

He looked at her. "Right now, I can't imagine anything I'd rather be doing, anyplace I'd rather be, than with you two."

She put her arm around him. "I love to see you with Ryan. I don't think he's ever been as happy as he has been since you came into our lives."

"He's a good kid."

"You make a good father."

"And you make a good mother."

Jennifer smiled at him. "Do you think we could handle more than one child?"

He looked at her. "Is this a 'what if' scenario, or something more immediate?"

She leaned her head against his shoulder. "Not immediate. But give it six months."

Dan had not considered the idea of their having a child. He had assumed marriage would come first. He felt both delighted and terrified. "Oh my God, I can't believe it. Is this what you want?"

"Yes, if it's what you do."

"I do! I do!"

Suddenly he hesitated. "What is it, honey?" she asked.

"I always had the idea my parents were thrilled with the idea of each of us, and not so thrilled once we actually got here."

"Dan, you are not your parents. You are you. I've seen you with Ryan. I'm going to go out on a limb and say you are already a much better parent than yours were."

He pulled away from her. "Don't you go criticizing my parents!"

She looked at him closely, wondering whether she had said the wrong thing. He smiled and they both laughed.

"So, here's to another generation of Sheehans!" he said. "If it's a boy, let's call him David. I don't think the Sheehans have ever had a David."

"Neither have the Gehls. And if it's a girl?"

"Well, I'm open to suggestions. But not Margaret. Definitely not Margaret."

# Karaoke and Mizuwari

## 1984

"Sheehan-san, tsugi-da!" Sato-san shouted, reaching over and slapping Tim Sheehan on the knee. Tim waved his hand to clear some of the cigarette smoke from in front of his face. He and Sato-san and three other men were sitting on zabuton cushions around a low table in the Rokubankan bar. On the table sat a bottle of Suntory whiskey with Sato-san's name on it (he was a Rokubankan regular), a pitcher of water, and a bucket of ice, the necessary ingredients for the two hostesses to keep the mizuwari flowing smoothly. The table also held dishes of edamame, nuts, and other snacks, and a large glass ashtray the hostesses emptied frequently.

This group, men with different professional backgrounds but a shared school history, met regularly for dinner and drinks, as described in the name, which translated to "The Second Tuesday of Every Other Month Club." Besides Sato-san the dentist, it included Nishi-san the shoochu exporter, Miyazaki-san the newspaper columnist, and Nagasawa-san the kimono shop owner. Tim became an honorary member shortly after his arrival in Japan six months earlier, introduced by an American friend of Sato-san's.

Tim had arrived for a two-year assignment at the American Consulate in Hakata on the southwestern island of Kyushu just a few days after the Soviet Union had shot down KAL flight 007 when it strayed into Soviet airspace. He came with a few months of Japanese language training at the Foreign Service Institute and previous assignments at the American embassies in Korea and Lower Volta.

Tim admired many aspects of Japanese culture. The frequent drinking bouts constituting such a large part of men's social activity were not among them. There was too much truth to the stereotype of Japanese businessmen working all day and drinking all night, not getting home to their wives and families until after midnight. It amazed him how quickly many men became inebriated on mizuwari. The drinks contained barely enough whiskey to give the watery liquid color. He appreciated that the members of the Second Tuesday Club didn't try to outdo each other in their drinking, and almost always ended the evening by ten o'clock.

At least karaoke provided an alternative to the inane conversation with the hostesses sitting there tittering with hands over their mouths. Tim just hoped no one would ever introduce karaoke to the United States.

Sato-san had told Tim it was his turn to sing, and so he would. "'Ue-o Muite Arukoo,' onegai shimasu," he said to the hostess.

"Sugoi!" She handed him the microphone and punched the buttons to bring up the video.

When he had first arrived in Japan, Tim had resisted singing karaoke. He knew the limits of his own voice, and he quickly learned the limits of English-language karaoke selections ("My Way" and "San Francisco" and a few others). But his approach proved frustrating for both Tim and his Japanese drinking partners. So, he chose a different tactic. Not only would he sing when called upon, he would do so enthusiastically. And not only would he sing Japanese songs, he would sing enka, the sentimental ballads described as the Japanese counterpart to American country music.

The TV sitting at the end of the table began displaying the video, a kimono-clad geisha under a bamboo umbrella walking in a garden as snow gently fell around her. As the musical introduction finished, the words began to scroll across the bottom of the screen. Tim held the microphone in front of his mouth, mimicking the enka singers he had seen on TV, and began to sing. His whiskey tenor voice came out of the speakers from all parts of the room.

"*Ue-o muite, arukoo . . .*" He relished the effect. Patrons at the other tables turned to see the source of this strange voice singing Japanese with such a thick accent. How could a foreign gaijin show such familiarity with a yamatodamashii song?

"*Namida-ga kobore nai yoo-ni . . .*" He pictured himself as a boy twenty years earlier in Detroit—that kid never imagined one day he would visit Japan.

"*Nakinagara aruku . . .*" One year earlier he would not have imagined how lonely he would be tonight.

"*Hitoribochi-no yoru.*" One year earlier he would have thought Japan would give him one more grand foreign adventure without regrets.

When he finished, there were shouts of "Subarashii!" and "Ankooru!" He nodded politely and took a sip of mizuwari. He passed the microphone to Nishi-san for the next song.

He would be on the hook for another song soon enough, so he leafed through the songbook for his next number. It allowed him to ignore the hostess gushing in his ear about how wonderful it was to hear him sing enka and praising his Nihongo.

None of the songs caught his fancy. He got to the back of the book where the English language songs were and unexpectedly found himself looking at "Unchained Melody," a long-time favorite he had not previously seen in a karaoke book. He had a rule never to sing a song he had not already practiced privately at home. He decided to ignore it for "Unchained Melody." He would sing this.

He leaned back against the couch. Already the thought of singing "Unchained Melody" had made the evening more enjoyable, the mizuwari more satisfying. The conversation flowed around him like a babbling brook. His friends politely tried to conduct it in a mixture of English and Japanese, given his limited Japanese. But as the evening wore on, the Japanese always increased and the English almost vanished. That was fine. He would just sit here and feel all mellow, enjoying life.

"Sheehan-san, tsugi-da-yo! Moo ichido!" Sato-san shouted, reaching over and slapping him on the knee again, waking him out of his reverie.

He sat up. "'Unchained Melody,' onegai shimasu," he said to the hostess. She pressed the buttons on the karaoke machine. The whole bar went quiet in anticipation of what wonders the gaijin would produce this time. Posing with the microphone, he rose to his feet so they all could see him better. The video began.

"*Oh, my love, my darling, I've hungered for your touch a long, lonely time,*" he sang, and he almost choked to a stop. He looked at the faces watching him expectantly: his friends, the hostesses, the other customers. He thought of how miserable he had been since his arrival in Japan. He remembered that last day at National Airport when he had said goodbye to Michael. Somehow this song captured his mood and made his heart feel lighter than it had in months. "*Time goes by so slowly . . .*"

Tim had returned to the United States from his Lower Volta assignment in the summer of 1982. Foreign Service Institute classes and Japanese language classes kept him in Washington for a year. Along the way, he got fed up with his nonexistent social life. He had accepted the difficulty of meeting other gays during his time in Korea and Lower Volta. What a stain on the United States if he were caught up in scandal! And if the State Department found out he were gay, he would lose his job. But he thought being in the United States, just one American among all Americans, rather than being one oddball American among foreigners, he could live his life as Tim Sheehan and not as the Face of the Government of the United States of America.

He placed an ad in the *Blade*, Washington's gay newspaper. "GWM, 30, 6'1". 165, professional, likes backgammon, tennis, hearts, folk music, opera, pre-1964 rock and roll, Orient, travel, good wine, cuddling." His intention was simply to meet some guys to pass the time until he went off to Japan. He was successful. He did meet them. He also met Michael O'Flaherty.

Tim had always questioned the corny sentimentality of the story of his father's falling in love with his mother the first time they met. Who in their right mind would do that? But that was the effect Michael had on him. Within a month they were living together in Tim's Alexandria townhouse. Suddenly going to Japan did not seem so appealing. But then neither did quitting his job with no obvious employment prospects. So, he dutifully went off to National Airport, Michael at his side, to leave on his assignment as scheduled. It felt like a nightmare. He had met the man he wanted to spend his life with, and he had to leave. They had a numb farewell. Was he sleepwalking? Fifteen hours later he got off the plane in Tokyo for an overnight stay before going on to Hakata.

Tim had visited Japan several times previously, while he was stationed in Korea, so his arrival felt almost like a homecoming. Except for the fact that the man he loved was half a world away. That fact had now hung over him for months. The regular exchange of letters and the occasional phone call did little to alleviate the isolation. No matter how much he enjoyed his experiences in Japan, he always wished Michael were there to experience it with him.

*"I need your love, I need your love, God speed your love to me."* Tim finished the song and sat down, the room applauding his performance. For some unfathomable reason singing this song had given him the strength to persevere until the end of his assignment. Michael would come to Japan for a two-week visit in a couple of months, and Tim would go home to America for a two-week visit at Christmas. And then the following summer he would go home for good. And they would be together.

"Sheehan-san, daijobu-desu-ka?" Sato-san asked with concern.

Tim forced a smile and waved his hand dismissively. "Hai, daijobu-desu. Ikimashoo-ka?"

"Hai, let's go."

*Titanic* wreck found / Palestinian terrorists hijack Italian cruise ship / *The Golden Girls* tonight on NBC, 9 Eastern, 8 Central / US performs test at Nevada nuclear test site / Audiences everywhere are flocking to *Back to the Future!* / *I was beat, incomplete, I'd been had, I was sad and blue* / 22nd space shuttle mission successfully launched today / Introducing the new Yugo, a paramount engineering achievement from Yugoslavia! / "We Are the World" tops music charts around the globe.

# A Morning Coffee Break

1986

Margie carried her breakfast dishes to the sink. Hearing a knock at the front door, she went and peered through the peephole. Mabel from across the hall was standing there. Margie's car was in the carport, so Mabel knew she was home.

They had known each other years earlier when they both lived on Darby Street. Even then, they had not been close, the Sheehans being Catholic and Mabel and her husband Lutheran. Mabel, recently widowed, had come to Somerset Park a year earlier and decided the coincidence of their living across the hall from each other and their common widowhood bound them together like soul sisters. Margie did not share the sentiment.

She opened the door. "Oh, Margie!" Mabel said, beaming. "What a relief to see you! I was so worried!"

"Worried? About what?"

"Didn't you hear the police helicopter overhead last night? I didn't know what was going on! Did you see anything on the news this morning?"

"Yes, they were looking for a thief and they caught him."

"Oh, thank God!" Mabel stood there expectantly. As usual, Mabel thought she needed to offer some excuse to justify a visit. Last week it was the *Challenger* shuttle explosion, but that news had been so distressing Margie had welcomed her company. "Would you like to come in for a cup of coffee?"

"Don't mind if I do!"

Margie pointed Mabel to the small dining table and went into the kitchenette to pour out two cups. "Black, right? No cream or sugar?"

"Black, please." Mabel tittered. "Oh, that reminds me of that naughty joke in the movie *Airplane*, 'I like my coffee like my men, strong and black.'"

Holy Mother of God, Margie thought, thanks for reminding me why I was happy to leave Darby Street. She put the cups on the table, her disgust hidden behind a blank face. "What do you have planned for the day?" she asked conversationally.

Mabel looked surprised. "Planned? Me? Well, I need to do some shopping, and I'm playing bridge later with some of the girls at the clubhouse. You should join us some time."

Margie took a sip. "No, thank you, my bridge playing days are over. Dan and I used to play all the time with our friends Guy and Toni. Dan's gone, Toni's gone, and I never see Guy — he lives over on the eastside now. No more bridge playing for me."

Mabel put her hand on Margie's. "You need to have some interests, you know. You can't sit around the apartment all the time."

Margie pulled her hand away. "I don't sit around the apartment. You know that. I volunteer at Beaumont. And I go to book club every week."

"How are your children?" Mabel asked, stirring the coffee with her finger.

Margie considered her answer. Well, there's Peggy, she's divorced now and she stopped speaking to me — what? — ten years ago. She lives in Washington, so I wouldn't see her even if we were speaking.

"Peggy's a very successful businesswoman. She has her own consulting business in Washington. She works with a number of major corporations, advising them on how to improve their business processes."

"Such a dear," Mabel said. "I remember when she used to babysit my little ones. Too bad she's divorced. Hopefully she'll meet another man."

And then there's Jane, Margie thought. She's divorced, too, of course, with twelve-year old Anne to take care of with no help from that good-for-nothing Oldman, making the best of it as a pharmaceutical salesman — saleswoman? — in Pennsylvania. As mother and daughter, we always get along better with a few hundred miles between us.

"Jane works in pharmaceuticals now. She finally decided she had had enough of nursing. She said after her year in Vietnam nursing in the 'real world,' as she calls it, hardly seemed like work at all." Margie reached over to the shelf behind her. "Here's a picture of her and her daughter Anne."

"What a beautiful child!" Mabel gazed at the photo with appropriate fondness. "I can see both you and Jane in her features!"

She's the spitting image of her deadbeat father, Margie thought, a daily reminder for Jane of her failed marriage.

Mabel set the picture back on the shelf. "Jane was our babysitter too. And Dannie used to deliver the *Free Press* every day to our house. Such memories!"

Dan, so much like his father. He finally settled down

with a divorced woman—Jennifer—in California. When I was young, divorce existed only in risqué novels and Hollywood movies. Now it surrounds me.

"Did I tell you Dan lives in San Francisco? He has a very good job in telecommunications. He keeps telling me in another ten or twenty years telephones will be nothing like we have now! We'll even carry them around with us."

"How interesting! But I already have enough clutter in my handbag. Do I remember he's married?"

No, he's not. What do young people have against marriage? But he and Jennifer have children. Jennifer already had a son from her marriage. I was thrilled when the little boy asked if he could call me "grandma." I wasn't as thrilled when Dan called to say Jennifer was pregnant with their baby, and no marriage on the horizon. When I told Jane, she didn't help. "Well, she could always have an abortion," she said. That shut me up! I just want them to be happy.

"Yes, he and Jennifer have two boys."

"Oh, my," Mabel said. "Two babies! Time does fly, doesn't it?"

"Yes, yes, it does."

And then Tim, my baby. He will never get married. He's gay. I guess I probably always knew that—don't all mothers? He'll never get married, but he and Michael have been together a few years now. I had known they were

358

roommates. Michael even stayed in Tim's house when Tim went off for those two years in Japan with the State Department. I finally got clued in when I asked Tim where Michael would live once he came home from Japan, and he sent me a letter that read, "Michael is homosexual and so am I. When I come home, we will live together, hopefully for the rest of our lives."

"Tim has a very successful career with the State Department. He travels all over the world. He just got back a few months ago from an assignment in Japan, and now he'll be in Washington for a few years."

"It must be so hard to have them so far away," Mabel clucked sympathetically. "Lucky for me, my children never left Detroit. They've got good jobs at Ford and Chrysler. I see them and their children all the time."

"Yes, that must be very nice." Was that what Margie had wanted for her children? At this point, she didn't even know. She took another sip of coffee. "How are your children doing?"

# Jane Does an Interview

## 1991

Jane sat ramrod-straight on her sofa answering questions, legs crossed at her ankles, her conservative business suit itching just a little, a cigarette in her hand. It surprised her how strange her own living room felt, occupied as it was with this reporter and a cameraman. They had come at her invitation, the recent Gulf War the hook on which to hang the interview. She felt sure this young woman and her crew had no idea about war. Vietnam was twenty years in the past. The recent Gulf War had offered a surreal demonstration of American power against an overwhelmed Iraqi opponent, with few American casualties. A few weeks and victory.

Why could Vietnam not have been like that?

Jane had done many interviews, trying to make the public understand the Vietnam War and its effect on veterans. Sometimes she felt she was beating her head against a wall. No, all the time she felt like she was beating her head against a wall.

She forced a smile to remain on her lips as she responded to the interviewer's interminable questions. What was her name? Katie Winters, or something. She wasn't good with names. Katie probably had been in kindergarten when Jane had served in Vietnam. Her questions showed it. It wasn't the Middle Ages, honey. It was twenty years ago.

And then Katie-or-whoever-she-was asked, "What's the single strongest memory of your time in Vietnam?"

Jane snapped back to the present, to the woman in front of her. The heat? The humidity? The blood? The grinding workdays? She answered, "My rape."

Katie looked flustered. "I'm sorry. What?"

"My rape?" Why did she say that? And why did she call it that? It sounded so intimate. My hair, my arms, my eyes, my rape. What could be more intimate than a man and a woman – but nothing was less intimate than "my rape." She was a hundred million light years away at the time.

"Yes," she said, answering herself more than the interviewer. "My rape."

361

"Do you want us to stop filming?" Katie asked, signaling uncertainly to the cameraman.

"No," Jane said decisively. "Let's go on." She crushed her cigarette in the ashtray and lit another one, stealing a glance at the clock. How soon would Anne be home from school?

"So, um, so," Katie said, "please tell us about your rape. I mean, if you want to. I mean—I don't like the way that sounded."

Jane looked at her, taking a deep drag on the cigarette. "I don't want to tell you about my rape. I don't want to have a rape to tell about. But here we are." She realized she had sat forward stiffly. She relaxed back into the sofa and looked out the living room window. Snow lay on the ground, a beautiful, fresh snow still unspoiled by shovels and footprints and dog pee.

"I have many memories of Vietnam, some happy, most not. As I said, I was a nurse in the emergency room, so you can imagine what we had to deal with. During night attacks, the Viet Cong 'walked the rockets in.' As each shuddering thud hit closer, we scrambled to get patients under their beds for protection. These were patients who shouldn't be out of their beds at all in the first place, but what choice did we have? The sound of small arms fire was even scarier. That meant the Viet Cong had penetrated the perimeter and might

362

be outside our ward door. American military policy didn't let us nurses have firearms, and our patients were in no condition to handle them." She waved the cigarette smoke out of her face.

"Oh, my," Katie murmured.

"But none of that compared to my rape." There's that "my rape" again. "One night, late, I was on duty in the ward. I was by myself, not the best arrangement. But one of the other nurses was sick with the flu or something and my friend Dottie wanted to have a date with her flyboy so I said, 'Sure, go ahead. I've got everything under control.'" She laughed. "Yeah, I thought I had everything under control. What a fool."

She took another deep drag before continuing. "So, the night went on, quiet, I was so thankful. No mortar attacks, no shooting. I'm standing at one end of the ward looking at these beds full of men who've been through so much. Always in quiet moments like that I just wanted to sit down and cry. What was the point of all this? Please, God, never let my brothers be here." She put the cigarette out and started a third one. "I had just recently gotten back from the States from my father's funeral, you see, so family was on my mind and both my brothers were at the age to become potential Vietnam victims."

"You didn't want them to serve?" Katie asked.

Jane paused with the cigarette she had been about to put in her mouth. "No. Hell, no."

"Please go on."

"I'm looking out over the ward, checking to see who needed meds when, and in came Captain—no, I won't say his name." She blew a smoke ring as she remembered. "He's a general now. What's the point? I knew the man; we had talked many times previously. So, I wasn't surprised he was there. Well, maybe a little, because it was the middle of the night. But why wouldn't a captain be concerned about his men? We chatted a little, nothing strange, and he went to look at a few of the patients. They were all sleeping, either naturally or with enough drugs, so we were essentially alone. When he came back up to me after walking through the ward, the banter got—curious? strange? Definitely uncomfortable." She looked at her cigarette with distaste and put it out. They had been sharing a smoke that night, right before. She remembered.

"It's been more than twenty years now. I liked to think then I was a sophisticated woman who knew what was going on. Now I look back and see a little girl fresh out of sixteen years of Catholic school who thought her exposure to a little medical gore had made her wise to the ways of the world. Suddenly he had me in the supply closet, not knowing how I got there, and all I could think about were my boys out in

364

the ward, as if what was happening in the closet wasn't. Wasn't happening, I mean." Jane looked at Katie. "Do I make myself clear?"

"Yes, I understand," Katie answered, ashen.

Oh, honey, Jane thought, if you're going to succeed in the news business, you'll need a better poker face. She started to reach for another cigarette but decided against it.

"And then he left. He was finished with me. He never bothered me again."

Katie asked, "You never reported this? You never told anyone?"

Jane looked at her. "No, of course not. I didn't report it. Who would they believe, a lieutenant or a captain? A woman or a man? And only the sleeping wounded as my witnesses? Reporting it never crossed my mind. I've never even told anyone about it. Till now, for some reason." What made her decide to blurt it out now?

"Have you thought about this much since then?"

Again, Jane looked at her. "No, I never 'think' about it," she answered with more asperity than she had intended. "I never think about breathing, or putting one foot in front of the other, or raising my hand to scratch an itch. It doesn't require thinking. It's part of me."

She heard the back door open.

"Mother, I'm home!" Anne called.

"We're in here, honey!" She explained to Katie, "It's my daughter, Anne. She's a high school senior."

Anne entered the room wearing a Catholic high school uniform of plaid skirt and white blouse. She paused when she saw the reporter and the cameraman. They looked at her without saying anything. "I'm sorry, Mother," she hesitated. "I didn't know you had company."

Jane laughed. "Oh, they're not company, dear. They're from WCAU. I'm just doing one of my interviews about the good old days." She turned to Katie. "Do you have enough material? Are we finished?"

"Yes," Katie said, standing up. The cameraman started to put his equipment away. "I'll call if I have any other questions, and to let you know about when we'll air the segment. Thank you for your time."

"My pleasure," Jane said as she escorted them to the door. Once they were gone, she turned and faced her daughter.

"Are you alright, Mother?" Anne asked.

"Yes, of course, dear, I'm fine. Just a little tired, I guess. Even I get tired of talking about Vietnam."

## Peggy Leaves for Good

### 1992

Tim looked up from the book he was reading as Michael came into the living room. "How was bridge?" Michael looked at him unhappily. "What's wrong? You look like you lost your best friend."

"Tim, I have bad news."

"Yes? What? What is it? What happened?"

"Philip was at the game tonight. I hadn't seen him there in several months."

"Philip?" Tim had to think a minute. "You mean Peggy's hairdresser?"

"Yes. He told me—he told me Peggy is sick. Peggy is dying. She has breast cancer."

367

"What? Oh my God. She's not even fifty."

Peggy. She never really did come home after she left that April afternoon in the early sixties. There was a reconciliation of sorts a year or so later, but her relations with the family remained brittle. She had married Anthony Fiorentino. She divorced him a year after their father died.

After Dan Sheehan's death, she found a reason in the following years to break with the family one-by-one. First with their mother, then Jane, then Dan, and finally with Tim. Now, by a twist of fate, she and Tim lived only a mile apart from each other in Arlington, Virginia.

Michael continued, "Philip said when she got the diagnosis, she told the doctor she had known about the lump for a while. Why wouldn't she do something about it?"

"I've got to tell Dan and Jane and Mother."

The next day, Tim talked to Dan and Jane. None of them wanted to break the news to their mother until they had a better sense of what was going on. They agreed to see if they could first reestablish contact with Peggy. At a friend's suggestion, they each sent her a single red rose with a note reading, "Thinking of you."

A few days later one of Peggy's friends called Tim. "I understand you and Margaret are going to get together. That would be wonderful."

He wondered how she had gotten that idea. He didn't

want to get together. He wanted her to see their mother.

Then, two nights later, Peggy called. "Thank you for the rose and the note." Her voice sounded weak, as if the act of talking were an effort. No, the act of talking *was* an effort.

"Peggy, I was very sorry to hear about your illness."

"I would like to see you."

"I was hoping you would agree to see Mother. Even briefly."

A silence at the other end of the line. "Tell her I'll see her in heaven."

Tim counted to three. "Well, I will do that. Thank you for calling, Peggy. Take care of yourself." He hung up.

The question of what to tell their mother resolved itself when her brother Joe — having heard the news from Jane — said if one of the Sheehan children didn't inform their mother he would. So, Dan used the opportunity of a business trip to Detroit to break the news to her.

A few months later Peggy went into hospice care. Within days she was dead. Philip the hairdresser called with the news. "She told them there were no next of kin. She said she had no family."

Warsaw Pact disbands / United Nations Security Council issues cease fire with Iraq / Space Shuttle Atlantis launched this morning on a weeklong mission / *If you're thinking about my baby, it don't matter if you're black or white* / Given his 90% approval rating, the pundits expect President Bush to win reelection handily next year / Saint Louis Blues come back from 3-1 deficit to win Stanley Cup, beating the Red Wings 3-2 in Game 7 / Dow Jones average closes above 3,000 for first time / Bill Clinton, Arkansas governor, running for president / Cellular One: we're making cellular sensible!

# Homecoming

## 1993

In the chill April drizzle Tim surveyed the tarp covering the ground.

"Mister Lynch," he asked, turning to the funeral director, "where's my father's grave?"

Mr. Lynch considered. "I think it's just about here." He lifted the corner of the tarp. "Yes. Here it is. You're standing on it."

"Well, at least I'm not dancing on it."

Tim had not seen his father's grave in more than twenty years. Then it was just a raw hole in the ground. Now it was part of the cemetery's mature landscape, with a marker reading: "DANIEL JOSEPH SHEEHAN BELOVED HUSBAND AND FATHER 1911-1970," and a new empty hole next to it. Tim knew that somewhere nearby was another stone for "PATRICIA ANNE SHEEHAN BELOVED DAUGHTER OF JOSEPH AND MARY 1943–1965."

Until Margie Sheehan became sick, Tim had not visited Detroit in years. What had seemed just a troubled big city in his youth proved itself different: a city in terminal decline, surrounded by a ring of suburbs, some prosperous, some fading. All his life, Detroit's population had steadily dropped. The upper class, the middle class, whites, blacks: they all fled, until it seemed the only people left behind were those too poor or too rooted to get out.

Now in 1992 only about a million people remained within the city limits, half its mid-century peak. Downtown had become a ghost town. Even Hudson's Department Store had closed its downtown building, its twenty-five stories standing empty with the other derelict skyscrapers, shuttered hotels, and boarded-up storefronts looking out on empty sidewalks. Beyond the downtown, whole neighborhoods resembled war zones of deserted and burnt-out buildings. Other empty neighborhoods, their buildings long since leveled, had begun to revert to grassland, broken up by the decaying street grid. Everywhere stood abandoned police stations, fire houses, schools, and libraries — the infrastructure a vanished population no longer needed.

The city had never recovered from the riot. The summer of 1967 might have been the hippies' Summer of Love in other parts of the country. In Detroit, the radio stations, even CKLW across the river in Windsor, stopped playing the Doors' "Light My Fire" while the city burned and people died and the 82nd and 101st Airborne Divisions moved through the streets.

Tim looked at the crowd gathered under a canopy of umbrellas around his mother's grave. He compared their faces to those who had stood here for his father. Many of the same faces, now twenty years older. His siblings, Jane and Dan. His father's brother Joe and his wife, Mary. His mother's last surviving brother with his wife. His mother's two sisters. His mother's nephews and nieces. Long-time family friends like the Blacks and Guy Alfieri. Father Hill, who had said the funeral Masses for both parents. Other faces were new: Dan's wife and children and Jane's daughter.

Tim had the sense that each death brought him one step closer to his own, each passing moving him closer to the head of the line. His father, his mother's dead brothers, Mr. Alfieri's wife, Toni, dead ten years, and now, his mother. Once, all these people stood between him and death. Now, there were fewer to shield him.

Only eighteen months ago Margie Sheehan had called Tim. "I saw Dr. Weiner today. I thought it was the flu or a cold. I've had it ever since I was Back East last summer. But it never went away. So they did some tests. Now, don't get upset. Dr. Weiner says it's lymphoma. But not to worry, he said, there's no cause for alarm. He says they can treat it and something else will kill me first! I think he thought that was funny. I wasn't so sure."

"Well, our family sure does love cancer," Tim replied, thinking of the various cancers other relatives had had. "Or, I should say, cancer seems to love us."

"That's what I told Dr. Weiner. He says that's the wrong way to look at it. There're all kinds of cancer. My brothers didn't have lymphoma. Neither did your father's brother Ed. They each had different cancers, so it's not correct to say cancer is our family disease."

"Maybe not. But we sure get our share. What happens now?"

"I start treatment next month."

The doctors did treat the cancer, with radiation and chemotherapy, and the cancer did kill her. For eighteen months, her family and friends watched the roller coaster, each high point lower than the previous high point, each bottom of the trough a further descent to the end. Radiation.

Chemo. Radiation. Chemo.

Jesus hung on the cross for three hours and saved the world, Tim thought. Cancer crucified my mother for months. She must have saved a whole universe.

He remembered his last visit to her bedside in Beaumont Hospital. He was flying in every other week from Washington, for a short visit. He would get to Metro Airport, rent a car, and check in at a hotel just off I-75 in Troy, near his mother's apartment.

One weekend she was home in her apartment, enjoying one of her deceptively healthy upswings. Two weekends later Tim came, and she was back in Beaumont. He entered the room the woman at the information desk directed him to, and found a shrunken wraith, her uncombed white hair half hiding her wrinkled face, her eyes drifting between vacant and terrified, meaningless slurred words coming out of her mouth, and no recognition of his presence. How could this be his mother? How could she have changed so much in two weeks?

He went out to the nurse's station. "Excuse me," he said to the young woman at the desk. "I just wanted to check which room my mother Mrs. Sheehan is in."

"Right there, sir," the woman replied cheerily, pointing to the room from which he had just come.

He went back into the room and sat by her side, his eyes

idly watching the beeping machines and IV drip they had hooked her up to. This wraith was his mother? He was wasting his time here. She didn't know he was here. She didn't know she was here. But even as he rose to go, he sat back down. He had worked as a janitor at the Little Sisters of the Poor Nursing Home during his college summer vacations. Most of the home's residents never had any visitors. A few family members came and stayed such a short time that even the habitually charitable sisters would make critical remarks after their departure. So he sat. Occasionally he looked out the window at the view from the sixth floor. He could even see the old neighborhood from here, screened by trees, with the house he had not set foot in for two decades. Finally, when he thought he had stayed long enough to satisfy the judgment of the Beaumont nursing staff and the sisters at the old folks' home, he got up. "I'll be back in two weeks, Mother," he said as he kissed her on her forehead. "I'll be back for Easter."

"Buh la um na," she answered.

Margie Sheehan died three days later.

Tim believed his mother gave up months earlier, gave up that night six months ago when he phoned her, after first arranging to have the Blacks drop in "out of the blue" to make sure she wasn't alone. "Mother, you can guess why I'm calling. Peggy is dead." Silence. "Mother, do you hear me?"

More silence, and then, "Yes, I hear you. I was just thinking about that day in the hospital when they put Peggy into my arms for the first time. My first baby. I remember thinking, 'You are beautiful, I will love you until the day I die, I don't care how many more come along, you will always be special to me.' I never thought I could love anything as much as I loved her at that moment. And then your father came into the room, and I thought, 'This is heaven. This is happiness. Will I ever be this happy again?'" She cried.

"Mother, are you all right?"

"Yes, I'm all right. It's just hard to understand, to comprehend, then and now."

Father Hill finished the graveside prayers. "To You, Lord, we commend the soul of Your servant, Margaret. Being dead to this world, may she live unto You. In Your most merciful goodness, forgive whatever sins she may have committed in this life through human weakness: through Christ our Lord."

The mourners responded, "Amen."

Tens of thousands of demonstrators march through Baghdad, demanding end to US occupation / Lance Armstrong wins a record 7th straight Tour de France / Hurricane Katrina strikes US Gulf Coast / *Revenge of the Sith* is tops at the box office / Space shuttle *Discovery* returns to earth, first shuttle flight since the *Columbia* disaster / *I don't wanna be lonely no more, I don't wanna have to pay for this* / The Civil Marriage Act makes same-sex marriage legal throughout Canada / *Harry Potter and the Half-blood Prince* sells 9 million copies in 24 hours.

# Kanturk

## 2005

Be a dear and light the fire?" Liam asked Cináed as he ran a duster across the table.

"A fire?" Cináed asked incredulously. "It's too warm for a fire."

"They're Americans. They won't think so." Liam brushed away a couple of cobwebs hanging on the candelabra overhead. "And they'll love the smell of the peat. It'll bring back all their ancestral memories."

Cináed chuckled. "Very well. You always have been the nicer one when it comes to accommodating the wants of the returning prodigals."

Liam waved the duster at him. "You be quiet. We have met some very nice people because of this house. If they hadn't been nice, we wouldn't do it. And you know you enjoy it too!"

"Yes, I grant you that. But if you die before me, I'm selling this place—to the O'Sullivans. It's time they paid for their family shrine!"

"And please stick to American English. Don't get all paddywhackery with the fake brogue and every other word Hiberno-English. It's only funny for the children!"

"Yes, macushla. And while I'm lighting the fire, why don't you put on the water so we can offer them a cuppa? They'll just be off their long flight and still in a daze."

Tim and Michael had landed at Shannon Airport early in the morning, their exhaustion from the transatlantic flight from Phoenix balanced by the adrenaline rush. Once they got their rented car, they headed south on the road to Cork. "The house doesn't look like it does in the old photos," Uncle Joe (his mother's brother) had warned Tim. "The people who own the place have added on another wing." Tim hadn't bothered to explain that he had looked the house up on the internet and wouldn't be relying on a century-old photo to find it.

"All this green!" Michael said. "I can't stand it!"

"They don't call it the Emerald Isle for nothing," Tim said.

"Yes, but, this is incredible! Maybe we've been in the Arizona desert too long?"

As they neared Mallow, they took the turn west towards Kanturk ("Enter the roundabout and take the third exit," the GPS commanded). When Michael had suggested at the airport setting the GPS language to Irish, Tim had looked at him in disbelief. "I don't need local color," he said, "I need directions." The Kanturk road was characteristically narrow, lined on both sides with verdant hedges concealing tall stone walls.

"Jesus Christ, fuchsia hedges!" Michael exclaimed. "I'm not sure I've ever seen fuchsia outside of a flowerpot."

It was still early enough in the day that they had encountered little traffic. The Kanturk road had even less. Still, Tim kept a firm grip on the steering wheel. "In five hundred meters, turn right," the GPS said. Tim wished for the day when the GPS would also warn him about any oncoming lorry about to appear around the curve. "Turn right here." Tim did as directed. "You have arrived at your destination."

In front of them stood a two-story, whitewashed stone farmhouse, looking little different from so many others in the Irish countryside, with a door and a few small windows cut into its face. Shingles had long since replaced the thatched roof. The addition his uncle had warned him about stood perpendicular to the main structure and was of almost equal size. The builder had made only a vague nod to the old house's historic features, presumably catering to the clients' wishes for a modern structure.

"How long have they been together, did you say?" Michael asked.

"My uncle said since the late sixties, so almost forty years," Tim replied.

"And they've owned this house the whole time?"

"Just about. When they bought it, it had been abandoned for twenty years or so. We can thank them for its still being here."

As Tim and Michael exited the car, two men emerged from the house's front door. "They make me feel young!" Michael whispered. The two Irishmen looked to be in their seventies, healthy but frail, the taller of the two with a full head of white hair and the other with a glassy bald dome. "I'll bet in his day the taller guy was quite the looker."

Tim whispered back, "In our day we were all quite the lookers."

Michael suppressed a laugh. "It is kind of amazing how at a certain age all young people become Adonises."

By now the two couples had reached each other. Tim

extended his hand. "I'm Timothy Sheehan, Timothy O'Sullivan's grandson, Margaret's son," he said. "And this is my husband, Michael O'Flaherty. Thank you for letting us visit your home."

"Fáilte abhaile! I'm Liam Keane," the taller man said, "and this is my partner, Cináed O'Malley."

As the four shook hands all around, Cináed asked, "Are you in fact married? It's not legal in the States, is it?"

"Only in Massachusetts," Michael answered. "But we got married in Canada, in Ontario, in 2003, right after it became legal there."

"We're hopeful someday to marry here," Liam said. "The times, they are a'changin'. Please, come into our house, into the O'Sullivan house." He turned to usher them toward the door.

"I am so glad we got here in one piece!" Tim said to Liam. "These Irish roads are nothing like the United States."

"It's true the roads were designed for sheep, not cars, just paved-over boreens," Liam answered. "It's just a fact of life. When we were younger, we took the narrow roads as a given. At least then the automobiles were small enough for the roads! But now with all the big Benzes and Lexuses the nouveau riche favor, even I hesitate to go for a drive. I come home shattered."

"I understand you've lived here for more than thirty

years?" Michael asked.

"Yes," Cináed answered. "We bought the place for the value of the land. The house had been abandoned so long the owner considered it a knock-down. Unlike every other young person in our generation, we weren't determined to emigrate. I mean, of course, we did spend a summer larking around America. What Irishman hasn't spent a year or two there, or if he hasn't himself, doesn't have a brother or a cousin over there? But we always planned to make our lives here. I guess that's just one more thing that makes us so quare."

Liam added, "It's only in the last few decades that Ireland's population has started to grow again. Even today the island has fewer people than it did at the start of the Great Famine. Eight million in about 1840, seven million today. That's including both the Republic and the North. How many other places on this beautiful planet of ours can say that? And now they all crowd into the big cities like Dublin, so the countryside is emptier than it has been in centuries. Well, except for all the holiday bungalows the Dublin lawyers and bankers are building everywhere."

"Are you both from around here?" Tim asked.

"Yes," said Liam. "Just a pair of muck savages. My family has been in Cork for several generations, even though the Keane clan originates from farther north. The family still has a local just south of Mallow. Cináed grew up in Kilkenny, which is not all that far from here (nothing in Ireland ever is) and we met in university in Cork. And here we are!"

They stepped into the old house's parlor. "Is this your first time in Ireland?" Cináed inquired.

"Yes, for both of us," Tim replied as he looked around. He knew the good-sized room had once been both the family parlor and kitchen, with two bedrooms above it, up the narrow staircase.

The room looked as he expected. The walls were whitewashed. At one end stood a fireplace with a small fire burning. "Ah, the fire feels good!" exclaimed Michael, moving to stand near it. "Takes the chill off. And I love the smell of peat!" To one side of the fireplace stood a built-in kitchen cupboard, and on the other a gas stove, a modern improvement over the open fireplace, with a kettle set over a blue flame. Old-fashioned wooden tables and chairs were scattered around the room.

"We try to keep this part of the house looking more traditional," Liam explained. "We tend to do our actual living in the annex we put up a few years back."

"Perfectly understandable," Tim said.

"As I said, we've lived here donkey's years, Cináed and I," Liam continued. "Back then Ireland was still a land of priests and nuns and assorted other busybodies, so we knew

385

better than to advertise ourselves as a couple. Just two bachelor farmers keeping to ourselves. Ireland has changed so much since then. Of course, the Church can blame itself for most of that, with all the stories of the good fathers diddling the little boys and the holier-than-thou nuns no better with the children in their tender care."

He looked at Tim. "Your mother was the first to visit, shortly after we bought the place. Only a year or so after your father's death, I believe. She came with two of her brothers — the priests — and her younger sister Madeleine."

"Yes," Tim said, "they were on their way to visit my sister Jane and her husband in England."

"Ooh, were we nervous," Cináed recalled, "the middle of the day, this shiny auto showing up with four people in it and us working around the property, cleaning it up — we had only moved in a few months earlier. Who were they? We didn't know. We knew nothing about the history of the house."

Michael asked Tim, "How did they know how to find it?"

"My mother had a cousin in Mallow who told them where it was. But she thought it was still abandoned! So they were all as surprised as these guys."

"It was too funny!" Liam laughed, and Cináed joined him. "We don't know who they are, they don't know who we are, and then one of your uncles says, 'This was our father's house. This is the house he lived in before he emigrated to America.' Well, I had sudden visions they had come to claim the house as theirs. But why pick our derelict farmhouse? Ireland had plenty to choose from!"

"We straightened it out all right," Cináed continued, "and soon enough we found ourselves entertaining these fine Americans in their father's family's home, wondering when one of them would finally ask the question, 'So, what exactly is the relationship between you two?' But not a one did. They spent the time reminiscing about the family and recalling the stories their father had told them of growing up here. They treated us as if we were just a regular couple. We had a grand craic! That's the way it was then, the seventies. I still don't know whether they had no clue we were gay or whether they just chose to avoid the subject. Please, have a seat," he said, as the tea kettle began to whistle. "We'll have us some tay."

The two hosts bustled around the room, placing cups and saucers and plates, napkins, soda bread, jams, and butter on the table. When they were all settled and beginning their repast, Liam continued. "We all had a grand time, your mother and her kin, right here in this very room at this very table. They arrived midday and we had nothing to offer them, being the poor Irish we were at the time. But we insisted they stay for supper. They agreed without too much hesitation, since they were passing the night in Mallow."

"That was the other thing," Cináed said. "Everywhere they stopped for the night the innkeeper assumed they were two married couples and tried to pair them off that way in their rooms. By the time it was all straightened out and it was understood they were brothers and sisters, and none of them married, and two of them priests, everyone had a good laugh."

"Although I wonder if it were still as amusing the fifth time as the first," Liam observed. "Anyway, Cináed laid on a fine supper of fresh trout that I was able to fetch out of the river, with vegetables out of our own garden. I think we surprised your people with the food. They had already been in Ireland almost a week, and naturally had grown used to a steady diet of overdone meats, vegetables boiled to mush, three kinds of potatoes with every meal, and plenty of the Black Stuff to wash it all down."

"He means Guinness," Cináed explained.

"This was the seventies! They told us they had eaten the night before at an alleged Italian restaurant in Killarney, where the plates arrived piled with pasta on one side and boiled potatoes on the other, and catsup all around as a sauce. So, our feast delighted them no end. That and the healthy doses of Jameson's we toasted each other's health with. Sláinte! Jameson's was one thing we had well-stocked. By the end of the night we were all shattered."

"Ireland's so much less insular now," Cináed said, "much more cosmopolitan, what with all the wealth we've come into between the EU and the Celtic Tiger years. Now you can get a fine meal in the meanest pub at an empty crossroads! Well, perhaps I exaggerate."

"They were our first O'Sullivan tourists, as I say," Liam resumed, "and since then we've been a prime stopping point for the others who've followed looking for their roots. Nowadays we usually get the younger generation, the grandchildren and great-grandchildren on European holiday after graduation. And now we know when to expect them, by email or letter or whatever, like with you. No one shows up unannounced anymore."

"What about your father's side, Tim?" Cináed asked. "What is their story?"

"I don't know much. When I was growing up, I just knew we were descended from Irish immigrants. Ireland being such a small place, it never occurred to me to ask where from. My mother's side of the family always knew a lot more about their ancestors. By the time I was old enough to take a real interest in Sheehan family history, all the people who could have given me any answers were dead. But I've been doing some research the last few years, especially now with the internet. It's amazing what you can pull up on ancestry.com, for example. But I still have no idea about my great grandfather John Sheehan before he got off the boat in 1870 or so. I've traced my father's mother's family back to Tipperary. I've got their birth and baptismal records, and their names on an 1885 passenger list out of Queenstown. But I have no idea how or why they came to leave Ireland. Or, really, who they were."

Liam stood up and pushed his chair back. "You'll be wanting to see it, I'm thinking." He reached behind them and opened one of the kitchen cupboard doors. "Here, Cináed, will you take these, please, dear?" he asked, handing his partner a stack of plates out of the cupboard. Cináed transferred them to the table. Liam beckoned Tim and Michael over.

Tim peered into the cupboard, into the corner where the dishes had been. Using the flashlight Liam handed him, he made out the lettering, "TO'S May 1912."

Michael looked over his shoulder. "What is it?"

Tim ran his finger over the carving. "The O'Sullivan version of the Lascaux cave paintings. My grandfather carved it the night before he left Ireland."

"We didn't know it was there," Liam said, "until your mother and company came. We'd only been in the house a short while, just. But they all knew the story of how your grandfather carved it the day before he went down to Cobh and sailed away."

"I never met my Grandfather O'Sullivan. He died before I was born." Tim turned to them. "It's so hard to imagine he did this almost a hundred years ago, to accept this as real. For that matter, I hardly knew any of my grandparents. They lived in Pennsylvania and I grew up in Michigan. They all died when I was a boy."

He turned back to the carving. The dancing light of the flashlight caused him to look slightly to the right of his grandfather's initials, farther into the cabinet. "It looks like my grandfather wasn't the only one to deface the O'Sullivan family property." He peered more closely. "But I can't quite make it out."

"Let me see," Michael offered. He looked over Tim's shoulder. "Looks more like chicken scratches than anything else. Maybe it's not lettering at all."

"It is lettering," Liam said quietly. "It reads 'M, M, S, F, May 1990.'" Tim looked at him quizzically. "Your sister was here."

"What?" Michael asked. "What does 'M, M, S, F' stand for?"

"Margaret Mary Sheehan Fiorentino," Tim answered, dwelling on each word. "I never knew." He looked more closely to make it out.

"She came with your mother's sister Madeleine and another woman whose name I do not recall. At first, I

391

thought the three of them were all sisters. It had been twenty years since Madeleine's first visit, so we didn't recognize her."

"Madeleine and Peggy were only ten years apart in age," Tim said.

"Your sister was very sick, very weak. She had an oxygen tank with her. I can't imagine why she chose to make the journey."

"Well, Aunt Madeleine is — was, before she retired — a nurse," Tim said, "so that would have helped. But still. And for someone who spent her whole life running away from the family — " He didn't know how to end the thought. "But then I guess even I've spent most of my life more interested in my dead relatives than the living ones."

Cináed said, "When Margaret asked — and it was hard for her to speak and hard for us to understand — whether she could carve her initials, Liam could see me over her shoulder, vigorously shaking my head and mouthing 'No!' at him." He laughed.

"But what were we to say to a dying woman with such a request?" Liam said. "I fetched a knife and sharpened the blade. In the end, I did most of the carving, guiding her hand, she with no strength at all at all. But she dictated the letters. It's been there fifteen years. You are the first visitor to notice."

"A last message from my dear departed sister beyond the grave," Tim said. "Whatever the hell it means." The room was quiet for moment. "Well," he said, "standing up, "I think jet lag is catching up with me and we should go find our bed and breakfast and get a few hours' rest."

"Probably a good idea," Michael agreed.

"But we'll expect you back for supper about six?" Liam asked with a note of alarm.

"Yes," Tim agreed, "and thank you for everything." The four men moved outside to the car.

As they drove off, Michael looked at Tim with concern. "Are you all right?"

Tim waved at him dismissively. "Yes, I'm fine. It's just — it's just —" He slammed on the brakes and turned to Michael. "It's just I cannot for the life of me understand my family, or why I should care about understanding my family. It just seems like our whole lives we pulled apart from each other. And then I look at other families and see nothing but normal people, people whose families work."

Michael put a hand on Tim's shoulder. "Maybe other families are not the normal people, or maybe they just hide the warts. Maybe in the scheme of things it's the Sheehans who are like most families. I don't know — I think my own family falls in between. But living together is not easy, whether as families or married couples. Life is hard, Tim. All we can do is do the best we can. We can pile up the regrets for all the things that went wrong, but every day is a new day. And it's easier to face it if we don't let the past drag us down."

Tim rested his hand on Michael's. "I don't know whether I believe that, Michael. We have so much pain in our lives, and we cause so much of it ourselves."

"No argument there. Now, let's find our bed and breakfast and get some sleep!"

## Leaving on a Jet Plane

### 2006

I think I will miss you most of all," Anne Genovese said to David Sheehan.

He smiled. "Well, I'm flattered. We're cousins and all, but in point of fact we hardly know each other. We did grow up on opposite sides of the continent."

Anne smiled in turn. "Well, it's not like I have a lot to work with. I mean, I'm not talking about friends and memories I have from here. I'm talking about family."

They were sitting at the end of a row of plastic chairs at San Francisco International Airport. Their four children—

two of hers, two of his, all aged three to six years — played quietly on the floor around them. David's wife Anita sat on his other side, casually watching the children and hushing them when they got too active. He had insisted on coming to the airport to see them off when he learned Anne and her family were transiting San Francisco on their way to Australia.

"I know she's your cousin," Anita had said. "But why do we all have to go? You hardly know her. She's never met me or the boys."

David looked at his wife. "I can't explain it, novia. For some reason I just feel it's something I have to do, to acknowledge a Sheehan family connection, no matter how tenuous."

"I didn't know your mother well," David said to Anne. "I only met her a few times. I was so sorry when she died."

"Thank you, David. Your father gave such a wonderful eulogy at the funeral. She's the only reason I stayed in the United States until now. Now that she's gone, I'm ready to move to Australia with Bob and the kids at last. His family has looked forward to that for a long time."

"So, this is goodbye, I guess forever. I mean, maybe we might come to Australia sometime, or you might come back to the States for a visit, but we're not likely to see each other more than once or twice the rest of our lives."

Anne looked away. "That's true. I don't have any family here. There's you, and Anita, and your family, and your father and Jennifer, and Uncle Tim. That's it. Of course, Uncle Tim and my mother stopped talking to each other years ago. I haven't seen him since our grandmother's funeral."

"What about your father and his family?" David asked uncertainly.

Anne's face twisted with displeasure. "My deadbeat dad, the man who dumped my mother — and me — for some woman he then dumped a few months later? Little newborn me got lobbed back and forth across the Atlantic before that got straightened out. How many people do you know who've flown across the Atlantic three times before they're six months old? I've never met my father, not at any age that I can remember. I have no idea where he is, what he's doing, whether he's alive. And I don't care."

David looked at this composed woman, speaking so calmly about a life his own experience of two loving parents could not comprehend.

"I have a half-brother," Anne continued. "I remember meeting him one time, kind of, when I was a little kid. My grandmother — my father's mother — had me for a week one summer. She arranged the meeting at a highway rest stop in Illinois with the boy's mother, my father's first wife. My mother was fine with us meeting. For some reason, it was a

397

problem if my father knew about it, even though he was long out of the picture. Both my grandmother and his mother spent the whole time looking around as if the police or somebody was about to swoop down."

"I didn't know that. What's your brother's name?"

"Chris. That's all I know. I'm not even sure about his last name. It might be Oldman, like his father's, or maybe he took his stepfather's name. I suppose by now he's married with kids, just like us."

"Are you still in touch with your grandmother, your father's mother?"

"I don't even know if she's still alive. She tried to stay in touch, no matter how many times we moved and my mother didn't bother to let her know. When she'd call, my mother would pretend she was the babysitter and say she wasn't home. I never understood that. Well, I guess there's a lot I don't understand."

David kept his face expressionless. "I only have a few memories of your mother, when she would come visit us."

Anne looked pensive. "I loved my mother. I owe so much to her. Growing up with her wasn't easy. Maybe no kid growing up with her mother finds it easy. But Jane Sheehan Oldman had her own peculiarities. For example, she was obsessed with the year she spent in Vietnam. That defined her more than anything else in her life. I can imagine — I think I can imagine but imagining is not the same as living it — how a year in a war zone might become the focus of your life. After the Vietnam Memorial opened in Washington, she visited it at least once a year. At first, she hated it. When she heard they were going to build it using a Chinese American's design, she'd scream, 'We don't need a gook designing a memorial for Americans!' But then she went to see it a couple of years after it opened, and — I don't know, it was magical, it enchanted her. It became her temple. She visited there as often as possible and hung out with other veterans, some she knew and many she didn't. She often took me with her, but I knew once we got to Washington, I was on my own."

"That didn't bother you?"

"No, it didn't bother me. It was important to her. I accepted that."

"You were very understanding."

"I didn't think so. It was the way life was. I accepted it. It's funny, I remember hearing our Uncle Tim saying, during one of the arguments he and my mother had when they thought I couldn't hear, 'If there's any justice in the world, Anne will treat you the way you treated Mother.' I guess life was different when they were growing up."

"I've heard stories from my father about the Sheehans in those days."

"Well, we don't have to repeat our parents' mistakes, do we?"

"Let's hope not."

"When I was young, I had respiratory problems, asthma almost, but not quite. My mother was convinced it was the result of her exposure to Agent Orange in Vietnam. We went to one doctor after another as she looked for someone to validate that opinion. She didn't like it when one by one they suggested that, no matter how bad Agent Orange may have been, my breathing problems were more likely due to a house full of her cigarette smoke."

She smiled at David. He hesitated before asking, "Did you resent that? That she would dismiss an obvious explanation—or at least a contributing factor—to your breathing issues?"

Anne thought a moment. "No, I didn't. Isn't it human nature to react the way she did?"

Anne's husband Bob walked up to them. "We're all checked in. I've got the boarding passes."

"Time to go then," Anne said. She stood up and looked at David and his family. "And time to say goodbye. Thank you so much for coming. It was a pleasure to meet you, Anita," as she hugged David's wife, "and your two handsome boys," as she kissed them on their foreheads. She looked around. "Come on, kids, say goodbye to your cousins," she called to her children. "We're off to Australia!"

The family walked toward the security checkpoint. David and his wife gave a final wave and turned to go.

An hour later the Qantas flight lifted off the ground, rising sharply and then banking to the West. Anne looked out the window, the Golden Gate Bridge far below her. Somehow its two towers made her think of twin sentinels holding upright swords, standing guard against her return.

"Do you think you will ever regret leaving?" Bob asked from his seat across the aisle.

"What?" His question jolted her. She turned from the window to him.

"Do you think you'll ever be sorry you've left the States?"

She looked at the two children in the seats next to her. "I don't think so. I have my memories. I've got you and the children. Everything else is history." She rested her head against the seatback, settling in for the fifteen-hour flight.